ONE ONLY KID

ONE ONLY KID

Manny's War & Peace
Book 1

David Brown

AESOP Modern Fiction
Oxford

AESOP Modern Fiction
An imprint of AESOP Publications
Martin Noble Editorial / AESOP
28 Abberbury Road, Oxford OX4 4ES, UK
www.aesopbooks.com

Second edition published by AESOP Publications
Copyright (c) 2014 David Brown

A catalogue record of this book is
available from the British Library.

Second edition 2014

ISBN: 978-1-910301-14-2

One only kid, one only kid
Which Father bought for two zuzim

Chad Gadya (Passover song)

To Gus and Freda,
who encouraged me,
and helped me to
publish this book.

David Brown

Cast of main characters

Manny Grenfeldt	Austrian Jewish teenager
David Grenfeldt	Manny's father
Martha Grenfeldt	Manny's mother
Hannah Grenfeldt	Manny's sister
Joshua Grenfeldt	Manny's brother
Mark Grenfeldt	Manny's paternal uncle
Doris (Dot) Grenfeldt	Mark's wife
Sam Grenfeldt	Son of Mark and Doris
Saul Fleischmann	Manny's friend
Joan Withers	Assistant at British Embassy in Vienna
Hans Mäeller	Manny's friend
Frau Mäeller	Hans's mother
Helga Mäeller	Hans's sister
Konrad Meinhoffer	Nazi blackshirt
First Lieutenant Grubber	SS officer
Dr Wiez	Family doctor
Mrs Wiez	His wife
Joseph Rosenblatt	Professor of Economics
David Spiegel	Manny's friend
Isaac Steinberger	Manny's friend
Zachary Bergman	Commando
Dominique Bergman	Zachary's wife
Sarah Faulkner	Sam's girlfriend
Rita Krantz	Hannah's friend
Mr White	Works for Haganah (Jewish Agency)
Mr Amber	Works for Haganah (Jewish Agency)

Prologue

27 March 1938

THEY STOOD in a circle; the voices of abuse, and the sound of truncheons, clubs and other weapons on breaking bones had disappeared as the circle of people looked silently down at the man on the ground who somehow turned his broken body onto its back looking up at the sky. Through blooded mouth and broken teeth, his voice loud and clear, he said, 'Hear o Israel, the Lord our God, the Lord is—'

His prayer was cut short as a man wearing a kepi cap and brown shirt with a Swastika armband ran forward, raised his club, bringing it down on the man's head so violently that he overbalanced, falling to his knees, and cannot escape looking into his victims' deep brown eyes that for a second smiled, then glazed over in death.

The brownshirt got to his feet, and the silence was broken by the crowd cheering and waving weapons, and as one, moved down the street yelling at the top of their voices, 'Jew bastards, we're coming to get you.'

Hitler's triumphant entry into Vienna fifteen days earlier had given Austrian Nazis the incentive for pogroms against Jews to begin. The newspaper headlines called it *The Great Spring Clean.*

PART I

Chapter 1

MANNY Grenfeldt stared thoughtfully through the carriage window as the countryside sped by. He looked at his watch: If they're on time... he smiled. Austrian railways were always on time. Another thirty minutes and he'd be back in Vienna. It had been over a year since he said goodbye to his parents and went to live with his Aunt Doris and Uncle Mark in the East End of London. It wasn't from choice, for him, or his parents.

With the closure of the borders between Germany and Austria, on the orders of the German Chancellor, Adolf Hitler, life in Vienna for Jews had become very difficult. Overnight, a boy who shared Manny's desk no longer sat there or spoke to him. Because of the discrimination against them by their fellow pupils and teachers, Manny and his siblings stopped going to school. Neighbours they had known all their lives, shunned and spit at them, calling them names, threw stones and picked fights. Because of this, Manny's father, David, decided that both his sons should be taught the art of self-defence, and enrolled them in the Haganah, which meant 'defence'. The Haganah taught people unarmed combat and the use of ordinary, everyday items as weapons, such as pens, pencils, hatpins and door keys.

Up until then Manny's life had been a happy one, with skiing or hiking holidays in the Swiss Mountains, mixed with those spent in the sun of the French Riviera with his parents, sister, Hannah and brother Joshua. Aunt Doris and Uncle Mark would often join them on these holidays with their son Sam, who was a month older than Manny.

David Grenfeldt's tailoring business suffered as his clients, who for many years had encompassed most of

Vienna's elite, suddenly stopped coming. His non-Jewish workers left, not because they wanted to, but because they were ordered to. One of his workers, Frau Mäeller, defied the order and was badly beaten and threatened with death if she didn't obey them. David knew that by 'them' she meant Austrian Nazis.

That was when Manny's parents decided to send their children to stay with Mark and Doris in London. One reason was for their safety, the other their education.

With the children settled in their new school, Martha and David returned to Vienna to sell their shop and apartments, but it wasn't as easy as they thought and weeks turned into months.

Without a word from his parents for two months, and disturbing newspaper reports from Vienna, a very anxious Manny decided to speak to his uncle who was in the study going through the accounts. Manny knocked on the door.

'Come in,' said Mark, smiling on seeing his nephew. 'What can I do for you?'

Manny walked towards the desk, a worried frown on his face. 'Four days ago there was a march on the city of Graz by 20,000 Austrian Nazis.'

His uncle nodded. 'I knew that.'

Manny leaned towards him, face grim. 'It's frightening, especially as we haven't received a letter or telephone call from my father for some time. I'm afraid for my parents' safety,' he said fearfully, stepping closer to the desk. 'I'd like, with your permission of course, to return to Vienna and find out what's happened to my parents.'

Mark stroked his bearded chin. 'Mmm, I don't know if I should let you go, it would be dangerous.'

'Apart from the people who knew me, I don't look Jewish.'

Mark nodded his head in agreement looking up at his five-foot ten, broad-shouldered, blond, blue-eyed nephew, who was wise beyond his years. Pushing back the chair, he stood and walked around the desk to face Manny, placing a hand on his nephew's shoulder saying seriously, 'Manny, you're in my care. If something should happen to you I would never forgive myself. Can you imagine what your father would say if I let you go? And your mother! Well, that doesn't bear thinking about. I've written to a friend of mine—'

Manny knew his uncle was right but couldn't wait any longer. 'Please, Uncle. Let me go. We may not hear from your friend in weeks, maybe longer. The uncertainty of not knowing was...'

His voice trailed off and for a moment there was silence between them. Mark took a deep breath, letting the air out through his nostrils like a sigh. Turning suddenly, he walked with thoughtful strides back to the chair behind the desk and sat heavily down.

Manny could see his uncle was wondering what to do for the best, and knew he was also worried about Manny's parents. Mark leaned back against the chair, looking down at his fingers, tapping on the desktop, and then looked up at his nephew. 'Let me talk it over with your Aunt Doris.'

*

That evening over dinner, Manny was told that he could go to Vienna. Hannah and Joshua wanted to go too, but Uncle Mark said a strong 'No!'

That was three days ago. The train slowed down as it entered Vienna's central station on time. Manny pulled his suitcase from the rack above his head, taking a deep breath, heart beating a little faster than usual and exited the carriage.

The station was full of noisy people as he quickly made his way to the bus stand, looking furtively around, making sure he wasn't recognised, changing the suitcase from right to left hand.

Looking through the window of the bus, he was shocked to see Austrian flags and banners with the swastika emblem fluttering in the slight breeze hanging from windows of houses and businesses. Two men, faces hard and unsmiling, armbands on their left sleeve with a red swastika inside a white circle, walked slowly along the bus looking at each passenger, unconsciously slapping truncheons into the palms of their hands. One glanced for a second at Manny, whose blue eyes stared back, wondering if the person next to him could hear his heart beating.

Leaving the bus he strode eagerly towards Herndlgrasse, turned the corner, coming to an abrupt halt, a look of amazement on his face. The windows of his father's shop were boarded up, swastikas and other obscene graffiti daubed all over them. He quickly crossed the street taking a key from his overcoat pocket, and opened the front door, closing it quickly behind him. He leaned his back against the door, hands shaking as he lowered the suitcase onto the floor. With his head tilted to one side, he listened for the slightest sound, but there was only an eerie silence. Iciness gripped his heart as he raced up the stairs two at time calling loudly, 'Mama, Papa,'

But there was no answer.

He hesitated on the landing, and then moved apprehensively over to the partly opened sitting-room door, pushed it fully open and stepped into the room. He stopped on seeing his father standing beside his mother, who was seated in an armchair.

Before Manny could say a word his father said harshly, 'What are you doing here?'

Manny was silent for a moment, unable to reply, shocked on seeing his parents' appearance. His mother was thin, face white and drawn, looking older than her years. Her usually well-groomed fair hair was now a dull grey, hanging limply over her shoulders. His father had also aged; the once-trim beard long and streaked with grey. The shoulders of this usually proud, upright, six-foot frame were stooped; the hazel eyes that normally sparkled with good humour, dull and downcast, and instead of the energetic stride, he shuffled towards Manny.

'Papa, I—'

'You should have written and asked my permission,' his father interrupted angrily. 'You must return to London immediately.'

Manny spreads his hands, astonished by the outburst, saying defiantly in a strong voice intent on making his point, 'I'm sorry, Papa, I've written but we hadn't received a reply from you for such a long time, and the telephone had been disconnected. We were worried that something had happened to you and Mama. Why didn't you answer me when I called?'

His father brushed the question aside. 'I've been too busy looking after your mother to write. She had pneumonia. Things, to say the least, had been rather hectic.'

Manny, concerned, strode quickly over to his mother, looking back at his father and saying resentfully, 'Why didn't you let us know what was happening? We could have helped.' He knelt, placing an arm around his mother's thin shoulders, and kissed her on both cheeks. 'How are you now, Mama?' he asked softly, looking anxiously into her eyes.

She gave a tired smile and sighed. 'I'm a lot better now, thanks to your father's nursing.' Her head jerked up, a startled expression on her face; eyes showing fear as outside in the street people were shouting.

Manny moved across to the window but came to a halt as his father ordered harshly, 'Don't go near the window.'

Manny turned a bewildered look on his face, to see his father move over to his mother, who was crying. He knelt cuddling her to him, the tears wetting the side of his face as he rocked her backwards and forwards as one would a child. Manny silently vowed that somehow he would get his parents back to London.

*

The following morning, Manny made his way to the railway station to buy tickets to Paris, knowing that once in France they could obtain passage to London. The station was full of German troops and young Austrians travelling to Germany to enlist in the armed forces. Manny waited patiently in the queue. On reaching the ticket window he was told, 'I'm sorry, but unless you have a travel permit, or are a party member, you're not allowed to travel.'

Disappointed, he left the station. Heading for the bus stop and came across a ticket agent on the opposite side of the road, and quickly crossed over.

'I'm sorry, sir, but you need a travel permit.' The agent smiled slyly, 'but I can sell you a ticket to Germany if you want to enlist.'

Manny foolishly offered him a bribe. Just his bad luck, there were two policemen outside checking people's papers. The agent moved quickly around the counter to the front door, shouting for them and explaining angrily about the bribe.

The two policemen beat Manny up a little before throwing him into a cell. Luckily for him, they don't ask for his papers. Sitting on the floor, knees under his chin, he recognised how stupid he was, but more to the point, what would his father say? He stood and walked slowly around the cell to ease the pain from the beating. He had been lucky: they hadn't broken anything.

*

That night, having paid a substantial amount of money, Manny's father obtained his release. On the way home David said, 'I want you to leave Austria and return to your aunt and uncle in London. As you know, at the moment your mother's unfit to travel.'

Manny was about to interrupt his father, but David ignored him and carried on speaking.

'Do you remember after your barmitzvah, I gave you a document to sign?'

Manny nodded.

'The Midland Bank in Whitechapel Road has that document.' David withdrew an envelope from his pocket and handed it to Manny. 'This letter instructs the bank to give you complete autonomy over my account. They'll verify who you are by matching your signature. As you know, in the last few years I had put all my assets into a Swiss bank account.' He gestured towards the papers. 'With those documents there's an introduction to my Swiss banker, Herr Schouler, at the Eisiedeln Bank in Zurich. I want you to remember some numbers, so if anything should happen to your mother and me, you, Hannah and Joshua must share equally what's in the bank.'

'Nothing's going to happen to you and I'm not going to leave without you,' Manny said emphatically, wondering if his father had given up all hope of ever leaving Austria.

Ignoring the remark, his father began telling him the numbers to the Swiss bank account; getting Manny to recite them over and over again and asking him to respond to him with the digits in all kinds of variations, until he was at last satisfied that Manny would never forget them.

*

The following day, Manny was on his way to see his rabbi to ask for help in getting his parents out of the country. Hat low over his face to cover the black and blue bruises he had sustained the day before, he turned into Shotten Ring, and found it crowded with people.

He tried turning back, but was swept forward amidst the men women and children, who repeatedly shouted and chanted viciously and aggressively at the top of their voices, '*Sieg Heil, Juden*, we are coming to get you...'

Feeling sick, helpless and scared in case he was recognised, he watched helplessly as Jews, no matter their ages, were dragged from their homes. Their tormentors whipping them, forcing the luckless victims to dip clothes torn from their backs into buckets of hydrochloric acid with their bare hands to scrub out anti-Nazi slogans from pavements and walls, while at the same time being continuously shouted at, spat on, and stones thrown at them by the baying crowd; eyes wide-open and intense, faces distorted, no longer human, gloating sadistically with repugnant pleasure at the expense of someone else, and relishing in the destruction and pillaging of Jewish shops and homes.

Entering the apartment, Manny found his parents listening intently to the radio. The announcer describing the tumultuous, enthusiastic. welcome Adolf Hitler was receiving as he entered Vienna. The man on the radio describing enthusiastically what he was seeing. 'Old people were weeping with joy and young girls threw flowers into the Fuhrer's car. Some teenagers were trying to break through the police cordon shouting "We want to see our Führer." I had never seen anything like this before.'

Through the open window Manny and his parents could hear the *Sieg Heils* and *Heil Hitlers* shouted by the thousands of voices lining the route to the Hotel Imperial. The ringing of church bells added to the noise. Neither of them realised the horrors to come.

*

Within days, Jewish professors, doctors, teachers and other high-profile professionals, including artists of the music hall and theatre, were dismissed from their place of work. Jewish shops were ordered to display placards in their windows with the words, 'Jewish Concern'.

Since returning to Vienna, Manny resumed his unarmed combat training with the Haganah. One of his friends, Solomon Katz, said angrily, 'Last night some doctors, professors and rabbis, including my father,' (Solomon's father was a professor of science at the university) 'were dragged from their homes and taken to a slaughterhouse—'

He unceremoniously dumped Manny onto the floor. 'They were forced onto their knees kicked and punched,' Solomon twisted his friend's arm, 'then made to lick pigs' blood from the soiled floor.'

Solomon released Manny, and smashed his hand against the wall, tears of rage and frustration running down his face as he turned to look at his friend, the dark brown locks falling across his red cheeks as he added vehemently, 'I'm going to kill those Nazi scum if they touch another member of my family again. My father lost his right eye from the beatings.'

*

Three days later, Solomon was dead. He attacked an SA trooper, stabbed him to death with a kitchen knife, stole his gun, and somehow got into the barracks, shot six more, and then charged the others with a cavalry sword that belonged to his father. In his rage he took no notice of his wounds, yelling obscenities at them in Yiddish and killing two more before slumping to the ground eyes defiantly staring at them and with his last breath praising God. Earlier that morning his sister had been raped and killed that morning by two troopers. Solomon was sixteen.

Manny's blond hair and blue eyes enabled him to walk about the streets unmolested, while brown-shirted troopers and Hitler Youth searched for Jews and Communists, but he must still be ever-vigilant in case he was recognised by a neighbour, or someone who was a pupil at his school.

Herman Goering warned Austrian Jews to quit the country. Manny and his father tried unsuccessfully to do just that, knowing that any journey they made would be a hazardous one as without proper papers it was impossible to leave Austria. What they needed was affidavits proving they had been offered work in another country.

David wrote to his brother telling him the only way they would be able to leave the country was if there was proof they had employment in England. Could he please send them as soon as possible?

Manny was angry at Goering's radio announcement. 'It's easy for him to say quit Austria, but how do we leave without the proper papers? Not with any dignity, that's for sure, or with our possessions.'

His father didn't reply, eyes staring at nothing in particular, deep in thought. David's lips suddenly formed a tight, straight line as a look of determination gripped his face. Getting up from the chair he gazed down at Manny.

'I remember a students' meeting I attended in 1931of a Pan European organisation dedicated to fermenting unity in Europe. For some unknown reason there were a large number of pro-Nazis in the audience who heckled and whistled every time a Jewish speaker came onto the rostrum, so that no-one could hear what they were saying. It was the turn of another Jewish speaker.'

David frowned in thought. 'I can't remember his name. The organisers asked him to miss a turn and be the last to speak, but he refused and walked onto the rostrum. Placing his written speech aside he looked steadily around the audience for a moment, and then said, 'I came here today, not as a Rotarian, vegetarian, liberal, socialist, mason, or barefoot walker, but as a Jew. One who's proud of being one, who doesn't pretend to be anything else, and doesn't give a damn about not being Aryan.'

Without another word, David turned, and with a renewed spring in his step, left the room, entering the bedroom where his wife was confined to bed. There were muffled voices and then silence.

*

An hour later his parents entered the dining room where Manny was studying. His mother's grey hair was tied neatly back from her face, there was a touch of lipstick on her lips and rouge on her cheeks. Manny smiled, and got to his feet, walked over to her, kissing both cheeks, and then stood back, holding her at arm's length.

'Mama, you look beautiful.'

She smiled, blue eyes sparkling with delight stepped forward, placed both hands on his cheeks and kissed him.

Manny's father was dressed in a business suit, beard neatly trimmed, and there was a new look in his eyes, one of defiance.

'Papa I—'

His father held up his right hand to silence him. 'Until we find a way out of this hellhole, we will act normally. Well, as normally as can be expected under the circumstances. The shop will open as usual. If they break our windows, we shall board them up. If they paint slogans on our doors and walls we shall paint over them.' He turned to his wife. 'Martha, a nice plate of gefilte fish with your usual trimmings, and, of course, apple strudel for dessert.'

Martha bowed slightly and smiled, 'Yes, my master.' She giggled.

David took a step forward wrapping his arms around his wife and kissing her on the lips. Manny gasped. His parents had never kissed in front of him before. They separated, Martha blushing and patting her hair into place.

Her husband noticed her embarrassment and smiled. 'Martha, things have changed. We live in a different world now.' He clapped his hands. 'Off to the kitchen with you, woman.' As she turned towards the kitchen he patted her on the bottom and she giggled again, which turned into laughter, a sound that hadn't been heard in their home for a very long time.

'Come on, Manny, help me open the shop.'

Together they took down the shutters, placing the 'Jewish Concern' placard in the window.

*

Neighbours and passers-by peered inquisitively through the shop window, surprised to see David Grenfeldt at his workbench, head down, and sewing. From time to time he would look up to see them stare at him and Manny. Most of them avoided eye contact, but when they did, David would smile and wink, or beckon them to come inside, holding out the garment he was working on.

When he did this they turned quickly and walked away, or openly made faces and rude gestures. Some stopped for a moment on the other side of the street to look across, and then proceeded on their way. Others, mostly Jews, passed with heads bowed, eyes moving furtively left and right like windscreen wipers, seemingly embarrassed by the Grenfeldts' open defiance.

Two wooden clubs stood behind the counter. Father and son having agreed they would not cow down to any Nazi thugs and were determined to defend themselves to the best of their ability.

Suddenly the street was silent and void of people. Six brown-shirts and two Hitler Youth, faces expressionless, stood silently in a line across the middle of the road facing the shop. As one, they began chanting in a singsong voice the usual obscenities and swearing against Jews, at the same time slapping rubber truncheons or wooden clubs into the palms of their hands to the rhythm of the chanting.

Manny and his father recognised one of them, a neighbour they had thought a friend. 'That's Otto Schreiber on the right end of the line,' said Manny. 'We were in the same class at school. Look, Papa, isn't that Konrad Meinhoffer?'

'Yes, you're right.' David shook his head. 'All those years he'd worked for me and I never knew he was a Nazi.'

The chanting stopped and the line of men threw stones at the window. Broken glass showered the two dressed window dummies. One toppled to the floor as a stone hit it on the head.

David hung up the garment he was working on, and joined Manny behind the counter. Father and son reached for their wooden clubs, holding them out of sight as the eight men walked silently and ominously towards the shop, their faces ugly, eyes staring unblinkingly with hatred as they begin chanting again, entering the shop through the broken window, jackboots crunching on the broken glass. Meinhoffer slammed his truncheon against the still unbroken shop-door window, shattering it before stepping through the empty space.

Father and son stood tall, looking silently at their antagonists. David glanced quickly at his son, two months short of his eighteenth birthday.

Sensing his father's gaze, Manny looked at him, gave a nod and a tight smile, then turned to face the menace walking towards them, chanting the same things over and over again. He swallowed back the bile of fear, licking his dry lips.

'Don't show fear,' muttered David. 'Don't say anything – just look at them with the contempt they deserve; if they say anything to you stay silent, and do not hesitate to kick them where it hurts the most. I can assure you they'll do the same to you without hesitation. If you fall to the ground, roll into a ball and protect your head and testicles.'

'Yes, Papa, I know. The Haganah taught me a few tricks.' Manny's chest expanded with pride that his father treated him as an adult, and was surprised that he no longer felt afraid.

As they practised earlier, father and son stood back to back behind the counter. This way the Nazis would have to come around the counter to get at them. One tried to reach Manny across the counter, feeling the full force of the young man's club on his head, while his compatriots attacked from the sides.

The SA troops and Hitler youth were surprised by the expertly wielded clubs; cursing at the pair in frustration, unused to having a Jew fight back. Father and son swung their clubs with great effect against the bodies and heads of their assailants, keeping them at bay for some time. Manny thought the Nazis were losing their zest for the fight, and were about to retreat when reinforcements arrived.

Superior numbers overwhelmed father and son, and they were pulled to the floor. Manny rolled up in a ball, covering himself as best he could, trying to think of something other than the pain, as he was beaten and kicked mercilessly, especially by those blooded earlier.

Tired of their sport, the Nazis turned to vandalising the place, but Meinhoffer yelled, 'Don't destroy the shop.'

While his friends made jokes about Jews, and ransacked the shop, Meinhoffer unbuttoned his fly and urinated on Manny and David, saying in his high pitched voice, 'Jew pigs, all the years I worked for you this was how you treated me.'

Laughing and holding their noses, Meinhoffer and his friends left through the broken windows.

Bruised, battered and blooded, father and son checked each other's wounds. Manny's finely chiselled nose was broken and left hand swollen where his ex-schoolfriend Schreiber had stamped on it; he didn't think it was broken. His body ached from the kicks and blows from clubs and truncheons, his arms and legs having taken the brunt of them. The shirts of both father and son were in shreds and there were red welts across their backs.

'I think my ribs are broken,' David said hoarsely, the right side of his face covered in blood from a gash on his scalp.

Slowly, painfully, helping each other to their feet, they climbed the stairs to the apartment, David bent slightly forward to ease the pain of his broken ribs.

Martha ran to help her husband, lowering him slowly onto a chair. 'Manny, while I go and get Dr Wiez, strip of your clothes and run a bath.'

While Manny ran a bath and helped his father undress, his mother knocked on the doctor's door, which was opened just wide enough to enable the doctors' wife to see who it was.

'Mrs Wiez, can I speak to the doctor please?'

Mrs Wiez, a small tubby and usually jolly woman, hair tied in a braid at the back, gestured for Martha to come in; stood to one side as she opened the door just wide enough for Martha to enter, then moved to the slightly opened door, poked her head out, glancing quickly up and down the street before closing it.

As a Jew, Dr Wiez wasn't permitted under Nazi regulations to practise medicine. But he ignored the rule, caring for his patients, both Jew and non-Jew. Martha explained her husband and son's injuries to the doctor.

'I've a patient in my surgery at the moment, once I've finished, I'll be right over.'

By the time Manny and his father had bathed, the doctor arrived to examine them. Binding David's ribs the doctor said, 'Your scalp needed four stitches, you've been lucky, there's no concussion and your ribs, with rest.' He smiled grimly. 'And no more fighting, would soon heal.'

He handed his patient a small bottle of tablets. 'Take one at night before retiring, they'll help you sleep.' He turned to Manny. 'Well, young man, let's have a look at your nose.' The doctor tried to readjust Manny's nose but it wouldn't set completely straight. 'I'm sorry, but that's the best I could do for you.'

Manny looked at his reflection in the mirror, smiling ruefully to see his nose a little flat, bending slightly to the left. 'I look more like a Nazi than a Jew.' He pointed at his nose. 'This would always remind me of today.' He turned to his father. 'We did well, didn't we, Papa?'

His father nodded, they both knew that Meinhoffer and his cronies would be back, and next time they would not allow them to escape so lightly.

The following morning, unable to find someone to replace the glass, a sore Manny boarded up the windows and front door, nailing 'Jewish Concern' onto one of the boards and the Open sign on the door, even though he didn't expect any customers. He smiled at the people who stopped for a moment to see what he was doing, and as usual avoid eye contact before walking away.

*

Two weeks had passed since the attack. The bruises around Manny's body and face; black eye and welts around his and his father's arms and torso had all but disappeared. David was now able to get around the house and shop without too much discomfort from his broken ribs. For some strange reason there had been no further incidents from Meinhoffer and his friends, who may have something else planned for them.

Martha was clearing away the dishes after the evening meal, when David said to Manny, 'Before those thugs return we need a secure hiding place for your passport, where is it?'

'It's in my room.'

'Please bring it here and follow me.'

Manny fetched his passport, trailing behind his father as they descended the stairs, entering the shop through an adjoining door in the hallway.

David pointed to some boxes under the counter. 'Move those boxes for me, please.'

Once the boxes had been removed, his father, holding his side, face screwed up in pain, knelt and pulled up one of the floorboards, reached inside and withdrew a long wooden box placing it onto the counter before getting slowly to his feet.

David opened the box. 'Mama and my passports are in here, and now yours.' He took Manny's passport, which had the envelope of introduction to the bank in Zurich his father had given him. Placing them inside the box, David withdrew a buff envelope up-ending it. American dollars, English pounds, French francs and Austrian schillings, all neatly bound with rubber bands dropped onto the counter. 'If anything should happen to your mother and me—'

'I told you before Papa,' Manny interrupted, 'nothing is going to happen to you.' He picked up a cloth-covered object from the box, and carefully unwrapped it to reveal his father's favourite cutting shears, the edges sharp as a samurai sword.

David shook his head and sighed, saying in a quiet, cogent voice, 'If something should happen to us—' He quickly held up a hand, stopping Manny from protesting once again. 'If it does, you must use this money to get out of Austria and back to London. I'm afraid this madness will not stop overnight. In fact I'm sure it's going to become more serious and degenerate as time goes by.' They placed the box back into its hiding place and returned to the apartment.

Chapter 2

20 June 1938

H IS EIGHTEENTH birthday had come and gone, and Manny was no nearer to helping his parents leave Vienna than when he first arrived. He needed to come up with something he hadn't thought of before, or speak to someone who might be able to help, but who?

There were very few people he trusted in Vienna, including Jews. He could think of only one person, Frau Mäeller, and he hadn't seen her for some time.

It was becoming more and more dangerous for his parents to stay. The tranquillity, fun and laughter had gone from their lives, which had now been taken over by the fear that at any moment Meinhoffer and his gang would return. Manny was determined to try everything in his power to get them out of Vienna. He decided that tomorrow he would call on Frau Mäeller.

It was a bright sunny day when he left the apartment, taking the bus to Döbling in the Nineteenth District. Alighting at the junction of Billrothstrasse and Schegagrasse, he decided to walk the rest of the way, stopping from time to time to make sure he hadn't been recognised or followed. On the corner of Frau Mäeller's street, Reiderbergrasse, he glanced around once more before walking up to number twenty, reached for the knocker and hesitated for a moment, wondering if this was a good idea, then knocked on the door.

Frau Mäeller's daughter, Helga opened it. She stared at him for a second, surprise on her face and voice, 'Manny?' She grabbed his arm pulling him into the house, quickly slamming the door shut.

'Are you mad?' she said angrily.

Smiling Manny said, 'It's nice to see you too.' He noticed the wedding ring on her finger and saw she was pregnant.

Helga's face softened as she reached up, placing her arms around his neck and kissing him on both cheeks and then the lips.

Helga, like her mother, worked for the Grenfeldts, but as a domestic. One night, while his parents were at a late dinner party, he had lost his virginity to her. He was fifteen and she seventeen. Their liaison lasted a year, and then Helga left to work as a secretary.

'In different circumstances it would be nice to see you, let's go into the parlour. Would you like a drink?'

'Coffee will do nicely, thank you.' He pointed to her left hand. 'I see you're married.'

She looked down at the ring and then at him with an impish dimpled grin. 'I couldn't wait for you, could I?'

'I'm—'

The sound of the front door opening and a voice saying loudly, 'I'm home', interrupted what he was about to say.

'I'm in the parlour. We have a surprise guest,' Helga yelled back.

'Who is it?' Frau Mäeller entered the parlour. Her hands flew to her cheeks, the ruddy face breaking into an enormous smile, brown eyes sparkling with joy. 'Manny.'

Manny stood to greet her as she moved towards him with open arms, crushing him against her ample bosom and kissing him on both cheeks before stepping back, the smile now replaced by a look of concern. 'Manny, you must be careful, someone might recognise you.'

'No one saw me. I was very careful. The bus was crowded and I sat between two Hitler youth.' He pointed to his hair and nose. 'With my blond hair, blue eyes, and now this, no one would know they're sitting next to a Jew.'

Frau Mäeller gave a slight smile. 'You must have grown at least three feet since I last saw you.' She touched his arm. 'How are your parents?'

Helga handed them both a cup of coffee and sat next to her mother as Manny related all that had happened to him and his parents since his arrival in Vienna, including Konrad Meinhoffer and his friend's attack on the shop.

'I must get my parents out of Austria. I have tried—' He stopped speaking. 'I'm sorry, Frau Mäeller, how rude of me. Here am I going on about my troubles and haven't thought of asking how you were.'

She gave a wry smile. 'I'm fine.' Her expression changed to one of sadness. 'But I'm unhappy with all that's happening here in Vienna and Austria. The world seems to have gone mad.'

'How's Hans? Are you working?'

'Yes, I'm working at the telephone exchange. There are very few non-Jewish tailors that are in need of an old buttonhole and felling hand.' She smiled ruefully and was about to say something else, but looked quickly down at the cup of coffee held between her hands, then up at him saying quietly, 'Hans is in the SS. He went to Germany a year ago and enlisted, he's an SS-Obersturmführer in a tank regiment.' She placed a hand on his arm. 'Please, Manny, do not think ill of—'

'Perhaps he could help Manny and his parents,' Helga interrupted.

'Do you think so?' Manny asked eagerly.

'I won't tell him you're here in Vienna,' Helga said, 'but I'll ask him in a roundabout way if he knew how the Jews were getting out of Austria. As soon as I know something I'll be in touch.'

'Thank you, but please be careful. If anyone knows that you're helping me, you'll get into a lot of trouble.'

'Don't worry about us, we'll be careful,' Helga replied.

Manny left Frau Mäeller's house, confident that he'd done the right thing in going there, and boarded the bus home. He left the bus at the Augatren Bridge, walking the rest of the way home.

The front door to the apartment was open. His mind raced with a terrible thought as he ran up the stairs two at a time panic, in his voice as he called, 'Mama, Papa,' but there was no reply.

The flat was a mess. The sideboard doors were open, its drawers on the floor and their contents strewn everywhere. His mother's best china tea and dinner service were missing, as was their entire silver cutlery service, which they used on special occasions.

He walked slowly towards his parents' bedroom, fearful of what he might find, giving a sigh of relief on seeing it empty; the bedclothes were torn and the mattress was cut open. The wardrobe doors lay at an angle where someone had tried to wrench them from the hinges. The dressing-table mirror was broken, its drawers upside down; even the curtains and drapes were missing.

His bedroom was a replica of his parents' room, with most of his clothing gone and what was left strewn around the room. He ran downstairs and knocked on their neighbour's door.

'Who is it?' Mr Bloomberg asked, too frightened to open the door.

'It's me, Manny. Do you know what happened to my parents?'

'SS and Gestapo took them away,' came his shaky voice.

'Do you know where?'

'I don't, but if I were you, I'd go back to the flat and lock the door. There's nothing you could do. You'll only get yourself into trouble and end up with your parents. My advice to you is wait a couple of days. If they haven't returned by then, go and see the rabbi. He's on the elders committee. Perhaps he could help you.'

'Thanks, Mr Bloomberg.'

Manny returned to the apartment, trying to think of what to do next. He had never been a violent person, but the frustration of not knowing what he could do about his parents' disappearance made him want to lash out at someone. He shook his fists in the air, while holding back his scream of rage.

Trying to think of a way to help his parents, Manny cleaned up the apartment, replacing drawers and clothing as best he could. By the time he'd finished, darkness had fallen.

Gathering up some bedclothes, he made up a bed on the couch, placing a bread knife under the pillow and fell into an exhausted sleep.

The apartment was in darkness when suddenly Manny's eyes opened in alarm; his heart skipped a beat on hearing the front door open and close.

Pulling back the blanket, he grabbed the knife from under the pillow and tiptoed to the top of the stairs, looking anxiously over the banisters as the climbing footsteps grew louder and heavier.

His mother appeared as if carrying a heavy weight. Manny moved forward, but quickly stepped back, placing a hand over his nose and mouth so as not to inhale the terrible smell coming from her; he swallowed back the bile that welled up in his throat when she reached the landing.

His mother's eyes were wide-open with horror, holding the top of her torn dress against her breasts that like her hands and face were smeared with faeces. The obnoxious smell of vomit and urine clung to her, tears ran down her face, forming rivulets amongst the dirt.

Manny's features changed from abhorrence and revulsion, to anger, and then sorrow. He wanted to embrace her, but instead said gently, 'Mama, get out of your clothes while I run a bath. Where's Papa?'

'Soldiers took him away,' she replied tonelessly. 'I don't know where as I was taken in a separate lorry to the barracks and made to clean the toilets and—' Her eyes showed her heartache as her body rocked from side to side. 'You must find Papa and bring him home.' Her voice was little more than a faint whisper.

'The first things you must do, Mama, is get out of those filthy clothes and have a bath.'

While his mother was bathing, Manny picked up her dress and underwear with a poker, placing them into an old bag, and then took it down to the small back garden situated behind the shop and buried it.

By the time he'd cleaned the banisters and stairs, his mother was out the bath. Manny helped her into the armchair before going into the kitchen to make a cup of coffee and a sandwich.

Between mouthfuls she whispered, 'If Papa hadn't returned by the morning, you must go to SS headquarters and find out where he was and bring him home.'

'Yes, Mama,' he said quietly, thinking that before going to SS headquarters he'd chance another visit to Frau Mäeller's house and see if Hans could be of assistance.

He was in luck. It was Frau Mäeller's day off.

'Hans was on manoeuvres,' Frau Mäeller told him. 'He should be back next week. As soon as he returns I'll ask him if he could help, but if in the meantime your father was released, you must let me know.'

As they kissed goodbye Manny wondered if she knew about Helga and him, but didn't dwell on the thought.

Once again, from the bus he witnessed offences against Jews. Half the bus moved across to one side to see the spectacle, jeering and mocking the luckless victims through the bus windows, while some passengers, embarrassed by the brutality, looked away. Manny was amazed that even though they were being beaten and forced to do menial tasks, or any sadistic thing Austrian Nazis could think of to humiliate them, many Jews did not cry out or whine about their lot. One rabbi said, 'That it's the will of God and a test of our faith.'

Manny didn't tell his mother where he had been. It was better she didn't know in case the SS or Gestapo questioned her at any time.

'Mama, if I'm going to SS Headquarters I think it would be a good idea if you dye my hair a darker colour.'

She didn't reply, but nodded her approval.

*

The following morning, with his hair now a dark-brown colour, mouth dry, heart beating, Manny entered SS headquarters and was told to fill in a form, place it in a tray and go to the end of the queue which stretched around the building. He learnt that those in the front had been waiting for over a week. He decided to go home, tell his mother about the waiting period, and return the following morning more readily prepared for a long wait.

Like many others, whose families waited in line, Martha came every day to bring her son food and water to drink and wash.

It had taken Manny eight days to reach the head of the queue. There was a lump in his throat, the hands inside his jacket pocket a tight fist trying to stop them from shaking as he waited outside the first-floor office of the SS officer he needed to see.

The door opened, and the woman who was in front of him in the queue came out of the office crying, and tearfully told him to go in.

Swallowing nervously, taking a deep breath and letting the air slowly escape through his slightly open mouth, he unclenched his fist, took his hands from his pockets and entered the office, closing the door behind him.

A strong smell of sweat and stale tobacco filled the room. A filing cabinet stood against the wall to his left. A Nazi flag adorned the wall behind a bald-headed, bull-necked SS-Obersturmführer, sitting behind a desk with file trays piled high with papers.

The SS-Obersturmführer looked up from a file he was reading; red veins prominent on his ruddy cheeks and bulbous nose. Small grey eyes stared contemptuously at

Manny as he leaned back in the chair and lifted a jackbooted foot onto the desk. Reaching for a cigarette packet, the officer took one and lit it, deliberately blowing the smoke through thick lips towards Manny, who stared calmly (although he didn't feel it) back at him.

'What do you want, Jew?' he snapped.

'My name is Manfred Grenfeldt.' Manny pointed to a file on the desk. 'You've my request in front of you, sir.'

The officer inhaled deeply on the cigarette, releasing a slow trickle of smoke through his nostrils, dropped the booted foot onto the floor leaning across the desk picking up the file. Glanced at it, then threw it back onto the desk, leaned back once more into the seat arms folded across his chest, looked out of the window to his right for a second, then back at Manny.

'Jew, I ask you again, what do you want?'

'My father, David Grenfeldt, was taken from our home on the 20th of this month. My mother and I don't know where he was, or what he'd been charged with. Can you please tell me, as there have been no formal charges against him, when will my father be released?'

'He's a Jew, that's what he's charged with,' the SS-Obersturmführer sneered, swivelling his chair from side to side as though thinking what else to say. He stopped the chair's movement, leaned forward elbows on the desk.

'So...' he played with the cigarette lighter, staring unblinkingly up at Manny, '... you want me to find out where your Jew bastard of a father was and return him to you.'

Manny wanted to reach over and strangle the arrogant officer, but instead replied, 'Yes please, sir.'

'And what do I get for giving you this information, you son of a Jew whore, and returning the piece of shit you called a father to you?'

Manny's face reddened under the insults, clenching his fists in anger so tightly that the nails of his fingers dug into the palm of his hands breaking the skin. He suddenly remembered his father standing relaxed and unafraid against Meinhoffer and his crew, and his words, *'Don't show fear, treat them with the contempt they deserve.'*

Manny stared unflinchingly into the Nazi's grey, lifeless eyes, inserting his right hand into his jacket pocket, extracting a neat bundle of notes that he had taken from its hiding place under the counter of the shop and placing it on the desk.

The Nazi rose quickly to his feet, both hands on the desk, and leaning menacingly forward, glanced down at the bundle and then at Manny, eyes slit. 'Are you trying to bribe me, Jew?' he hissed between clenched teeth, with just a hint of a smile on his thick lips.

'No, sir.' Manny looked into the German's eyes, gritting his teeth, knowing the officer was toying with him and enjoying it.

'The money's a donation to the SS orphans fund.'

The officer sat back into the chair, stubbed out the cigarette into a full ashtray and picked up the money. Flicking through the bundle, he tucked it inside the top pocket of his tunic; then he picked up a pen and signed a piece of paper, offering it to Manny.

'This allows you to come straight to this office without queuing. Return here tomorrow and bring another donation, and in the meantime I'll try and have the information you require.'

Manny reached for the slip of paper. The Nazi didn't release it at once, but stared into Manny's blue eyes, then his hair, and smiled, releasing the paper.

Manny nodded. Turning towards the door, he opened it, wondering if the Nazi had noticed his dyed hair. White with anger at the SS-Obersturmführer, he ran blindly down the stairs, bumping into an SS officer who grabbed his arm, turning Manny to face him. Surprise showed on both their faces – it was Hans Mäeller.

'Jew bastard,' yelled Hans. 'Why don't you look where you're going?' Hans slapped Manny across the face. It was not a hard slap, but caught Manny by surprise, and he slipped down the stairs, grabbing frantically at the banister to stop himself from falling any further.

Hans followed him down the stairs, grabbed his arm leaning close whispering in Manny's ear, 'Meet me at Villantag ten tonight,' and then for the benefit of the people standing around looking at them, he yelled. 'Are you blind or stupid?'

'No.' Manny tried not to laugh.

'No, just no. Don't look at me, Jew bastard,' screamed Hans, his face close to Manny's as he pointed at his shoulder insignia. 'When you speak to me scum of the earth, you address me as "SS-Obersturmführer" or "sir". Do not look at me, pig, you're unworthy to look at me. Kiss my boot.'

Hans was taking this a little too far, but Manny knew he must comply as the consequences if he didn't were too severe to contemplate. He knelt and kissed Hans's shiny boot, but when he met him later he would avenge this humiliation. He looked up and winked at Hans.

*

The moon played hide and seek amongst the clouds as Manny, his hair now back to its normal colour, walked towards the lake in Villantag Park. Hans hadn't arrived yet, so he climbed a tree besides the lake, perching himself onto the first thick branch, gently running his fingers along an outline of his and Hans's initials.

Although they came from different backgrounds, and Hans was two years older than Manny, they had been friends for many years.

Hans's father worked for David Grenfeldt, but had a heart attack and died. Manny's father helped the Mäeller family survive their loss by offering his widow a job at the same wages as her husband, so that she could support her two children.

Manny stiffened as he spotted Hans in civilian clothes coming along the path towards their meeting place. Hans stopped by the tree, looked around, and then paced up and down for a couple of minutes, looked at his watch and then towards the entrance to the park.

Manny waited until his friend was standing directly beneath him, and then dropped from the branch onto Hans back, pulling him to the ground.

'Kiss my boot, kiss my boot, you can kiss my arse.'

Hans laughed. 'Good improvisation, don't you think?'

'Have you been practising?'

'Don't be silly, I may be in the SS, but I draw the line at certain things, especially when it comes to defenceless people. Get off me, you idiot.'

Manny removed himself from Hans back, offering a hand to assist his friend to his feet.

'What about your friend at headquarters?'

'Grübber, he's no friend of mine. I'm sorry about today. I had to do it. Grübber and some of his cronies were watching. I see your hair's back to its normal colour.'

Manny patted his hair. 'I thought it might be a good disguise. I understand you shouting at me, but the "kiss my boot" was humiliating – a bit over the top. I could have killed you for that stunt.'

Hans laughed. 'Yes, I thought that was a good touch. I was having fun with you and got carried away.'

The two men moved towards each other and hugged. 'It's good to see you, Hans.'

'And you, even under these circumstances. I thought you were in London.'

'I was, but when I hadn't heard from my parents for some time, I and the rest of the family were worried that something had happened to them, so I came back to make sure everything was OK and to take them back to London.'

'My mother told me about your father, and I've made a few enquiries. He's in Dachau.'

'Where's Dachau? Can I go and see him?'

Hans turned away from his friend, walked a couple of paces head bowed slightly, then turned back to stand in front of Manny, placing a friendly hand on his shoulder. 'Manny, please don't do anything rash, just leave it to me. You know how I feel about your father. My family and I would always be indebted to him.'

'What's Dachau?' Manny whispered.

Hans looked away, removing his hand from his friend's shoulder. 'It's a concentration camp,' he whispered.

The colour drained from Manny's face. 'What! Oh my God. I must get him out of there.'

'I'm telling you leave it to me. If for some reason I'm unable to help, I'll let you know.'

'What on earth made you join the SS? You're not like those other thugs. I know you – you must have your reasons.'

'Yes, I do, but I'll not go into that right know. Perhaps another time when all this stupidity and madness is over, and we can talk openly again.'

'I hope so, Hans, I truly hope so.' The two friends hugged then parted.

*

Two days had gone by since the meeting with Hans, and Manny wondered if his friend had been able to do something about releasing his father. He'd give Hans a week. If nothing happened by then he'd have to think about going back to SS headquarters, and Grübber. He sighed, praying it wouldn't come to that.

Food for Jews was scarce, unless you wanted to buy on the black market. All Manny had been able to buy today was a few potatoes. If things didn't improve soon, he and his mother would have to go to one of the soup kitchens the Jewish Agency had opened in Vienna.

Entering the apartment he was greeted by his tearful mother.

'What's the matter, mama?'

She grasped his arm, pulling him towards the dining room. 'Two men arrived with Papa. They didn't say a word, just carried him up the stairs, sat him in his chair and left.'

Manny entered the dining room to see a man, shaven head bowed, who at first glance didn't resemble his father; the clothes that hung like rags on his body were filthy and torn. At Manny's approach, he slowly lifted his head.

David's ashen face was thin and drawn. There was congealed blood down the ragged beard and around his mouth. Some of his teeth were missing, the jagged ends protruding through the gums. The fingers of the right hand resting on the arm of the chair were caked with blood where the nails had been torn from the fingers. His bare feet, like other parts of him, were covered with excrement, urine and vomit.

Anger boiled within Manny. Trying not to show his feelings he turned to his mother, saying quietly, 'Mama, go run a bath.'

She didn't move, her face a white mask of dismay. Staring at her husband, tears streaming down her face, she silently mouthed, 'Why?'

Raising his voice a fraction, he ordered, 'Mama, go run a bath.'

His mother flinched, replying dolefully, 'Yes, Manny.'

While his mother was in the bathroom, Manny entered the kitchen, put on the kettle and then returned to his father.

'The bath's ready,' Manny's mother said from the doorway, seemingly afraid to enter the room.

'Mama, I've put the kettle on. While I help Papa bathe, make some soup.'

Martha looked at her son for a moment, a frown creasing her forehead as if trying to understand what he said, and then nodded, turning slowly away.

Being as gentle as he could, Manny picked up his father's emaciated body, holding him close as one would a child, trying not to gag from the smell as he carried him into the bathroom. He   lowered him gently onto a stool and carefully stripped off the ragged clothes. Manny's mouth set in a grim straight line on seeing the red welts across his father's back and buttocks, but when he came across the cigarette burns around his father's testicles he wanted to scream with anger and lash out at something or someone, but he didn't say a word as he helped him into the bath.

David gasped with pain as his wounded body entered the hot water, then sighed and closed his eyes, settling his head onto the end of the bath.

'I don't want to talk about it,' he whispered hoarsely.

'OK, papa.'

After the bath, Manny helped his father into bed, and while his mother fed him potato soup, he went to fetch Dr Wiez. The doctor was as usual with a patient, but promised to be over as quickly as he could.

Twenty minutes later the good doctor arrived with his wife, and while her husband examined his patient, Mrs Wiez took Martha into the kitchen to make coffee, trying to take her mind off her husband's injuries.

'David, you'll need to rest in bed for at least a week,' said the doctor. 'Here are some tablets for the pain and ointment to put on your burns. I'll return in two days to see how you are. If you need me before then, you know where I am.'

Gradually, as the days passed, David's body healed, and he was able to get out of bed and fend for himself.

*

Three weeks after his return, David said to Manny, 'Your mother and I have decided that it would be safer for you to stay at the apartment in Kloster Gasse.' This apartment was in the district of Währing, and was used by the Grenfeldts on High Holy Day Festivals.

The affidavits from Uncle Mark had still not arrived by mid-July. With the shop permanently closed and no money coming in, and wanting to save what little cash they had left, the Grenfeldts resorted to using the Jewish soup kitchen. Sometimes, when his parents were not feeling well, Manny picked up a family dinner.

At last, on 22 July, their affidavits arrived. Manny, with their passports and other documentation went to the British Embassy, where as usual with anything official in Vienna, there was a long queue.

After six boring hours, Manny stood in front of a bespectacled man in his early twenties, sitting behind a desk piled with papers. He didn't look up from writing and without a word held out his left hand. Manny placed the documents in the hand of the young man, who inserted them in the left-hand tray still without looking up. He then put his pen down in a straight line on top of the desk and picked up some papers from a right-hand tray. Clipping them together, he looked up at Manny for the first time as he handed them to him, and in a bored tone said, 'Fill those in and take them to the young lady over there.' He pointed to a desk on the right, and without another word picked up the pen and continued writing.

'When would we be able to leave for London?'

The young man looked up in astonishment, taking off his glasses, blinked a couple of times and said hesitantly 'I'm ... I'm sorry ... I don't know.' He made a motion with his hands. 'Perhaps two ... three months ... maybe more.' He picked up the pen adding, 'We'll let you know. As you can see—'pointing to the papers on the desk— 'you're not the only one with affidavits.' Seeing the look of despair on Manny's face, he added softly, 'I wish I could tell you exactly when, but I really don't know.'

As he left the Embassy, Manny turned to stare with an unseeing eye at the entrance. He wondered what he should do: wait for the bureaucratic cogs to get into motion or try and get out of the country by other means.

In the last few months he had grown, not only in stature, but in age, no longer a teenager but a man. He frowned, turned and headed for home, still wrestling with the dilemma.

Chapter 3

'I'M FED UP with all this waiting.' Manny said to his friend Saul Fleischmann, as Saul lunged at him with a knife. Manny parried the thrust. 'It's been two weeks since I left the documents at the Embassy.

'Two weeks isn't a long time when you're dealing with bureaucrats. It'll probably be more like two months,' replied Saul with a grunt as Manny in one fluid motion stepped forward, grabbed Saul's wrist, hooked his foot around his friend's leg and flipped him onto his back, at the same time going down on one knee, twisting Saul's wrist.

'That's not what I wanted to hear,' Manny said, staring into his friend's green eyes behind brown mottled wire spectacles.

'Hey, careful, that hurts,' Saul released the knife.

'Sorry.' Manny helped his friend to his feet.

'I'm worried about my parents, especially my father. Since his ordeal he has become withdrawn. If only he'd talk about it.' He shrugged his shoulders. 'I'm going to wait till the end of the month. If we haven't received our papers by then I might do what Shulom did and try and get them over the Swiss border.'

'You don't know if Shulom succeeded.'

'We would have heard if he hadn't.'

Manny left the centre for home. Entering the apartment, he found Dr and Mrs Wiez with his mother.

'Mama, why are you crying?'

'They've taken your father away again.'

'What! Who are they?'

'It was Konrad Meinhoffer and his cronies,' the doctor replied, handing Martha a tablet and a glass of water. 'Martha, this should help you relax.'

Manny looked helplessly down at his mother, wondering what he should or could do now. Inwardly fuming, as usual he showed an outwardly calm face to his mother, Dr and Mrs Wiez. There was only one person who might be able to help him.

'Dr Wiez, could you and your wife stay with my mother for a little longer? I won't be long.'

Mrs Wiez patted Manny arm. 'Take as long as you like,' she said compassionately.

There was no reply when Manny arrived at the Mäellers' home, so he decided to leave a message for Hans.

*Is it possible for **Him** to contact **Me** regarding the **Paper**?*

Posting it through the letterbox, Manny hoped Hans would understand the bold letters, which of course stood for Hans, Manny and Papa

*

The following morning while Manny and his mother were having breakfast, there was a knock on the door. Thinking that Hans had helped once again, and it was his father, Manny leapt down the stairs and opened the door to be confronted by Konrad Meinhoffer in SA uniform. Three bulging dented suitcases with string holding the lids closed stood by his right foot and behind him was an elderly couple.

'What do you want, Meinhoffer?'

Meinhoffer's deepset beady brown eyes glared at Manny. His partial baldness hidden by a flap of light-brown hair combed from right to left. The little Hitler moustache twitched. 'Don't use that tone to me, Jew bastard. As of now I'm appropriating your property.'

Manny clenched his fists, eyes narrowing, and took a menacingly step forward. Leaning over Meinhoffer and looking down into the face of the rotund, five foot seven Nazi, he said coldly between tight lips, 'Meinhoffer, you've caused my family enough trouble. I think you'd better go back to whatever hovel you crawled from. I'm waiting for my father to return home.'

Meinhoffer giggled like a girl. 'You could wait till time has frozen over,' he sneered, 'but your precious fucking papa isn't coming home. He's dead, so piss off, Jew. This shop and apartment belong to me now.' He rocked backward and forward, arms folded across his chest and smiling sinisterly. 'If you want to cause trouble I'll go, but rest assured I'll return with some friends, and then we'll see who stays and who goes.'

'You're lying,' Manny said in disbelief.

'Why would I want to lie about a piece of garbage like your father?' Meinhoffer picked up two of the cases, sidestepped Manny and climbed the stairs, followed by the elderly couple.

'Who was it, Manny? Is it papa?' his mother called from the top of the stairs.

'No, whore, it's me, Konrad Meinhoffer.' He reached the top of the stairs, pushing roughly past her.

'What's the meaning of this, Meinhoffer? Where's my husband?'

Manny rushed up the stairs. He didn't want Meinhoffer telling her that his father was dead, at least not until he could confirm it. He moved between his mother and Meinhoffer, who nodded, a tight, knowing smile on his face.

'Could we pack some clothes?' Manny asked, trying to control his anger but wanting to punch the smirk of the little Nazi's face.

Meinhoffer waved a hand as if dismissing Manny. 'Just a small bag,' he replied with tight-lipped impatience.

'Mama, come with me,' ordered Manny.

His mother turned her head to one side, spreading her hands as if asking a question. Manny gestured for her to follow. She hesitated, looked distastefully at Meinhoffer, who stared back, his thin lips drawn back in a sneer.

'If you don't hurry, Jew whore, I'll throw you out without any clothes, and that includes the ones you're wearing.'

Manny stepped in front of the little man, face and lips white with anger at the way Meinhoffer was speaking to his mother, voice and eyes turning to an icy coldness.

'Be careful, Meinhoffer, you're treading on dangerous ground,' he whispered between clenched teeth.

Meinhoffer laughed in Manny's face, his fat belly dancing beneath the black shirt. 'No, Jew bastard, you piece of shit, you worthless piece of snot!' he screamed in Manny's face. 'You be careful, otherwise I'll send your mother to a concentration camp, and then we'll see who treads on dangerous ground.'

Manny turned and, gently taking his mother's arm, steered her towards the bedroom. 'Manny, what's going on? What's that filthy pig doing in my home?'

Softly, as if talking to a child, he replied, 'Mama, under Aryan rules, any Aryan can appropriate any Jewish property.'

'How much money was he giving us?'

Manny sighed. 'Mama, he doesn't have to give us anything. Please pack some clothes.'

Packing a few essentials, Manny walked out of his bedroom to find that Meinhoffer, feet astride, thumbs hooked through his belt loops, had now been joined by a half-dozen of his cronies.

'Fuck off, Jew,' he said, a satisfied smile on his fat face. 'Before I have you thrown down the stairs.'

The troopers laughed and jeered at them as they descended the stairs. One of them placed a booted foot on Manny's back, pushing him down the stairs, but he managed to grab the banister, stopping himself from falling on top of his mother.

As Manny closed the front door, someone bumped into him, palming a piece of paper into his hand. He put it into his pocket as they boarded the bus to Closter Gasse where the apartment the family used on high holidays was situated.

Once safely inside the apartment, Manny took the note from his pocket.

*Sorry to inform you that the **P**aper has ceased to exist. Unfortunately the **M**anservant **K**ept it in the wrong place and his **G**uard set it alight. **H**e cannot be contacted again.*

Manny wiped the tears from his eyes. His father was dead. The capital **P** was his papa. He knew who killed him by the capital **K** and **M**, Konrad Meinhoffer, but could not fathom who or what the **G** stood for, and it seemed that **H**ans had gone somewhere.

Manny knew that, by just looking at his face, his mother would know something was wrong and there was no easy way to tell her of his father's death.

Manny knocked on her bedroom door and entered. His mother was unpacking. Taking her hand he gently pulled her down beside him on the edge of the bed. Martha looked sadly into her son's eyes. 'What is it?'

'Mama, Papa is dead,' he whispered.

Her eyes widened and she shook her head in disbelief, thrusting the knuckles of her hand into her mouth to stifle a scream as tears ran down her cheeks.

Manny hugged her to him. 'Mama, you must be strong for the others. We must leave for London as soon as possible.' She moved slightly away, his shirt wet from her tears, not saying a word as she stroked his face.

'The affidavits are at the British Embassy. I'll go there first thing in the morning and tell them what's happened. I'm sure they'll help us leave now,' he said reassuringly.

She shrugged and lay on the bed facing the wall, curling into the foetal position, body racked by her sobbing. Covering her with a blanket, Manny shook his head, wondering when this nightmare would end.

'Mama, get some sleep, I'm going to the soup kitchen to get some food.'

On the way to the soup kitchen it felt as though there was a black cloud following him, and a new dark world that day by day seemed to grow increasingly evil, more than he or anyone else could ever have envisaged. A sense of humiliation overwhelmed him. He had always considered himself Austrian, but because he was a Jew, he was now scorned, ridiculed and surrounded by hatred, with no place in society, a non-person. The transition from normal life to this incredible abomination seemed to have happened overnight.

*

It was dark by the time Manny returned home to find the apartments in darkness, the fire in the grate giving off an eerie glow to the room. He entered his mother's bedroom, moving towards the bed.

'Mama, mama, I'm home,' he whispered, but she didn't stir. He moved closer, a feeling of foreboding sweeping over him, and said a little louder, 'Mama, wake up, I'm home.'

He knelt and his knee touched something. Looking down, he picked up an empty bottle of sleeping tablets. He took her hand, it was cold, and felt for a pulse even though in his heart he knew there wouldn't be any.

'Oh! Mama, why? We needed you.' Tears rolled down his cheeks cuddling her to him. After a few moments he lowered her head gently onto the pillows, stroked her face tenderly, turned and walked heavily from the bedroom, quietly closing the door.

As dawn broke, Manny left the apartment to make funeral arrangements.

*

He took no notice of the SA and white-socked teenage Nazis who cheered, threw stones, earth and bags filled with faeces at the small funeral procession proceeding towards the Jewish cemetery at Seperstrasse.

The funeral over, Manny decided he would sit the week of mourning when reunited with the family in London. His thoughts were interrupted by a knock at the door. He opened it to find Frau Mäeller, cheeks wet with tears.

Manny stepped aside. 'Please, come in.'

'I'm very, very sorry for your loss. Your parents were wonderful, good-hearted and loving people, and—'

Tears fell down Manny's cheeks. Frau Mäeller cuddled him to her, the heartrending sobs shaking their bodies as the sadness and despair of the last few days and weeks finally overwhelmed him.

After a while, Manny released himself from the comfort of her arms. 'I'll put the kettle on,' he said.

'No, I'll do that, go and wash your face.'

He nodded obediently, turning towards the bathroom.

'Hans sends his condolences. He would have come, but he's been recalled to his unit in Germany,' she said pouring the tea.

'When you see him, thank him for all his help and information. How's Helga?'

Frau Mäeller's face broke into a broad smile. 'Oh, my goodness, how could I forget? She gave birth to a little baby boy. They named him Franz after my late husband.'

Manny smiled for the first time in days. 'That's wonderful news. Are they both well?'

'Yes, mother and child are fine.' Her smile disappeared. 'What will you do now?'

'Try to get to London.' For a moment there was silence between them, and then Manny said, 'Helga hasn't a home of her own, has she?'

'No, she can't afford it. Her husband's only a postman.'

'She can come and live here.'

'What?'

'She can come and live here.' He smiled.

'What about you?'

'I told you, I'm going to try and get back to London.' He turned towards a cupboard, taking paper and pen from the drawer and began to write:

I, Manfred Grenfeldt, being the eldest survivor, and heir of David and Martha Grenfeldt, have sold the property known as 62 Kloster Grasse and all its contents to Frau Helga Brau.

Signing it, he blotted the paper and asked, 'Have you two schillings?'

She nodded, opened her bag and handing him the money. Manny gave her the paper in exchange. Frau Mäeller put on her glasses to read it.

She looked at Manny, tears in her eyes. 'Are you sure about this?'

'Positive.' He gave a rueful smile. 'Anyone that's not a Jew could come in here and by law appropriate this apartment. I'd rather someone I know and love, live here than someone I hate.'

'What about all these beautiful ornaments?'

'I hope Helga enjoys them as much as my mother did.'

'Manny, you're a wonderful person, just like your parents. I'm sure that if Helga were here, she would thank you properly.'

Manny handed her the keys. 'I'm going to pack a few things and then I'll be on my way.'

'Where will you go? Stay here till you leave for London.'

'No, there are a few things I must attend to before I leave.'

Thirty minutes later, a knapsack on his shoulder, Manny took one last look around the apartment, kissed the old lady and left.

He went to see Dr and Mrs Wiez, asking, 'Please, may I stay here for a couple of days?'

'No problem,' said Mrs Wiez. 'You can have my son Aaron's room. He's in America, thank God.'

*

It was a warm night and the moon and stars shone brightly down on an unusually quiet Vienna. Manny, dressed in black, stood in the shadows opposite his father's shop. There was a grim, determined look on his face, eyes slit in concentration, head tilted to one side listening for the slightest sound. He glanced up and down the street, took a key from his pocket and then ran silently across to the other side facing the boarded shop-door and slowly inserted the key into the lock, while at the same time holding his breath. He slowly turned the key.

There was a click and he exhaled with relief: Meinhoffer hadn't changed the lock. He opened the door just wide enough to slip into the shop. Closing the door he leaned against it for a second.

Dust, swirling into the air from his quick entry, caught in a beam like a small searchlight that shone across the room from a hole in the corner of a board where it hadn't covered the entire window. Manny waited for his eyes to become accustomed to the darkness and then walked silently over to the counter, knelt, and carefully removed the cardboard boxes before lifting up the floorboard to take his father's box from its hiding place. Laying it beside him on the floor, he hesitated for a moment and then opened it.

Taking the money and the letter of introduction to the banker in Zurich, he dispersed them about his person. He uncovered his father's shears and got to his feet, but this time walked noisily across the room and stood with his back to the wall by the door that connected the shop to the hallway and stairs leading up to the apartment. He looked up at the ceiling, hoping to hear someone from above coming down to investigate, but there was only silence.

Moving away from the wall, he stomped around the shop, making as much noise as possible before moving back behind the door. A floorboard above creaked as someone walked across the room. A beam of light seeped through the bottom of the shop door as the hall light was switched on and heavy footsteps descended the stairs.

Manny held his breath as the door opened and light poured into the shop from the hallway. He couldn't mistake the bulbous shape of Meinhoffer's shadow on the floor as the fat Nazi plodded into the shop.

Moving like a cat behind the naked Meinhoffer, Manny wrapped his left arm around the Nazi's fat neck, placing the bone of his wrist against the larynx. Meinhoffer tried to pull away, but Manny tightened the grip, pulling back slightly, at the same time placing the points of the shears against the naked man's back and whispered ominously, 'Halloo, Meinhoffer.'

'Manny!' Meinhoffer recognised the voice. 'W-w-wha-what d-do you want?'

'I want to kill you, you fat pig,' Manny replied icily.

Meinhoffer's body shook with fear. 'P-plea-please ddon't kill me, it wasn't my fault.'

'You're lying.'

'No, no I'm not,' was the whimpered reply, adding quickly, 'I could help you.'

'Help me, how?'

'I could get you and your mother out of Vienna. Out of the country if you wanted.'

'You're a little late with that offer,' hissed Manny.

'What do you mean?'

'Because you murdered my father, my mother committed suicide.'

Meinhoffer began to cry. 'Please don't kill me,' he sobbed. 'I'll do anything you ask.'

Manny tightened the grip of his forearm around the Austrian's throat, pulling back, cutting off the sound of a shout. 'How does it feel to be as helpless as my father was when you took him away and tortured him?' Manny said in barely a whisper, relaxing his arm around Meinhoffer's throat just enough for him to reply.

'I never tortured your father.' Meinhoffer's voice and body quivered like jelly with fright.

Manny was nauseated by the pungent smell of the Nazi's unwashed body and his urine as Meinhoffer wet himself. 'I know it was you.'

'I swear on my parents' life it wasn't me.'

Manny held back the rage, wanting to beat Meinhoffer to a pulp with his bare fist, but instead said, 'You shouldn't say things like that, especially as I've been told by a reliable source that it was you. Why did you kill my father?' he asked between clenched teeth. Meinhoffer gurgled as the wrist tightened against his larynx. 'He never did anything to hurt you.'

Meinhoffer tried to say something. Manny relaxed his forearm a little so the Nazi could speak.

'I'll take you anywhere you want,' croaked Meinhoffer. 'I'll get papers for you and a visa for any country of your choice, please don't kill me.'

'Do you think for one moment that I'm stupid enough to believe what you say, you little toad?' Manny pulled him closer, digging the shears into his side just enough to break the skin. 'Have you ever read the bible, you peace of piss? No, probably not, you're too fucking ignorant.'

There was emotion, hatred, loathing, and venom in Manny's word as he continued, 'It says, and I quote, an eye for an eye, a tooth for a tooth, and a life for a life.' As he said 'life', Manny released his grip and spun the Nazi quickly around, pushing him forward and slamming his face against the wall. Then he turned the dazed Nazi about, ramming his forearm against his throat and knee into his groin, and leaning the full weight of his body against him.

In the dim light he could see Meinhoffer's eyes wide with fear; blood running from his nose where it slammed into the wall. Meinhoffer shook his head whispering, 'No, please no,' as Manny slowly thrust the razor-sharp shears into his body, cutting through skin like a knife through butter.

Meinhoffer's eyes widened and he silently mouthed the word 'No.' Blood trickled from the corner of his mouth, the eyes gradually glazed over and he went limp.

Manny withdrew the shears and stepped back, letting the lifeless body drop to the floor. He looked distastefully down at Meinhoffer, stepped over him and left the shop, climbing the stairs to the apartment.

The door to his parents' bedroom was open. A raging anger welled up inside him on seeing the old lady and man asleep in his parents' bed. He strode purposefully into the bedroom, the shears held blade down, and plunged them into the old man's chest. Blood spread across the sheets as Manny moved quickly around the other side of the bed, just as the old woman opened her eyes and was about to scream, but Manny clamped his left hand over her mouth, thrusting the shears into her throat. The body convulsed for a second, and was then still.

Breathing heavily, Manny took his hand from her mouth. He stepped away from the bed, the anger slowly subsiding as he walked out of the bedroom, emptied his pockets and stripped off the blood-soaked clothes. Placing the clothes and shears, still dripping blood, inside one of Meinhoffer's old suitcase, he took it down to the shop, hiding it with the now-empty money box under the floorboards. He replaced the cardboard boxes under the counter and left the shop, climbing the stairs to have a shower.

Meinhoffer's stale sweat lingered in the air as Manny walked into his bedroom in search of clean clothes, and was surprised and thankful to see some of his own still hanging in the wardrobe.

Twenty minutes later, taking a last look around the apartment, he placed the key on the table and left a place that has once been filled with happiness and laughter. He felt no remorse for what he had done, just the satisfaction that he had avenged two very kind, generous and gentle people whom he loved dearly and whom Meinhoffer and his cronies had taken from him.

The next morning at breakfast he said to Dr and Mrs Wiez, 'Thank you for allowing me to stay the night, but I must leave today. You do not want me staying here to attract attention to you.' He kissed Mrs Wiez's cheek and shook the doctor's hand, palming some money into it. The doctor went to protest, but Manny had walked out of the door, heading for the British Embassy.

*

The nameplate on the desk read 'Miss Joan Withers'. Manny waited patiently for her to finish reading the form he'd filled in. She was very pretty, with dark-brown shoulder-length curly hair that from time-to-time she brushed away from her face with a finger. Miss Withers looked up, blushing on seeing him staring at her. Without a word she stood, straightened her skirt, and with long-legged, high-heeled strides walked over to a filing cabinet against the far wall. Placing a pencil between white even teeth, she opened a drawer and finger-crawled along the folders until finding what she was looking for. She pulled it out, opened it, glanced quickly at its contents and then returned to the desk, tut-tutting as she sat down.

'What's the matter?' Manny asked, a worried frown on his face.

Miss Withers leaned slightly forward to reveal a little cleavage, as her dark-brown eyes looked into his. 'You've some papers missing.' Her German was good, with a slight English accent.

'What papers? I gave you everything. It's taken me over two weeks to gather all the documentation you demand.'

'There should be one from the police. It would be proof you weren't a criminal.'

He leaned forward slightly, 'Apart from that?'

'Everything's in order, but—'

'Look here, Miss—' he glanced down at the nameplate, even though he remembered her name.

'Withers,' she said quietly.

'My parents are dead; I need to get back to London so I can take my exams.'

'I'm very sorry for your loss,' she said tenderly, eyes under long lashes looking compassionately into his. 'I wish I could help, but until we receive the police report, we can't agree your affidavit.'

Manny's heart sank. He'd purposely avoided getting the police report because he wasn't sure if his arrest when he tried to bribe the travel agent was recorded. Now, because of that, the British hadn't even begun to check his affidavit. He looked down at her hand which covered his, and then up into her eyes, and for a moment was surprised by the warmth in them.

'Thank you, Miss Withers, for your condolences. I've been attending Davenant Grammar School in East London. I came back here because my mother was very ill, and had since died. Now I need to return to school and get on with my education.'

'I'm sorry, Mr Grenfeldt, what you say may be true, and I for one believe you, but we still have to check everything. You would be surprised at the stories we've been told by people wanting to get to England. I'm sorry, but there's nothing I could do for you at the moment.'

Manny whipped his hand away, leaping from his seat, leaning angrily across the desk.

'Look,' he said rather too loudly. 'I've just lost both my parents; my brother and sister are in London staying with my aunt and uncle, as I was. Why don't you people believe me? Surely something could be done to cut through this bureaucratic red tape?'

Placing a hand on his arm, concern in her face and voice, she whispered, 'Mr Grenfeldt, please do not raise your voice. Sit down, otherwise the guards will throw you out, and then we'll be forced to ignore your affidavit.'

Manny slumped helplessly back into the chair and asked quietly, 'So when do you think I'll be hearing from you?'

She smiled grimly. 'How long is a piece of string? I wish I could do more for you.' She looked down at his file. 'Are you still living at the same address in Hendlegasse?'

'No.'

'How will I be able to contact you?'

'Through my rabbi at the synagogue. I'll write down the address.'

*

The sun was shining, a slight breeze moving the leaves on the trees as though in dance as he walked away from the British Embassy, wondering what to do next. Going back to Dr Wiez was out of the question. He found himself walking along the chestnut-lined Hauptalle towards Prata and the Reisenrad.

Sitting on a bench Manny stared at the giant Ferris wheel turning lazily around, and remembered happier days with family and friends. Occasionally he glanced with trepidation at the soldiers, some with young girls on their arms as they passed by. Jews were forbidden to enter parks or other places of leisure, but they took no notice of him, taking photos of each other chattering loudly amongst themselves.

He looked up to heaven, thanking whoever was responsible for his blond hair and blue eyes, then turned to stare unseeing at the Ferris wheel to ponder his dilemma, but could not concentrate, as there was the ever-present fear that someone, perhaps a neighbour, might recognise him. He stood and quickly walked away, heading towards the Haganah training centre.

Arriving at the centre, he found Saul teaching a group of youngsters basic defensive moves. Saul spotted him standing by the door, and told one of the pupils to take over, then strode over to his friend.

'Why are you looking so glum? I thought you would be well on your way to London by now?'

Manny told him about his meeting at the British Embassy. 'Now I have nowhere to stay, and I can't go back to Dr Wiez.'

'You can stay at Schischnigg.'

'What! The Zionist camp? No thanks.'

Saul laughed. 'Are you afraid of a few Zionists, or afraid of becoming one?'

'I told you before. I don't want to go to Palestine. I don't want to dig ditches, build walls or mud huts. I want to finish my education.'

Saul held up his hands in surrender. 'OK, OK, so you don't want to be a Zionist.' He slapped Manny on the shoulder. 'Come, let's find you a place to sleep.'

Saul was helping Manny stow his gear when suddenly there was a sound of racing engines. Manny rushed to the window as an open-topped staff-car and lorry raced into the camp, stopping in a cloud of dust outside the Zionist office. Soldiers leapt from the rear of the lorry to stand in a line across the road. Their officer and a man in a leather coat and fedora hat, its brim low over his eyes, alighted from the car. The officer straightened his tunic and the two men entered the office. The soldiers dispersed amongst the buildings.

Manny turned to his friend in alarm, wondering if they're looking for him. 'What are the Gestapo doing here?'

Saul smiled wryly. 'Don't worry, they aren't looking for you, they're looking for money, or any other valuables we might have.' He placed a finger to his lips just before two soldiers entered their room.

After searching the room, opening drawers and cupboards, throwing their contents everywhere, the soldiers left.

'How often do they do this?'

Saul shrugged his shoulders. 'Whenever they're in the mood. We're lucky today, they usually come at night, preferring to wake us at three or four in the morning and keep us standing out in the cold while they searched the place. They sometimes wake us just for the hell of it.'

'Do they find anything?'

Saul burst into hysterical laughter, eyes sparkling through his spectacles. 'No, they're too stupid, they couldn't find it if it were under their noses.'

Saul jeered at the Gestapo as they drove away empty-handed.

Chapter 4

30 September 1938

MANNY leaned nonchalantly against the wall opposite the British Embassy, waiting patiently, with a slight feeling of apprehension in the pit of his stomach. He gave a slight smile as she appeared, nodding at the sentry as she walked through the gates, stopping for a moment to pull up the collar of her coat against the cold, and then walked on.

Manny moved away from the wall, crossing the street on a converging course. 'Good evening, Miss Withers.'

She looked round, a startled look on her face, right hand going to her throat. 'You scared the living daylights out of me. What do you want?'

'I'm sorry to have scared you, but I need a favour.'

She came to a halt. 'Look here, Mr Grenfeldt,' she said angrily.

'Manny.'

She ignored the interruption. 'If it's a visa you want, I couldn't get it for you.' She turned to walk away.

Resting a hand on her arm, he stepped in front of her, eyes looking intently into hers. 'Could I buy you a coffee? I'm not asking for any preferential treatment where the visa was concerned. As I said – I need a favour.'

'What sort of favour?'

'Can we discuss it over a coffee?'

She looked towards the Embassy, then back at him. 'OK, there's a little café around the corner.'

Once they were seated and had given their order, Manny said quietly, 'I need a package sent to an address in London via the Embassy mail.'

She leaned towards him, 'What! Are you mad? You accost me outside my place of work and then have the

audacity to ask me to send a package through diplomatic…'
She looked into his eyes and hesitated. The anger leaving
her face and voice as she looked around the café, she turned
back to him, and shook her head. 'It's against the rules. No
one but Embassy staff could send or receive mail through
the diplomatic bag.'

'Miss Withers, please.' He took her hand between his.
'If I send it through the normal postal service the Nazis
would confiscate it.'

'I sympathise with your problem, but—' She looked
down at their hands, gently taking hers away as the waitress
brought their coffees.

'It's nothing illegal, but what…' He looked away and
then back to her – playing with the salt pot for a moment
and then continued. 'When my parents died,' he said
sombrely, 'they left something for my sister and brother,
who as you know are in London. It might be many months
before I'm able to leave Vienna, if at all. If this package
was sent via your Embassy mail they would receive it.' He
covered her hands with his again. 'I'll pay for the postage
and your trouble. If you say no, I'll understand, but you're
my only hope.'

She stared thoughtfully at him, the pupils of her eyes
seeming to change colour. The sweet delicate smell of her
perfume filled his nostrils, he wanted to lean over and kiss
her, but didn't.

Taking her hands from his, she picked up the cup and
took a sip of coffee. She looked at him over the rim, then
placing it carefully onto the saucer, picked up her handbag
and opened it. She took out a pen and piece of paper, and
began writing. 'This is my address. Bring your package
here at eight o'clock tonight.' She smiled. 'Thanks for
coffee.' She stood and walked away.

Manny's gaze followed her as she left the café, thinking
how beautiful she was, and for a moment wondered what
she would have done if he had kissed her. He was happy

that she was going to do as he asked. The papers would be safe in his uncle's hands.

*

Later that evening, he stopped outside her apartment block, wondering why she wanted him to bring the package to her flat. He could have given it to her earlier outside the Embassy, or at the café. He nodded agreeing with his next thought, realising that they might have been seen, and that would have meant awkward questions being asked.

Climbing the stairs to her second-floor apartment, he felt quite excited at seeing her again. A bunch of roses in his right hand, and the package under his arm, he knocked on the door.

She opened it with a smile on her face. 'Come in.' She stepped back for him to enter.

'Well I was—' Manny hadn't intended staying, just giving her the package and go, but he couldn't be rude and not accept the invitation as she's doing him a big favour. He handed her the flowers as he moved into the hallway, waited for her to close the door, and then followed her into a living come dining room.

'Thank you, that's very thoughtful of you. I won't be a moment, make yourself comfortable while I put these in water.' She pointed to a settee, turned and disappeared into what he presumed was the kitchen.

Manny was still pondering whether to stay or go. One half of him wanted to stay the other to hand over the package and leave. 'I can't stay very long, Miss Withers.'

She poked her head around the corner of the door. 'Joan, will do Manny.' She disappeared again, but within seconds entered the room carrying a vase with the roses placing it on top of a sideboard.

'Would you like a drink?'

'Coffee would do nicely, thank you.' He didn't mean to say that, just excuse himself and go.

She pointed once more to the settee against the wall. 'Sit and relax while I make the coffee.' She disappeared once more into the kitchen, appearing a few minutes later with a tray, two cups of coffee and a plate of biscuits.

He smiled as she handed him the cup. 'Thanks.'

Joan made herself comfortable at the other end of the settee, legs drawn up under her.

Taking a sip of coffee, she pointed a finger at the package he was still holding. 'Is that the package you want me to send to London?'

'Yes.'

Setting the cup and saucer onto a small, glass-topped table beside her, she took the package, placing it next to her coffee and then moved closer to him. 'Tell me more about yourself.'

He smiled but didn't reply, instead asking, 'How long have you been in Vienna?'

'Two months.'

'Have you made many friends?'

She shook her head, lips drawn in a tight line. 'I'm afraid the Viennese are not at the moment in a friendly frame of mind. Most of the Embassy staff had partners, or are a little too old for me.'

Manny felt at ease by her closeness as she asked, 'If you're at school in London, how come you're here now?'

He looked at her and started talking, sometimes stopping with emotion as he told her all that had happened to him. Although his eyes were moist and speech solemn, his eyes wandered now and again to the blouse, the top buttons undone revealing her breasts as she leaned forward, wondering if she had done that on purpose and noticing how her closeness was arousing him.

'Your German's very good,' he said, adding, 'Where's your home in England?'

'I was born and raised in Leeds.'

'You don't have a Leeds accent.'

'Thanks, my elocution lesson seemed to have paid off. My grandfather was a German prisoner in the last war. He decided to stay in England, met my grandmother and the rest as they say is history.

'I left Leeds to get away from the norm, see the world and enjoy myself before settling down to have a family. So I took the train to London, joined the Foreign Office as a secretary, received a promotion, and here I am.'

He couldn't help himself as the urge to kiss her was now stronger than ever. Moving closer, he placed his right hand around her waist and kissed her. She didn't resist, wrapping her arms around his neck in response.

There was a hunger in their kiss, of two people needing the closeness of another and a moment of tenderness.

He kissed her neck, and then back to her lips, his hand sliding down till reaching a small round breast, caressing it, feeling the nipple harden. Their kisses become more passionate as his hand slid down her body to caress the inside of her thigh; halted for a second then continued its upward journey. She uttered a sigh of pleasure as his fingers found their objective, their kisses becoming more demanding until Joan pulled slowly away saying breathlessly, 'Please, wait a moment.'

She took his hand, kissed him on the lips saying huskily, 'Come with me,' leading him into the bedroom where for a split second they stood facing each other and kissed, a gentle, lip-caressing kiss. Then, as if by mutual consent pulled away and undressed, until they were standing unashamedly naked.

He touched her breasts. 'You're so beautiful,' he whispered and leaned forward to kiss her left breast. He didn't know how, but they were now on the bed and gently exploring each other's bodies, Joan gives a moan of pleasure as he slowly entered her. Their movements were slow at first, hips moving in rhythm, which became faster until, like a dormant volcano, they erupted as one. They lay, arms around each other, no words spoken, just soft kisses.

Joan pulled slightly away. 'Can you stay the night?' she whispered.

He stroked a tress of hair away from her face and kissed her eyes. 'Wild horses couldn't pull me away.'

*

Manny and Joan saw as much of each other as possible. He found her an inventive lover. There wasn't a place in the apartment they hadn't made love. She tried to obtain the visa he so desperately needed, knowing that every day he would be in danger of being recognised and taken away.

Although his file was still waiting for the police report, it was now in the Embassy's system, but Joan didn't have the power to find it.

They met at her apartment every weekend, but during the week he lived with Saul and the other Zionists at Schischnigg. Sometimes Manny and Joan ventured out to the other side of the city. They would sit at a café or walk hand in hand, laughing, kissing, and enjoying each other's company. They took a chance and went to Prata, and Reinsert, and in a fit of joyous madness took a ride on the giant Ferris wheel.

Manny wondered if at last things might be returning to some form of normality, as random violence and vandalism of Jewish property had died down. It seemed the Nazis had come to realise that if they were going to appropriate Jewish property for themselves, it was in their best interests if the property was undamaged.

Now and again the SS and Gestapo raided Jewish homes. It was an uneasy peace. At the Café Costner members of the Nazi party and SS played cards with Jewish customers.

Saul said to Manny, 'Some refugees had tried to get out on their own, but very few were getting past the border guards.'

This was valuable information, as Manny was toying with the idea of escaping to Switzerland, even though it meant leaving Joan. The short winter days made it an ideal time to try. He knew the terrain around the Austrian and Swiss Alps from family skiing and mountain climbing holidays. If he waited until the warmer weather, he might never be able leave Austria.

*

It was a little before four o'clock in the afternoon of 10 November before Manny could get away from the Zionist office, taking the bus to Albert Grasse in District Eight, where Joan's apartment was situated.

Manny frowned: there was a lot more people than usual on the streets, talking loudly, gesturing, and pointing in various directions.

Above the noise of the bus's engine could be heard a hubbub of sound that grew louder and louder. Suddenly, the bus was surrounded by men and women, even housewives carrying small children, all brandishing a variety of weapons. Their faces deformed into ugliness, eyes gleaming like demented madmen, their voices swelled into a crescendo of sound as they chanted over and over again, '*Juden rouse, Juden, Juden* Christ killers, *Juden* we're coming for you, *Juden, Juden.*'

The bus begins to move, but the driver stopped looking up at the roof of a factory building to his right. Manny like the others followed his gaze. A group of men and women had a woman spreadeagled between them, their faces masks of delight, as they swung her backward and forward and then suddenly let go. She flew screaming through the air like a human arrow and plunged to the ground.

No sooner had he closed the door to the apartment, than Joan was in front of him, eyes and cheeks wet from crying. 'Oh! Manny, I thought you would never get here.' She placed her arms around him, smothering his face with kisses.

'Do you know the streets are crowded with people doing the most atrocious things to Jews?'

'Yes I know. It began last night in Germany. It's a pogrom against the Jews of Germany and Austria. Please, Manny stay here till this blows over. Don't go out again,' she pleaded. 'I telephoned the Embassy and told them that I'm not feeling well. I don't have to return to work till Monday.'

'You could get into a lot of trouble if I stayed.'

'If someone recognised you, they'd kill you. Please stay here.'

Manny could see the fear for his safety on her face and voice, and knew she was right. He nodded. 'OK, I'll stay.'

She kissed him passionately on the lips. At least the weekend would not be a boring one.

*

The next morning Manny telephoned Saul. 'What's happening? The whole of Vienna seems to have gone mad.'

'Last night,' said Saul, 'in what seemed to be a coordinated attack, mobs rampaged throughout Berlin and Vienna, running riot against Jews and Communists. The Nazis have named it Kristallnacht, because of the amount of glass broken. I hear Goering is fuming; he said the rioters should have killed more Jews and broken less glass as most of the replacement glass must be imported and paid for in scarce foreign currency.'

In the weeks following the Kristallnacht, Jews from all over Austria were rounded up and transported to concentration camps.

Manny and Saul were as usual at the Haganah training centre, now situated in the synagogue hall, as their usual training facility was by this time a pile of ashes, having been torched three nights ago.

'I'm surprised your affidavit hadn't been processed yet,' Saul said with a grunt as he tried to throw Manny onto the floor.

'I was at Westbahnhof Station yesterday and saw the Kindertransport train leaving for England. Ouch! I'm young enough to be on that train. I don't know about you, but I feel like a caged animal, and Vienna's my cage.'

'You have Joan.'

Manny face brightened with a smile. 'Yes, I have Joan.'

'Can't she help you?'

'She's tried, but...' Manny hesitated. '... To tell you the truth my papers are not in order. There's one missing.'

'Let's call it a day,' said Saul. 'Why have you waited so long? What's missing?'

'Police,' was the clipped reply.

Saul shrugged his shoulders. 'So go down there and get it?'

Manny told his friend about the time he tried to bribe the travel agent and landed in a police cell. 'My father gave them money to release me. I'm not sure if I'm on their records or not. I've been too scared to go there, especially now.'

'Why now?'

'The policeman I have to see about the document is Sergeant Eisenbrüchmann. He used to be a nice, amicable policeman, but as soon as Hitler came to power he changed, donned a Nazi armband and overnight became a Jew-hater. I'm sure he would never give me the document I need.'

'I see.' Saul looked thoughtfully at Manny, and then said, 'Forge the documents.'

'How? I don't know any forger.'

'Yes you do.'

Manny frowned. 'You're crazy, how would I know anyone like that?'

'You know Isaacson. He was the man who forged our documents. He's the best forger in Austria,' smiled Saul.

'Any idea how much he would charge?'

'I don't know. You'll have to ask him yourself. He's at the office as we speak.'

That afternoon, Manny asked Isaacson how much he would charge to forge the police document that he needed.

The forger replied, 'A three-course meal with wine will do nicely thank you.'

*

That night as they lay close, arms around each other, the perspiration from their lovemaking still on their bodies, Manny said, 'They're rounding up more and more Jews every day.'

He disengaged his arms and leaned on one elbow, looking down at Joan stroking a strand of hair away from her face. 'I must get out of Austria. I don't want to leave you, but if I don't go, then one day someone will recognise me and I'll get caught. If I'm with you when that happens, you'll be in serious trouble with the authorities. I care too much for you to let that happen. So I've two options.'

'And they are?'

'I could forge the police document, or try and get into Switzerland without them.'

'Both are dangerous if you're caught.'

'Which would you choose?'

'That's easy, forge the documents. It's a much more comfortable ride to England and London than climbing the Alps.'

'And if I get caught,' Manny said philosophically, 'it's a concentration camp.'

'It's that, even if you don't try,' she said, rolling on top of him and kissing his right nipple and then the tip of his nose as his hand slid between her thighs.

'I'll go for the forgery,' he said, just before her mouth engulfed his.

Two weeks later, Joan cooked Isaacson his three-course meal with wine.

As the bells rung throughout Vienna to herald in the New Year, Manny handed Joan his forged police documents.

Chapter 5

'E VERYONE'S talking about Germany's invasion of Czechoslovakia.' Manny said to Saul, as they entered the synagogue for the Shabbat morning service.

'I heard the population booed and hissed as German troops marched into Prague, and when Hitler appeared they sang the Czech national anthem,' Saul said quietly as they sat in their usual seats.

The rabbi wagged a finger for Manny to come to him. Wondering what he wanted, he strode over to him.

'Manny, I've been told that your papers were ready at the British Embassy. You must collect them as soon as possible, as you leave for England on Tuesday.'

Manny could hardly contain his excitement; he thanked the rabbi and moved quickly back to Saul, whispering the good news. Throughout the service he couldn't stop smiling, knowing that he'd soon be with his family in London, but the mood changed at the thought of leaving Joan.

The service over, Manny and the other congregants left the synagogue. Suddenly, four trucks and an open-topped car screeched to a halt in front of them. German soldiers leapt from the rear of vehicles surrounding the congregant's rifles aimed at them, while others ran into the synagogue, pushing those still inside out into the street.

A thirteen-year-old boy, who was barmitzvah'd the week before, ran defiantly at a soldier pushing his mother with the butt of a rifle. The young boy was no match for the hardened trooper, who tossed him to the ground like a ragdoll and shot him. There was a scream like a wild banshee from the boy's mother as she broke away from the soldier holding her and ran towards her son. A shot rang out and she fell to the ground, tried to stand, another shot. She gave a sigh, arm outstretched towards her son blood seeping down her back onto the ground.

At the same time, three men, thinking the soldiers were distracted by the boy and his mother, ran in separate directions trying to escape. There was a fusillade of shots. The escapees are dead before their bodies hit the ground and the thought of escaping left Manny as quickly as it came.

An SS-Hauptsturmführer, the death's head emblem above the peak of his cap, stepped from the car. 'Filthy Jewish dogs get into the trucks,' he yelled. 'If you disobey or hesitate you'll be shot, *Rous* scum.'

'We must try and escape,' Manny whispered to Saul as they're herded towards the vehicles. A rifle butt slammed into Manny's back. 'Shut you're fucking filthy mouth, Jew bastard,' yelled a soldier, pushing Manny towards a lorry. '*Rous*, Jew.'

Two soldiers sat by the tailgate of the lorry as it moved off, their rifles resting across their knees. Manny, who's the last into the lorry, looked back along the road and unconsciously placed a foot onto the tailgate trying to think of a way to escape without being shot. Suddenly he felt the cold muzzle of a rifle against the side of his temple.

'Jew – please jump,' a voice pleaded.

Manny swallowed nervously turning slowly to face the soldier, the muzzle of the rifle now pointing at the middle of his forehead, and looked directly into the German's hard brown deep-set eyes that stared unblinkingly at him, the mouth drawn into a tight grin.

Quietly, trying not to show fear, his speech deliberately placed, with just a hint of a smile on his lips, Manny said, 'I wasn't going to jump. I'm steadying myself against the jolting of the lorry otherwise I might fall out.'

The soldier laughed, taking the muzzle away from Manny's forehead. 'You Jews have an answer for everything. Where you're going you won't have time to breathe, let alone talk.'

'Where are we going?' Saul whispered hoarsely, not able to control his body from shaking.

'Mauthausen Concentration camp,' sneered the other soldier.

Manny couldn't believe it, the very morning he had been told his papers were through and that he could leave for England he was on his way to a concentration camp. He had to escape, or somehow get a message to Joan.

Manny's heart sank as the trucks passed through the gates, and for the first time he saw the bleak, dark, dank, formidable granite walls of Mauthausen.

Saul looked despairingly at Manny as the lorry came to a halt and was immediately surrounded by Waffen-SS, their machine pistols and rifles pointing at them, shouting incessantly at the prisoners as they left the trucks in a crescendo of noise.

Some, who were too slow, were beaten with rifle butts or kicked. If they fell to the ground they were beaten till they got up, or lay dead in a pool of blood. Manny noticed there were no women in the group; they were probably taken somewhere else.

'*Juden* scum, line up along the wall,' shouted an SS-Rottenführer. Again, those that were too slow were pushed in the back, slapped or punched.

The SS-Rottenführer ran up to Glikman, a neighbour of Manny's, and punched him in the face. 'Shithead, I didn't say lean on the wall.' He punched Glikman again and again until he fell to the ground and then shot the helpless man in the head, and without another look, turned and walked nonchalantly along the line yelling, '*Juden* scum, you're all nobodies, a nothing. You're lower than a worm in the ground and as worthless as shit. Take off your clothes.'

'What! You mean right here?'

Manny knew the man. He was Zimmerman the diamond merchant. Before he could blink an eye, an SS-Schütze (private) kicked Zimmerman in the groin. The merchant doubled over from the blow.

'You don't speak to us, phlegm of a whore,' the SS-Schütze yelled, knocking Zimmerman to the ground with a blow to the back of the head with a cosh. While he was on the ground two other soldiers joined in. The jeweller tried to protect himself against the kicks and blows raining down on him until, unable to fend them off any longer, he resigned himself to the inevitable; giving a loud sigh, he died.

It began to rain as they silently undressed, and for the first time saw the inmates in their striped prison garb. Two of them stripped Glikman carrying him away, while two others did the same to Zimmerman. Manny noticed one of them taking something from the dead jeweller's jacket pocket, placing it in his mouth. The prisoner, seeing Manny looking at him, raised a finger to his lips and shook his head. Manny turned to face the front as the dead merchant was carried away.

Standing naked in the freezing rain, his mind was as numb as his body, he didn't know how long they stood there, but it seemed like an eternity.

Suddenly the SS-Rottenführer (corporal) yelled, 'Shit head slime, pick up your clothes and place them on the tables over there.' He pointed to a line of tables some yards away and smiling grimly added, 'And then you can shower, and we will give you some new clothes.'

Twenty minutes later, head shaved, sprayed with disinfectant and showered, Manny was given his prison clothes – a blue and white-striped cotton-twill suit with a yellow Star of David and wooden shoes. He still couldn't believe this was happening to him as he sat in front of an inmate who painfully tattooed a number on his arm, and then ordered him to line up with the others.

*

As darkness descended, Manny was tired, cold and hungry. He hadn't eaten since early morning; it was still raining and becoming colder by the minute. He chanced a glance in Saul's direction, whose thin body was shivering uncontrollably.

A stony-faced SS-Hauptsturmführer (captain) appeared with an SS-Unterscharführer (sergeant) either side of him, slapping a riding crop in his leather-gloved right hand against the palm of his left. The green angry eyes seemed to look directly at each prisoner as he paced up and down the line, slapping his crop portentously against his thigh. He suddenly stopped and turned to face them, saying menacingly through thin lips. '*Juden*, I'm your worst nightmare. My name is SS-Hauptsturmführer (Captain) Conning.' He paused to look along the line as he took a gold cigarette case from his tunic pocket, opened it, extracted a cigarette and lit it with a gold lighter. He rolled back his head, exhaling the smoke skyward, and then continued pacing along the line.

'In the future, you'll look down at the ground, when you're spoken to by a member of the superior Aryan race.' He suddenly, for no reason, lashed the riding crop across the face of a prisoner in front of him, and then continued as if nothing had happened, '—and call them by their rank or Herr.' Once again he slashed the hapless prisoner across the face, opening the skin. 'Do I make myself clear, you pathetic excuse for vermin?' Everyone immediately looked down at the ground as Conning struck the man again. 'Do I make myself clear, *Juden* bastards?' he yelled.

'Yes, Herr Conning,' the prisoners chorused.

Conning struck the man with his fists. 'I cannot hear you.' His voice was now an octave higher as he hit the man again and again while Manny and the others shouted as loudly as they could. 'Yes, Herr Conning, we understand,' hoping the SS-Hauptsurmführer would stop beating the prisoner.

Breathing heavily from his exertions, Conning gestured for the SS-Unterscharführers (sergeants). With sinister smiles on their faces, the two men moved forward beating the hapless man with their coshes until he laid unmoving, eyes wide in death. They gave him a final kick and rejoined their officer.

'Your life belongs to me,' a breathless Conning said, stamping out his cigarette and then took off his blood-soaked gloves dropping them onto the ground, brushed some imaginary speck of dust from his sleeve, straightened his well-fitting tunic, and once again paced up and down looking at each prisoner, their heads bowed.

'You're a nothing, a nobody, a no name, just a number,' he sneered, looking along the line, slapping the crop against his boot and saying arrogantly, 'I can assure you that no one has ever left Mauthausen alive.'

Manny's heart grew cold, suddenly realising that not only was he deprived of his name, but he was an anonymous, nameless entity. He looked down at the wooden shoes his mouth forming a determined line saying to himself, *I'll escape from here, how, I don't know yet, but I will somehow find a way.*

His legs ached and his feet were numb from the cold, but he dared not move them. Those prisoners who had stamped their feet, or waved their arms to get some circulation into them had been promptly beaten. He could see one of them out of the corner of his eye lying motionless on the ground, and heard the whimpers of others.

There was a sudden shout of '*Juden Rous*,' then quietly, 'Follow me, you can look up now.' The prisoners obediently and silently followed the man, another prisoner, into a barrack, where they were given watery turnip soup, a little potato and a piece of rye bread.

Manny and Saul sat close together, obtaining warmth from each other's bodies. 'We must get out of here; otherwise we're going to die here,' Manny whispered.

'I agree,' Saul replied, whispering back. 'But how?'

'Would you like some more soup?'

Manny turned to look at the man who knelt in front of him. It was the prisoner who had taken something from poor Zimmerman's pocket. Manny went to hold out his bowl.

'Leave the bowl where it is,' the man ordered quietly, moving closer, hiding the metal jug from the other prisoners as he poured half its contents into Manny's bowl and the other into Saul's.

'Thank you. What's going to happen to us now?' Manny asked.

'At the moment you're in a quarantine barrack.'

'I need to get a message to someone,' Manny whispered.

'Impossible. Forget it, unless you have some money or jewellery as a bribe, and even then there are no guarantees that the message will get through.'

Manny placed his hand down the front of his trousers. 'Will this do?' He handed the man his gold barmitzvah ring with a diamond in the centre.

'How did you manage that?' Saul asked.

'Call it magic,' Manny replied with a smile. 'Could you help me get a message out?'

The man looked at the ring. 'I'll try. Who's the message for?'

'Joan Withers at the British Embassy. Tell her I'm here, she'll know what to do.'

The man nodded and turned to leave.

'Could you tell me about this place, and what we must do to survive and escape?' asked Manny.

The man half-turned back. 'Here it's every man for himself. Have no friends. It's better to be alone and trust no one, because your friend may betray you for just a crust of bread. All you could do was surviving one day at a time, Escape?' The man's face was a grim mask. 'The only way to escape was to die. I'm only helping you this once because you kept silent.'

'What's your name?' Manny asked.

The man stared at Manny as if he were mad. 'I haven't been asked that for some time.' There was a slight tremor in his voice. 'It's Daniel Krantz.'

Manny pointed at his friend. 'Saul Fleischmann.' He held out his hand. I'm Manny Grenfeldt.' Krantz didn't shake hands, but patted Manny's arm and left without another word.

*

After five weeks of hauling stones for eleven hours a day up the stairs of Wienergraben Quarry – called The Stairway of Death by the prisoners – Manny's body had become lean and muscular. How long that would last on the meagre rations the prisoners were getting he didn't know. Sometimes, but not often enough, the kitchen smuggled extra food into the barracks.

Manny learnt very quickly how best to survive the hardships and brutality of Mauthausen, especially to avoid working on the wagons that hauled heavy loads up the quarry slope.

Those wagons had twenty prisoners pushing at the front; ten either side of a metal bar that ran through the front section of the wagon, and twenty men pushing from the rear. When the wagon neared the top of the slope, those prisoners at the rear were whipped and beaten on the back of the legs by the SS-guards, who laughed and joked, having bets on how long the prisoners would last before they were unable to sustain such punishment and fell to the ground, making it impossible for the men at the front to hold such a heavy load. They, with the wagon, hurtled to the bottom of the quarry to be crushed to death by the heavy stones. The injured didn't survive either, as the guards killed them.

Manny and Saul hauled the heavy stones in a hod strapped across their shoulders and chest by strong webbing. Every day there was the constant threat of being beaten or killed. Insults, humiliation and harassment were part of the day's routine. The camp was an arena of violence. The SS-guards and their officers were ex-jailbirds or thugs from the slums of Germany and Vienna. Their cruelties knew no bounds, having no inhibitions as they enacted and fulfilled every barbaric and sadistic thought each day at their will; having absolute power over life and death, pain or relief from pain. The prisoners, the recipients of these acts, lived in terror of punishment for transgressions they committed, or had been deemed to commit.

Manny was amazed by Saul's strength. His thin, wiry frame carried rocks weighing two or three times his own body weight. But, from the very first day in the quarry, and for some unknown reason, an SS-Rottenführer (corporal) named Edschmidt, with a mole on his right cheek and greasy, spotted complexion, picked on Saul, going out of his way to continually insult and abuse him, yelling at the top of his voice at Saul wherever he was. 'Hey 147212, your number was as long as your nose. I'm going to watch you die, there's going to be no quick way out for you, or parachutist wall.' He laughed. 'How did your whore of a mother get that nose through her fanny?'

*

One night, after Saul had received more than his share of insults and beatings by his tormentor, he said to Manny, 'I don't think I could take much more. I'm getting weaker every day. I would like to strangle that bastard before I go.'

'Saul, you mustn't do anything foolish. I'm sure my message got through to Joan. You have to keep going until we find a way of escape.'

'We've been here five weeks and haven't heard anything. What makes you so sure she received the message, or could do anything to help us if she had?'

'I believe she had,' Manny said with conviction, trying to keep his friend's spirits up. 'Things would be different in a week or two, you see.'

'Manny I want you to promise me something,' his friend said quietly.

'What?'

'If you get out of this hellhole, you must promise that you would go to Palestine and plant a tree for me.'

'Don't be stupid, you'll get there yet and plant a whole forest.'

Saul grabbed Manny's arm. 'Promise me,' he said earnestly.

Manny didn't like what he was hearing. It was as though his friend had given up, which wasn't like him. 'I promise, but—'

Saul leaned over and kissed him on both cheeks and smiled. 'Thanks.'

*

The next day Saul's tormentor was off duty, and he was in better spirits and joking with Manny. 'You're so skinny; if you stood behind a post the guards couldn't see you.'

But the following morning, as soon as Saul entered the quarry, Edschmidt was immediately by his side, leaning over him.

'Big nose, did you miss me yesterday?'

Saul tried to ignore him as he picked up a large stone.

'You could carry more than that,' Edschmidt yelled, bringing his truncheon down on Saul's back and pointing to a larger piece of granite that weighed well over two hundred pounds. 'Jew bastard, son of a whore, you worthless piece of shit, pick it up.'

Manny had a feeling of trepidation that clutched at his heart on seeing the look of hatred in Saul's eyes. Lips draw tightly together in a slightly grim smile as he slowly picked up the large piece of granite, he held it against his chest, then turned to face his tormentor, who was still yelling abuse at him. Saul straightened his back and suddenly lunged at Edschmidt. They fell to the ground with Saul on top.

'You Nazi scum, you'll never see me die.'

Manny didn't know how, but Saul lifted the rock into the air smashing it down onto the SS-Rottenführer's head, screaming, 'The only son of a whore is you, do you know who your father was?' He dropped the granite once again onto the Nazi's head, and was about to lift the rock once more when a shot rang out. Saul dropped the rock, which landed on the lifeless Edschmidt's already battered face. Blood spread across the back of Saul's shirt as he slowly got to his feet, turned and smiled at Manny, who heard the impact of the second bullet before the sound of the shot. Saul tried to say something, but fell to the ground. Manny quickly knelt beside him, thinking he was dead, but Saul gripped his sleeve uttering hoarsely, 'Don't forget your promise.'

A guard pushed Manny aside and shot Saul in the head.

Saul's death took all the fight and spirit out of Manny. He worked like a robot, numb to all and everything around him. The grim determination, and unrelentless desire to escape that had been strong within him since his incarceration, had disappeared.

'Oh God, what am I doing here?' he moaned to himself as he stood in Roll Call Square after another day at the quarry.

A completely drunk SS-Hauptsturmführer (Captain) Conning suddenly appeared with his mastiff held on a leash. Smiling, he turned on the nearest prisoner and hit him across the face with his riding crop until it bled, and then unleashed the dog on the prisoner. The ferocious animal pulled the man screaming to the ground, tearing an entire layer of flesh from his body, while at the same time his master beat the prisoner with the riding crop. Conning called off the dog that was gnawing at the arm of the dead inmate.

A wave of unspeakable horror and revulsion swept over Manny, to be replaced by a chilling hatred. Fists clenched tightly by his side, he wanted to rip out the dog and its owner's throat, but realised the foolishness of his thought as his face, that a few moments ago had showed despair and misery, was now set in grim determination to find a way to escape.

*

That evening as he lay on the barrack floor trying to rest, which was impossible on account of the noise in the block, someone said, 'You don't look too good, Manny Grenfeldt.'

Manny looked up. 'Daniel! What are doing here?'

'I came to tell you that tomorrow they would be transferred to my block, and you would start work with me in the kitchens.'

Manny leapt to his feet. 'How? Why?'

'Let's just say your Miss Withers had done the best she could to help you.'

Manny nodded understandingly. 'Thanks.' His heart skipped a beat; Joan knew he was there. He felt like leaping into the air and yelling at the top of his voice, but didn't.

'She knew I was here,' he whispered. He was sure that it would only be a matter of time before Joan was able to obtain his release.

*

The following day, as Daniel said, Manny was moved to another block and began working in the kitchens.

Life became easier with a little more food and warmth. Every day he remembered the promise Saul had extracted from him, but first he must escape.

Going over the wall was impossible, the fence was electrified, plus there were watchtowers with SS-guards ready to shoot anyone that approached the wall. He had thought of hiding in one of the barges that transported the granite down the River Danube but guards with dogs searched the barges before they left.

The week previously, a prisoner who had escaped was recaptured. The whole camp was awoken in the early hours of the morning and ordered to Roll Call Square. As the escapee passed between lines of guards, he was beaten with truncheons and iron bars, carrying a poster which read, 'Hurrah I'm back again'.

He was dragged up the stairs of the scaffold, where he stood for a moment looking at the sea of faces and smiled, pursing his lips in a kiss as the officer that captured him placed the noose around his neck. The prisoner began reciting the Shema: *'Shema yisrael adonai elohenu adonai echad.* Hear Oh Israel: the Lord our God, the Lord is one.'

There was complete silence in the square. Manny knew that like him, every Jew there wished they could cheer; many had tears rolling down their cheeks, while others folded their arms, slapping their hands against their bodies in silent applause at this brave act.

One man, overtaken by this show of defiance, punched his arms into the air shouting, 'Hitler's a shithead, Hitler is a bas—' He got no further as a red dot appeared on his forehead, followed by the echoing sound of a gunshot. He slowly crumpled to the ground, the smile still on his face. Everyone turned back towards the man on the scaffold, who was now swinging backward and forward, eyes bulging, as he slowly choked to death, to jeers and insults of the SS personnel.

*

Daniel Krantz took Manny under his wing, teaching him how to bake the coarse rye bread for the prisoners, and the special bread and rolls for the SS officers.

Whenever the camp commandant had guests for tea, Daniel made cream cakes and gateaux – his speciality.

Manny's nineteenth birthday was spent baking bread and cleaning the kitchen. Daniel surprised him with a small birthday cake, a rare treat. Manny wished, as he blew out the candle, that he and Daniel could somehow escape from this nightmare.

In each other's company they used their first names instead of a number, giving them a feeling of being normal amongst such unspeakable suffering and depravity.

Their stories were similar, except that Daniel was old enough to be Manny's father. Daniel and his family lived above his baker shop in Berlin. When the Nazis broke his windows and painted swastikas and other obscene graffiti on the walls and doors of the shop, Daniel decided to send his son Wilem and daughter Rivka to live with relatives in London.

He repaired the windows and defiantly carried on baking. Like Manny's father, Daniel had fought in the First World War, winning the Iron Cross, but this had no significance for Hitler's thugs.

*

Early on the morning of 2 April 1938 Daniel and his wife were arrested by the Gestapo and transported to Dachau Concentration camp where they were separated. Daniel had tried by every means possible to find his wife, not knowing whether she was alive or dead. He was transferred to Mauthausen in August 1938.

The officer in charge of the kitchens was SS-Hauptsturmführer (Captain) Willi Böhll. Manny had so far been lucky to avoid an encounter with him, although he'd seen him on a few occasions.

Böhll was a slim man with blue watery eyes under long, curling lashes that blinked whenever he was angry and yelling at the prisoners.

This unadulterated cruel person carried a birch which he used without warning and to great effect on prisoners. Thinking nothing of peeling the skin from a prisoner's face, leaving it hanging like wallpaper from a wall, or slashing the skin from an inmate's back until the flesh tore from his body, laughing hysterically as he did so, licking the blood that's dropped onto his hand, or his manicured fingers.

Daniel told Manny to avoid Böhll at all costs. When Manny asked why, Daniel's face turned red with anger. 'Manny, please just do as I say.' Manny was about to pursue the matter, but Daniel held up a hand saying, 'Böhll's bisexual, he likes men and women, although he preferred young men like you. How he had kept it from his fellow officers and superiors I don't know. My last assistant was about your age. Böhll wanted someone to clean his rooms and clothes.'

'Where's the boy now?'

'Dead, Böhll had no more use for him after he got what he wanted; the bastard killed the boy, mutilated his face and body with his birch. That's why I'm telling you to be careful. Stay away from him and be sure he doesn't see you when he comes into the kitchens.'

'I'll try,' Manny said grimly.

*

For a while Manny was successful in avoiding contact with Böhll, but how long he could keep up this cat and mouse game he didn't know.

Manny was busy cleaning the ovens and unaware that Böhll had entered the kitchen, nearly jumping out of his skin when there was a sharp pain across his buttocks and someone yelling, 'Turn around, boy, who are you?'

Manny's heart skipped a beat. Groaning inwardly, knowing immediately who it was, he turned his eyes down, seeing his reflection in the shiny jackboots of the SS-Hauptsturmführer, who placed the end of the birch under Manny's chin, lifting his head.

'I haven't seen you here before, how long have you been here?'

Manny stayed silent, surprised to find that he wasn't scared of Böhll. He tried not to yell in pain at the birch cutting into his flesh as the SS-Hauptsturmführer hit him across the shoulders, screaming into his face, 'Speak up, boy.'

For an instant, Manny stared with hatred into the Nazi's eyes, then he looked down, saying meekly, 'I don't know how long I've been here, Herr SS-Hauptsturmführer. Time means nothing. I don't know what day it is, except when it's dark it's night.'

'Mmm.' Böhll looked at him, slapping the birch against the side of his boot with a loud thwack, and then paced up and down in front of Manny. He stopped suddenly, placing the birch against Manny's left cheek. 'I need someone to clean my clothes and look after my room, you'll do nicely.' Without another word he turned and left the kitchen.

Manny's heart sank and a feeling of doom and utter helplessness engulfed him as he waited for Daniel to return from serving the commandant.

When he told Daniel what had happened, the baker shook his head, his face an angry mask of frustration. 'I'm afraid there's nothing I could do to help you.'

'I'll hide, stay out of sight whenever he enters the kitchen. Perhaps after a few days he will forget me.'

'Believe me, Böhll would not forget you, he would turn the camp upside down looking for you.'

That night, as he lay next to Daniel, Manny tried to think of a way out of his predicament. *I have to escape, it's better to die trying than wait for Böhll to kill me*, he said to himself as his eyes closed and he fell into a fitful sleep.

He dreamt that Böhll was standing over him, slapping the birch against his boot, while Manny looked up at the Nazi. Suddenly it wasn't Böhll's face but his own, their roles now reversed, and it was he who was beating the Nazi with the birch. He groaned in a restless nightmarish sleep as his and Böhll's faces kept interchanging. His subconscious mind told him that the dream was trying to tell him something, but what?

Manny was suddenly awake, leaping to his feet, eyes wide with excitement. 'My God,' he whispered in the darkness, 'it could work. It's dangerous, but what have I got to lose? Only my life.' He was breathless with excitement.

He woke Daniel, who grumbled that he should let an old man get his beauty sleep. Sitting close to the baker so he wouldn't be overheard, Manny told him his plan to escape.

The older man was instantly awake. 'You do realise what would happen to you if you got caught?'

Manny nodded. 'Yes, I also realise what that piece of garbage Böhll would do to me if I stayed here. In reality I've nothing to lose except my life.'

There was a moment's silence between the two men. Manny was the first to break it. 'Can you help me with the information I need, and could you keep Böhll of my back for a day?'

'In answer to the first question yes, but the second...' Daniel's voice trailed away, his forehead creased in thought, ignoring the sounds of the other prisoners' snoring or groaning of pain. He snapped his fingers, looking up at Manny with a lopsided grin on his face, 'Stomach ache.'

'What?'

'I'll give you something that would give you shits for the day; it would be painful.'

'I don't care, just give me a day or two to finalise my plan.' Manny laughed. 'I suppose this is what they call shit or bust.'

Daniel chuckled. 'You definitely won't be laughing tomorrow.'

For the rest of the night Daniel gave Manny the information he needed, with interruptions every now and again from Manny to clarify something. Once morning roll-call was over, all Manny had to do was to keep out of Böhll's way and finalise his escape plans.

Within minutes of drinking Daniel's concoction, Manny was running to the toilet, and by mid-morning it felt as though his insides were dropping out, but at the same time he managed to stay away from the guards and Böhll, who had come looking for him

That evening Daniel gave him something to stop the runs. He didn't ask what it was as it smelt and tasted vile.

Daniel and Manny went over the plan of escape one last time.

'Daniel, come with me?'

Daniel pursed his lips and patted Manny's knee. 'If only I could, but...' he hesitated for a second, his eyes sad and said in barely a whisper. 'What if my Miriam was still alive? I would never forgive myself if I abandon the search, and let's face it, I'm a little too old to go traipsing around Austria. You'll have a better chance of escaping on your own.'

'You know what would happen here when they found out?'

Daniel nodded.

'So why not take the chance and come with me?' Manny knew that if his escape was successful, it would mean a draconian collective punishment for all the prisoners.

'Manny, I love you like a son, and I wouldn't jeopardise his chances if he were trying to escape, so I'm damn sure I won't jeopardise yours. No, I'll take my chances.' Daniel gave a wry smile. 'Anyway, who'll bake the commandant's cakes if they kill me?'

Manny nervously waited with one eye on the entrance to the kitchen, and the other on extracting the bread from the oven. A shiver ran up his spine as Böhll entered. The other prisoners quickly looked down at the ground as he smacked the birch against the side of his right boot, ignoring everyone striding purposefully towards Manny.

'Ah! Good, you're better.'

Manny stared unafraid into Böhll's eyes. 'Yes, Herr SS-Hauptsturmführer, I'm feeling much better now.'

Böhll tapped Manny on the shoulder with the birch. 'Follow me.' He turned, and without looking to see if Manny was following, headed towards the door.

Manny glanced across at Daniel, gave a weak smile and waved. Daniel nodded and mouthed, 'Good luck,' as Manny followed Böhll out of the kitchen towards the camp exit.

While Böhll signed for his prisoner to leave the camp, a soldier manacled Manny's hands. The sentry opened the gate and saluted the officer, who returned the salute as he strode through.

Manny's guard yelled, '*Rous*, Jew,' slamming the butt of a rifle into Manny's back, forcing him to stagger forward as he followed the SS-Haupsturmführer.

Inside Böhll's quarters the guard unlocked the manacles from Manny's wrists, saluted, and left. As the door closed Böhll touched Manny's face with the birch pointing to a pile of clothes in a wicker basket. 'I'll return this evening. Make sure this place is clean and tidy and my clothes ironed.'

The watery eyes slit, voice cold, 'I warn you now, try and escape.' Without warning he smashed the birch across Manny's shoulders. 'That's just a taste of what you'd receive if you try.'

He took a step forward and grasped Manny's chin between thumb and forefinger and kissed him on the lips, then turned and walked out, locking the door behind him.

Stunned by the kiss, Manny stared with hatred at the closed door, spitting and wiping his mouth with one hand, rubbing the smarting shoulder with the other and decided to have a look around.

Böhll's living quarters consisted of a room with a brown-cloth settee and matching armchair; a table and two chairs stood against the far wall, with a well-stocked drinks cabinet next to it. The bedroom had a double unmade iron bed, a closet and dressing table.

Manny stood in front of the mirror and pulled off his shirt. There was anger on his face and a rage within him on seeing the red welt left by the Nazi's birch. Putting on the shirt, he resumed the tour. There was a separate bathroom and toilet. To the right of the front door, hidden by a cloth curtain, was a kitchenette with gas ring and a rusty kettle. Two cups hung on hooks attached to the wall above the sink. Manny smiled for the first time that day when he spotted a key on a hook by the kitchen window.

The rest of the day was spent cleaning the quarters and ironing the Nazi's clothes. Both men were the same height and about the same build, so he tried on Böhll's uniform, nodding at the reflection in the mirror. Removing the uniform, he hung it in the closet, took one last look around the quarters and then calmly waited for Böhll to return.

Manny faced the door as a key was inserted into the lock and the door opened. Böhll stood for a moment framed in the doorway, looked around the room and then entered. Without saying a word he closed the door and walked straight into the bedroom. The bed was made, shirts and uniforms hung neatly in the closet, underwear and socks folded in the chest of drawers. He nodded with satisfaction and then moved to the bathroom, gave a quick glance and then turned to Manny. 'Run me a bath, nice and hot.'

Manny bowed. 'Yes, Herr SS-Hauptsurmführer.'

Böhll took off his jacket throwing it across the settee, unknotted his tie, stripped off his shirt and dropped them onto the floor before entering the bedroom, closing the door behind him.

Having picked up the discarded clothes and run the bath, Manny knocked on Böhll's bedroom door. 'Your bath is ready, Herr Böhll.'

A couple of minutes later Böhll emerged from the bedroom, wearing a white silk dressing gown and walked towards Manny while at the same time untying the belt, letting the dressing gown slide onto the floor and stood unashamedly naked in front of Manny. Noticing Böhll's erection, he took a step back, fists clenched by his sides.

Böhll moved quickly towards him, placed a hand around the back of Manny's head, pulling it towards him. As their lips met, Manny lifted his right fist, the point of the key protruding through his knuckles and with all the force he could muster, slammed his fist into the side of Böhll's neck.

The point of the key entered the jugular, its jagged edges ripping into the artery. Blood spurted from the open wound like oil erupting from the ground. Manny pulled away from the stunned German, who tried to stem the flow of blood with his hands while at the same time, an anguished sound, somewhere between a scream and a sigh, was emitted from his lips.

The torment, fear and anger that Manny had seen and felt over the last few months, and the recent memory of the death of his friend, erupted as he swivelled his hips, stepped forward and, with all the power he could muster, slammed his fist into Böhll's body just below the ribcage.

There was a whoosh of air and frothy blood-bubbles from the Nazi's mouth as the force of the blow slammed him against the wall, a look of disbelief on his face as he slowly crumpled to the floor, blood forming a pool around him.

Manny knelt beside the Nazi, the birch in his hand, looking into Böhll's frightened eyes. 'This is for all those innocent people you've beaten and tortured.'

He lashed down on the dying Nazi's face until the skin peeled away like a flapping curtain. A gurgling noise came from Böhll's mouth instead of the intended scream as Manny whipped him again and again, until he was too exhausted to lift the birch.

Head bowed, hands limp by his side and breathing heavily, he walked slowly into the bathroom, shredding the blood-soaked prison clothes and climbed into the bath. Böhll was dead, and unrecognisable.

The curtains were drawn and the place in darkness, when a little after four in the morning, Manny left Böhll's quarters, attired in the SS-Hauptsurmführer uniform. Holding a small suitcase in his left hand, he smacked the birch, held his right against the shiny boot as he walked nonchalantly, which he didn't feel, across Access Road, passing the entrance to Mauthausen and alongside the wall until reaching the SS-garage courtyard.

Böhll's car was exactly where Daniel said it would be. He stood for a moment by the car, heart pounding like a bass drum, looking slowly along the formidable dimly lit walls, vowing that he would rather die than return here.

Opening the car door, Manny threw the suitcase onto the rear seat and slid behind the steering wheel, inserted the key he had found in the Böhll's pocket into the ignition, held his breath, saying a silent prayer and pressed the starter button, exhaling slowly as the engine fired.

Easing the gearshift into first, he let off the hand brake, lifted his foot slowly off the clutch and accelerated away from the courtyard, silently thanking Uncle Mark for teaching him to drive; smoothly changing gear he moved alongside the quarry and parachute wall, gaining speed and heading for the Swiss border and freedom.

Manny chanced a look back. A cold hand touched his heart on seeing the bleak, chilling granite walls and the huge Nazi eagle above the gate, symbolising the sanguinary, utter despair and gloom of Mauthausen.

Manny's plan was to drive in the direction of Grein, following the left bank of the River Danube, hoping the SS and Gestapo would think he was heading for Vienna. He glanced into the rearview mirror and then at the fuel gauge, seeing the needle pointing to the half sign.

Shrouded in mist, the high wooded cliffs stood silent and mysterious as he turned right at Persenbeug, its castle overlooking the Danube, and crossed the river towards Ybbs. The road narrowed, climbing steadily upward, the massive peaks of the mountains silhouetted like fingers in the moonlit sky.

Turning at the signpost for Heiflau, he impatiently hit the steering wheel in frustration as he was forced to slow down along the twisting mountain hairpin bends, the car's wheels skirting the edge of the road, which had no guard rails.

Crossing the bridge over the rushing tributary of the Enns, Manny had a close-up view of the formidable Hochtor, often used by enthusiastic climbers. A smile broke across his serious face as the road levelled out and he picked up speed, passing quickly through dark, silent towns and villages, glancing once more at the fuel gauge.

'I'm going to need petrol soon,' he said aloud.

Reaching Radstadt, he drove slowly through the town, looking for a garage, finding one at the end of the high street.

A beam of light glowed out of the darkness from under the workshop door; someone's an early riser. *At least I won't have to wake anyone*, he said to himself, braking to a halt by a petrol pump. Opening the car door, he picked up the birch and got out of the car. He stood for a moment, breathing the clear night air and then put on the cap, straightened his tunic, strode over to the garage door and banged on it.

'OK, OK, I'm coming, where's the fire?' someone shouted from inside the workshop. Manny banged impatiently on it again. 'Hey, stop that, you'll wake the whole neighbourhood, I said I'm coming.'

The door opened, the light from inside the garage spilled out into the courtyard from behind a small tubby bearded man, wiping grease from his hands with a dirty rag.

Manny whipped the birch against his right boot with a loud thwack. 'I need petrol.'

'I'm sorry, I'm closed.' He saw Manny looking into the workshop. 'I have a special job that needs to be finished this morning, that's why I'm here.'

Manny took a menacing step towards the man and leaned over him, his speech deliberate, menacing, and slowly paced, 'I-said-I-need-petrol.'

The mechanic looked for the first time at the death's head emblem on Manny's cap and his complexion turned ashen. 'Y-yess sssir,' he stuttered, and quickly walked over to the pump, unlocked it and proceeded to fill up the car.

As Manny drove away, he glanced in the rearview mirror to see the mechanic looking down at the money in his hand and then at the disappearing car. Manny smiled, he had given the man far too much, but who cared, it wasn't his money.

Passing the marked military milestones along the old Roman road, he wound down the window to let in the cool early morning air as he headed towards the Kapruner Valley. Here, the road cut into the steep, rocky mountainside, its jagged outcrop rising like huge whales' fins, the tips white with snow.

Through the open window Manny could hear a vibrating roar which grew louder and louder as the road became steeper. Having to change down a gear, he slowed down to see in the brightness of the moon the beauty of the Krimml Waterfall that cascaded downward, forming veils of foam and mist on the side of the wooded valley, the water glowing with bright rainbow colours that shimmered and change constantly as it dropped twelve hundred feet, sending up clouds of spray that for a moment hung suspended above the pine forests below. He knew from past journeys that this was the most scenic of routes, but also the most fearsome and treacherous as the road rose between steep glacial mountains, their summits sparkling like diamonds with steps of snow that hung over the edges.

Glancing once again into the rearview mirror, he allowed himself a slight smile: there was only the empty road sloping steeply downward. He changed down to second gear, gritting his teeth as the narrow road descended into a series of hairpin bends that coiled like a snake down the mountain. Letting out a sigh of relief on reaching a straight stretch, he put his foot down on the accelerator.

The rear wheels spun on the damp road and the car slid sideways, the front of the bonnet turning towards the edge of the road. He quickly counteracted the skid, crashing the gears to change down into first, and gently touched the brake, at the same time turning the steering wheel a touch to the left. The car responded, coming to a stop side-on an inch from the edge of the road. His heart beat like a trip hammer as with shaking hand he switched off the ignition, dropped his forehead onto the steering wheel, exhaling slowly from the near escape of crashing into the valley below

Before continuing, Manny decided to change his clothes. Taking the suitcase from the rear seat, he exchanged the SS-uniform for brown corduroy trousers, grey woollen shirt and jumper, tossed a dark brown raincoat onto the back seat and threw the suitcase over the edge of the mountain. He slid once more behind the steering wheel, placing Böhll's pistol in the glove compartment, started the engine and drove away, turning left at the signpost for Innsbruck.

*

As dawn streaked the sky Manny by-passed Innsbruck; he needed a respite from the tension of the escape and the constant vigil of driving on the mountain roads and decided to stop at the small elegant country resort of Seefeld in Tyrol, where he and his family had spent many happy times skiing on mountaineering holidays.

After a decent breakfast, he entered the store to change into something more appropriate for the area. Satisfied with his purchase, he threw a haversack into the boot and a white hooded anorak onto the rear seat, got behind the steering wheel and drove away from the resort.

Puffs of white cloud surrounded the summits of the ridge-topped glaciers of the Öztal Alps as once again the road zigzagged and progress was slow. Turning at the signpost for Imst, he picked up speed again on a straight stretch of road that followed the River Inn as it curved around Landeck. He changed down to take a bend as a man suddenly appeared in the middle of the road, waving him down. Manny had no choice on the narrow road but to stop, winding down the window as the man ran up to him.

'Thank you for stopping,' he said a little breathlessly. 'We've broken down; can you please give us a lift to the nearest garage so we could arrange to have the car towed? Damn thing stalled and we couldn't restart it.'

Manny had no choice but to help. 'OK, hop in.'

'Thanks, I'll just get my companion.' He ran over to a car parked at the side of the road a few yards further on, spoke to someone in the rear seat and pointing back towards Manny. The door opened and a large, bald-headed man alighted from the car.

Manny peered through the windscreen, a look of shock and disbelief on his face, gripping the steering wheel tightly to stop his body shaking, as he whispered, 'No, it can't be.' He wanted to drive away, but was frozen with fear. How could he ever forget Grübber? The red veins in the cold mountain air were prominent across the fat Nazi's cheeks and nose. Manny shivered, hoping that Grübber didn't recognise him.

Without a word, Grübber opened the rear door, throwing Manny's anorak on the floor and moved onto the seat, while his companion moved in beside Manny.

'Thank you once again for your help. I'm Stefan Shtick, my companion is Herr Bruno Grübber. I hope we aren't inconveniencing you in any way?'

'No, not at all,' Manny replied, trying to keep his voice normal, holding his left leg tightly to stop it from shaking, not giving his name, trying to smile, hoping his face didn't show his true feelings as he glanced into the rearview mirror at Grübber, whose grey lifeless eyes stared back. Manny looked quickly away, wondering if Grübber had recognised him – but then how could he, when hundreds of Jews passed through his office and Manny's hair had been dyed when they met? Shtick was saying something.

'We're staying in Imst. Herr Grübber wanted to see the eagle memorial at Pontlatzbrücke.'

Grübber was silent. A cold shiver ran down Manny's spine feeling the Nazi's eyes boring into his back. Trying to ignore this he turned to the man beside him. 'The nearest place with a garage would be Prutz. I could stop at the memorial if you like? It's on the way.'

Shtick smiled, turning to look at his companion who nodded. 'That's very kind of you, thank you.'

Manny stopped the car opposite the memorial, glanced in the rearview mirror at Grübber; their eyes met for a second, the Nazi's narrowing as he opened the door, tapped Shtick on the shoulder as he went to get out, inclining his head for him to follow.

Both men walked towards the memorial; Grübber stopped for a second, turning to stare at Manny, who was now sure that somehow the SS officer had recognised him. The two men disappeared behind the memorial.

Manny knew he should drive away, but instead took the pistol from the glove compartment and got out of the car, moving behind the front wing, the hand holding the pistol hidden from view. The coincidence of him and Grübber being at the same place at the same time had Manny thinking that for some unknown reason, this was meant to be.

He couldn't understand why, but when he first saw the Nazi he was scared but he was now calm and unafraid. The two men reappeared from behind the memorial, parting slightly as they walked towards the car. Grübber's right hand behind his back; Manny knew he had a weapon. Shtick's hands were empty as he moved away from Grübber, walking at an angle to come around the front of the car.

'Hey! Jew boy, did you think I'd forgotten you?' Grübber said with a sinister smile on his face.

Manny looked at the Nazi, glancing quickly at Shtick, and back at Grübber. 'I could never forget a piece of piss like you, or your father.'

He raised his left arm out to the side and a gold fob watch fell, swinging as it hung suspended by its chain held between the German's thumb and two forefingers.

Manny's mouth set into a grim angry line as he recognised his father's watch, and at last the puzzle of the **G** in Hans's note telling him of his father's death was now solved; it stood for Grübber. Manny's eyes stared icily at the bald-headed Nazi, and then quickly across at Shtick as Grübber taunted him once again.

'You thought that weasel Meinhoffer killed that worthless piece of shit of a father.' He smiled, swinging the watch backward and forward as he brought his right hand from behind his back, pointing a pistol at Manny. 'I thought you were coming back with more money...' He took a step forward. 'I wondered who you were driving my friend Böhll's car. Then I recognised you. I never forget snot heads like you, son of a whore. I've decided that I'm going to set you alight as I did your father. I wonder if you could scream as loud—'

Manny raised the pistol from behind the wing and fired two rounds at Grübber, then turned just in time to fire into the face of a leaping Shtick, who fell in a heap at his feet. Manny quickly turned back to fire once more at Grübber, but the German was lying face down in the middle of the road, a stream of blood flowing down the hill from under his body. Manny walked warily towards him, pistol ready in case he was playing possum. With a booted foot he turned the Nazi's body over, Grubber was dead.

*

Taking his father's watch from the dead man's hand, he walked back to the car, moving once more behind the wheel and drove away, leaving the two Nazis lying in the road and smiled grimly as a passage from the bible entered his head: *Vengeance is mine sayeth the Lord.* He looked up at the sky knowing it was a lucky shot and whispered, 'Thank you.'

A quick glance at the fuel gauge told him that he was nearly out of petrol. He wouldn't stop to refuel, but would continue till he ran out and walk the rest of the way. At least he was still alive.

Two miles from Pfunds the engine coughed, spluttered and then stopped. Manny steered the silent car behind some rocks at the edge of the road. Taking the gear he needed from the boot, he donned the white anorak, placed the pistol in its pocket and walked away from the car.

Avoiding Austrian army mountain patrols, Manny walked across the Swiss-Austrian border. A light breeze whispered through the mountains, blowing in his face. He turned to wave goodbye to the country of his birth, wondering, as he looked down the mountain, if he would ever return to see such magnificent sights as these, or climb and ski on its mountains again. He sighed disconsolately and descended towards Switzerland and freedom.

Having travelled about six miles, he stopped to have a breather; climbing onto a rock taking a bar of chocolate from his pocket, rotating his head slowly to survey the stunning scenic delights of Switzerland's untamed landscape, the breathtaking views of hills with forests of tall pine trees on its slopes with an orgy of alpine flowers. Herds of cows roamed lush pastures in the valley below as, high above, puffs of white clouds moved slowly across blue skies bordered by snow-capped mountains.

Tears filled his eyes and ran down his cheeks as he remembered those he had left behind; he fell to his knees, body shaking uncontrollably, looking up at the sky, arms outspread, letting out a scream of anguish that echoed back from the mountains around him.

At last the tension and depression he had felt for so long left his body and he rose to his feet, gathered up some snow, wiped his face and then continued his descent towards Scuol. He had been there once before with his grandfather to visit the mineral baths for his health.

Suddenly he heard his father's voice. *Go to my Swiss banker Herr Schouler at the Eisiendeln Bank in Zurich, and remember these numbers*. Manny recited the numbers as he wearily entered Scuol, heading for the railway station to catch the next train to Zurich.

Chapter 6

Zurich, 26 June 1939

FINDING a small hotel not far from the railway station in Niederdorfstrasse, and weary from his escape, Manny fell fully clothed onto the bed and within seconds was in a deep exhausted sleep.

The sun shining through the window awoke him. After a wash and breakfast, he walked the short distance to the British Embassy, giving a wry smile on entering to find the usual queue and form to fill in.

Three hours later, he sat waiting patiently for the woman, her grey hair tied into a bun, to finish reading his form. She looked up, light-grey eyes twinkling as she smiled, saying in a soft, caring voice, 'What can I do for you, Mr Grenfeldt?'

'Mrs...' He looked at the nameplate on the desk – 'Mrs Anne Reece-Davis' – and then up at her '... Reece-Davis. I need to get to London.'

'This isn't the Visa section.'

'I know. I also need a passport.'

'Oh! Is that all?' She looked at him for a moment, taking a breath, 'I'm—'

'I've just escaped from Mauthausen concentration camp,' he interrupted, continuing quickly, 'I was due to leave for London when I was arrested. Unfortunately all my papers, affidavit and passport were still in Vienna.'

Her face showed her concern. 'Oh dear! You poor boy you—'

'If you get in touch with Miss Joan Withers,' he interrupted once again, 'at the British Embassy in Vienna, she'll vouch for me, and in all probability still has my papers.'

'You know Miss Withers?'

104

'Yes.'

She stared at him for a moment, pushed back her chair picked up the forms saying, 'I won't be a moment.' She turned and left the room.

Twenty minutes later Mrs Reece-Davis returned with a big smile on her face. 'I've just spoken to Joan. Your papers and passport should be here in a couple of days. I'll have—'

'Is she OK?'

'Who?'

'Joan.'

'You'll see her in a couple of days. She's very excited about your escape, and has insisted on bringing your papers herself instead of the usual courier.'

He smiled. 'Joan's coming here?'

'That's what I said. In the meantime I'll get your travel documentation sorted out. It may take a week or two.' She pointed to the papers in front of her. 'I have your address; do you have enough money?'

'Yes, thank you.'

She patted his arm and handed him her card. 'If you need me, just call this number. You're a very brave young man. Would you like me to notify your family that you're here?'

'No thanks, I'll do that myself.' He stood and shook her hand. 'Thank you, madam, for your time and help.'

'My pleasure, I'll let you know when Joan arrives.'

While waiting for Joan, Manny located the Eisiedeln Bank and caught up with some sleep.

He was about to get dressed after having a bath, when there was a knock at the door. Wrapping a towel around his waist, he moved quickly across the room and opened the door.

'Yes—' The force of Joan hurling herself at him, kissing his eyes and lips, propelled him backward. Unable to keep his balance he fell onto the bed with her on top of him.

Between kissing his face she sobbed, 'I never thought I'd ever see you again,' but before he could reply she clamped her lips onto his once more.

Placing his hand on her shoulders and reluctantly taking his lips from hers he said softly, 'I think we'd better close the door, don't you?' Extracting himself from under her, he picked up the bag she'd dropped on the floor and closed the door, turning back to see Joan lying naked on the bed. Smiling, he stripped away the towel and returned to the bed and her arms.

*

After a bath, and something to eat from room service they lay entwined on the bed listening to the radio. Joan looked at him and said, 'I tried to get—'

He placed a finger on her lips. 'I know.'

They were silent for a while, content with each other's closeness. Manny kissed the top of her forehead. 'When do you have to go back?'

'Not for a week, I'm owed some annual leave.'

Lifting himself onto his elbow, he looked down at her, kissing the tip of her nose. 'I need your help once again.'

'If I could, I will.'

'I need a letter sent from London to Zurich, via the Embassy mail.'

'Why can't it go through the normal post?'

'It'll take too long. I need the letter and a copy of my signature from the Midland Bank in East London.' He explained about his father's Swiss Bank account. 'So you see I must get to the bank before my travel documents arrive.'

'OK, no problem, but how are you going to get a message to the Midland Bank and the letter to my office in London?'

'I still hadn't told my family that I'm safe, so when I heard that you were coming I thought I'd wait and see if you could help me before phoning them.'

'How could you ever think I wouldn't?'

He smiled sheepishly. 'You've helped me so much already; I didn't want to take advantage of you.'

Her arms went around his neck, pulling his face down towards hers. Before their lips met she said huskily, 'Before we phone your family, you can take as much advantage of me as you like.'

The shouts of joy over the telephone, Manny was sure, could be heard the other side of London. After speaking to each member of the family, Manny explained to his uncle why he needed to obtain the letters, and introduction from the Midland Bank.

'Don't you worry; it will be on its way before you can say Jack Robinson.'

*

Two days later, Manny and Joan received a message from Mrs Reece-Davis that a letter had arrived for Joan from London.

Inside the envelope was a short note from Uncle Mark, and the letters and documents Manny needed.

Arriving at the Eisiendeln Bank, Manny handed the letters to Herr Schouler's secretary, requesting an interview with him. After a short wait, they were shown into Schouler's plush office to be greeted warmly by the banker, a tall, slim man with thin blond hair. The grey cravat and white wing-collared shirt was bright against the black single-breasted jacket of his suit. The banker held out his hand.

'It's a pleasure to meet you Herr Grenfeldt and...' he looked down at the fingers of Joan's left hand, 'Miss...?'

'Withers,' Joan said smiling sweetly, as Manny took the offered hand.

Schouler gestured with his other towards two comfortable chairs in front of his desk. 'Please, sit down. How can I be of assistance?'

Schouler sat back onto his chair, fingertips making a bridge, nodding from time to time as Manny explained about the death of his parents, and that he, as the eldest member of the family, had the combination to his father's account. He pointed to the papers in front of Schouler. 'That's a copy of my father's will and his signature, and my signature and an introduction from the Midland Bank.'

'Yes, I see.' Schouler handed Manny a piece of paper. 'Please, Herr Grenfeldt, sign that.' As Manny signed, the banker said, 'I'm sure you understand, but I must check that the signature is authentic. Please return here tomorrow morning at ten o'clock.' He smiled, adding, 'With your passport.'

Manny nodded. 'I understand, Herr Schouler.' He and Joan stood and shook hands with the banker and left.

Walking hand in hand towards the hotel, Manny asked, 'What would you like to do for the rest of the day?'

'Find a decent hotel with a larger bed and a hot bath,' she replied happily.

*

At precisely ten o'clock the following morning, Manny and Joan were shown into Schouler's office.

'Everything was in order, Herr Grenfeldt,' said the banker.

Manny handed him his passport. The banker opened it, glanced at the picture and signature, and then handed it back. 'Do you want to continue with the same arrangements your father had with us?'

'Yes, please.'

Schouler pushed back his chair, stood and walked around his desk, placing a document in front of Manny, handing him a gold fountain pen. 'Sign here, please.' He pointed to a dotted line at the bottom of the page.

Manny quickly read the document and then penned his signature. 'I would like my sister and brother to have access to this account, just in case something should happen to me.'

'That could be arranged, just send me a copy of their signatures. If, and when they come here, all I need do is to compare signatures as proof of identity.' Schouler blotted Manny's signature. 'We have now completed our documentation, please follow me.'

They followed Schouler out of the office across a marbled hall, passing cashiers busy with clients, to the far corner of the bank.

'I'll wait here for you,' said Joan, as Schouler unlocked the door to a private lift with a key at the end of a long chain attached to a button of his waistcoat.

'You can come if you want.'

'No, it's better you go alone.'

He kissed her on the cheek. 'I won't be long.'

Manny followed the banker into the lift; the doors closed and they descended. Within seconds the lift came to a stop and the doors opened. Manny stepped out of the lift into a narrow corridor. Facing them was a two-foot-thick opened steel door. He followed Schouler through another door into a vault filled with numbered boxes with combination locks.

'I will leave you know, I'll be waiting outside.' The banker turned and left the vault.

Manny, his heart beating a little faster, looked around, his eyes coming to rest on the box he had been looking for; he stepped over to it, entering the combination. The box moved away from its housing. He pulled it fully out, placing it on a table in the middle of the room. For a second his hands rested like a caress on the box and then, taking a deep breath, carefully opened it.

Inside the box, neatly bound, were American dollars, English pounds, Swiss francs, a small cloth bag, and an envelope with his name on it in his father's familiar handwriting. He opened the envelope.

Dear Manfred,

If you're reading this letter, your Mother and I are no longer of this world. The contents of this box are to be shared equally between you, Hannah and Joshua.

You have been wonderful children and a joy in my eyes. Be good to your Aunt Doris and Uncle Mark. I wish you all a happy and long life.

Love, Papa

Tears rolled down Manny's cheeks at the thought of never seeing his parents again, but in his heart he knew they would always be with him. Wiping away the tears, he opened the cloth bag. Inside were six identical diamonds and another letter, this time from his mother.

My dearest children,

We've had some wonderful and happy times together. My greatest sorrow is that I'll never see you again, be at your wedding, or hold my grandchildren.

These diamonds are to be shared equally between you. I hope that you'll use them as engagement rings for my future son-in-law and daughters-in-laws.

I kiss your eyes and lips,

Mama

Manny read both letters again and then put them in his pocket. Taking a third of the Swiss francs and English pounds he closed the box, returning it into its housing. He stood motionless for a moment, hand still resting on the box as a mental picture of happy times with his parents passed through his mind.

Sighing, he turned towards the door, stopping in mid-stride, a thoughtful look on his face, running his teeth over his bottom lip. He nodded and opened the door. As expected, Schouler was standing just outside waiting for him.

'Herr Schouler, can I have a word with you please?'

Schouler nodded and followed Manny back into the vault. 'Yes, Herr Grenfeldt, what can I do for you?'

'Would it be possible to transfer everything in my box to a bank in America?'

'Why would you want to do that?' the banker said a little indignantly, a look of astonishment on his face.

Manny ignored the question. 'Can you?'

'Yes, but why? And which bank?'

'To tell you the truth, I don't know...' He entered the combination and pulled the box from its housing. 'Just a gut feeling, I really cannot tell you why.' He looked into the banker's eyes. 'Transfer it to the Bank of America.' Opening the box, taking out the cloth bag, placing it safely into the inside pocket of his jacket, he then picked up the box and walked out of the vault, followed by Schouler.

Although he smiled, Manny could see that the banker's demeanour was one of anger. Manny didn't dwell on it as he was surprised at the amount of money in the box, which added up to twenty thousand dollars.

The mid-morning sun threw their shadows onto the pavement as arm-in-arm Manny and Joan left the bank.

'You OK?' she asked.

He wrapped his arms around her waist and kissed her on the cheek. 'I am now.'

'Let's have some lunch.'

'Good idea, then I must do some serious shopping – these clothes are beginning to smell.'

Hours later, laden down with bags and boxes, Joan stopped to look longingly at a black slinky dress in the window of Bergman & Son, Couturiers.

'Would you like to try it on?' Manny asked.

'No, it's a wonderful dress, but way beyond my budget,' she replied wistfully.

'I'll buy it for you.'

Lifting the bags in her hands, she pointed a finger at a gold bracelet. 'You've bought me enough already. Let's get a taxi back to the hotel and then I will be able to thank you properly.'

Manny grinned. 'Miss Withers, I'm shocked. Are you trying to corrupt me?'

She giggled. 'Why, Mr Grenfeldt, I thought I had already.'

*

Time had flown by. While Joan was at the station picking up her ticket to Vienna, Manny was on his way to the British Embassy, having received a message from Mrs Reece-Davis that she wanted to see him.

The last few days with Joan had been wonderful. They toured the old city, sailed on Lake Zürich, climbed the tower of the Grossmünster with a distant view of the Alps, laughed and loved.

Mrs Reece-Davis greeted him with a smile. 'You look well, Zürich must agree with you. How's Joan?'

'She's fine, sends you her love.'

Mrs Reece-Davis handed him an envelope. 'Here are your tickets and travel documents. You leave on the 10.22 train on Thursday morning.'

He looked at the envelope then at her. 'Thank you very much for all you've done.' He bent kissing her on the cheek.

Her face reddened. 'Don't be silly. After all you've been through, it's the least I can do. Wish Joan a happy birthday, tell her to phone me some time, good luck.' She patted his arm and walked away, leaving Manny staring after her as she disappeared around the corner, an amazed look on his face. *It's Joan's birthday, and I didn't know it. I should have known, why didn't she mention it'*

An hour later, a smiling Manny entered their hotel room, placing a box on the floor by the door as Joan emerged naked from the bathroom. 'It must be good news.'

He held up the envelope. 'My tickets and travel documents.'

'When do you leave?'

'Day after tomorrow.' He moved towards her. 'This is our last day together till...' he shrugged his shoulders '... whenever. Let's do something special.'

'What do you have in mind?'

'Dinner at that place we saw the other day, north something or other.'

'North Star, that's dinner and dancing. I haven't anything to wear.'

He moved back to the door and picked up the box. 'You have now.'

Her eyes widened in surprise on seeing the name, *Bergman & Son, Couturiers* on the box. 'You didn't.' Unable to contain herself, she excitedly and carefully opened the box. 'Oh! Manny, you shouldn't have, it's so beautiful,' she whispered, and was about to step into the dress, but with an impish grin said, 'I'll wait till later.'

He moved closer to her, taking a round velvet box from his pocket. 'This is to go with it. Happy Birthday.'

'How did you know?' Taking the box from him, she lifted the lid. 'You're mad.' Her eyes shone with tears as he placed an arm around her waist and gently pulled her towards him.

'I'm mad – madly in love with you,' he said, just before their lips met, picked her up and carried her to the bed, quickly stripping off. 'I love every part of you,' he said, passionately kissing her mouth, and then moving down to her neck and breast. The pupils of her green eyes widened with desire as his mouth slowly slid downward.

They lay close, spent from their lovemaking. Joan moved onto her side placing her head on his chest. 'I love you,' she said, lifting her head slightly to look up at him. 'I have from the very first time I saw you in Vienna.'

He smiled, stroking a curl from her forehead. 'So you invited me to your flat and seduced me.'

'I'm pleased you did, because I love you too. What's going to happen to us now that you're returning to Vienna and me to London?'

'I have another leave in October, that's not too far away, and I'll write to you.'

'Once you're back into the glitter of Embassy life, you'll forget me. By the way, how old are you today?'

'Twenty-three.'

'What? Here am I thinking that I'm making love to an older, sophisticated woman and—'

She stopped him saying any more, grabbed the pillow and hit him over the head with it. He grabbed another, gently doing the same to her, and within seconds she was astride his waist, hitting him playfully with the pillow until he grabbed her hand and gently pulled her down towards him.

*

Two hours later, dressed in a dark-blue serge lounge suit, Manny waited in the bathroom for Joan to get ready.

'OK, you can come in now,' she called.

He opened the bathroom door. 'Wow,' was all he could say, mouth open. The thin diamante beaded straps glittered on the black, off-the-shoulder silk dress that clung to her ample breasts, fitting closely down to the waist and tapering out into a flowing skirt that ended just below the knee. She wore very little make-up, just a hint of mascara and lipstick.

'Well, what do you think?' She twirled around, the skirt billowing out.

'I'm speechless. You look absolutely stunning.'

Her face glowed with pleasure. 'Do I really?'

'Joan, you're the most beautiful woman in the world, and I love you.'

They danced till the early hours of the morning, and made love till dawn streaked the sky and Joan had to leave for the station.

*

As he waved goodbye to Joan, he reflected on the past and all that had happened to him since entering Vienna over a year ago. The violence he'd witnessed and participated in. He had seen at close hand man's cruelty to man at its most vicious. He had killed once in cold-blood, another in rage, again out of necessity. There was no regret or remorse, as the men he had killed were evil.

And amongst all that violence and fear, there was Joan. His features softened at the thought of her, and although it had been just a short time since she had left, his arms ached to hold her close and he could still smell the aroma of her perfume. Whatever the future held for him it included Joan. The train disappeared from view. He turned, head bowed. October seemed a long way away.

Manny wondered how his family would react when he told them he was in love with a non-Jewish girl; he smiled as if hearing their voices.

'This was the first girl you've known, why not a nice Jewish girl? What would your parents had said? This wouldn't happen if they were alive.'

His reply would be that both his father and uncle fell in love the instant they saw their prospective wives, so why couldn't it happen to him? He sighed, that bridge would be crossed when he came to it.

PART II

Chapter 7

VICTORIA Station was a cauldron of noise as trains arrived and departed to the south of England and the Continent. Puffs of white smoke from locomotive stacks sent smoke signals up to the blackened roof of this cavernous barn.

Hundreds of voices shouted to be heard above the noise of the Tannoy announcer, the guards' whistles and marching feet of the multitude of people that criss-crossed the concourse in their haste to be somewhere. Some wore worried frowns, anxious about being late, while others smiled, holding loved ones they had just met, or wept tears of sadness as they departed.

Children were crying, laughing, wheeled in prams, or held lovingly in parents' arms. Some sat on proud fathers' shoulders, or chatted away to their parents, trying to keep pace by running alongside them, their parents' replying automatically, 'Yes dear, I see, no, maybe later,' while their eyes were fixed firmly ahead, trying to protect their children from the oncoming rush of people.

A woman held her daughter's hand tightly, the little girl's legs working like pistons trying to keep up as they followed the porter with their luggage as he wove expertly through the throngs of people.

Platform sixteen was lined with those eagerly awaiting the arrival of the *Golden Arrow*. Porters, one hand on their trolleys, glanced at the clock and then moved towards the edge of the platform as the *Golden Arrow* appeared, blowing its whistle to announce its arrival.

Eyes moved from side to side, searching the passing carriage windows hoping to catch a glimpse of those they were here to meet. Arms waved excitedly when they spotted them; running happily alongside the carriage, weaving in and out of the bystanders and porters.

A door banged open against the side of the carriage, narrowly missing a porter as an impatient man stood with one foot on the step, balanced for a moment and then leapt from the slow-moving train heading towards the taxi rank.

Doris and Mark Grenfeldt and the three children, stood in a line along the platform, anxiously looking into the carriage windows as they passed.

'There he is, there he is,' shouted Joshua and his cousin Samuel together, racing excitedly alongside the carriage smiling and waving at Manny.

Manny stood by the carriage window, looking at the sea of faces passing by, wondering whether he would ever find the family amongst them. Two young men ran alongside the carriage, waving and smiling at him. He recognised Joshua and Samuel and waved back, turned and reached for his suitcase on the luggage rack above his head as the train comes to a halt.

He stepped from the train into the arms of a tearful Aunt Doris and Sister Hannah, while the others gathered around, engulfing him in their arms, their cheeks wet with tears.

'Come, let's go home.' Mark said, placing his arm around Manny's shoulders. 'You've grown taller young man, welcome home.'

Manny, a lump in his throat, couldn't answer, just hugged his uncle in reply.

That evening, with the family gathered around the dining table, Manny, in a voice that had to stop from time to time from emotion, related all that happened to his parents and him since leaving London. All were weeping, as one by one they retired for the night, until the only two left at the table were Manny and his uncle.

Manny stood, as did Mark, who grabbed him, holding him close, kissing his cheek, and saying softly, 'Manny, you're a brave young man, we'll talk again tomorrow.'

On Monday, 10 July the family began a week of mourning for David and Martha Grenfeldt.

Chapter 8

East London, 29 August 1939

O NCE the week of mourning was over Manny wrote to Joan, asking if she could obtain any information about Daniel, and send him a parcel through the Red Cross.

Joan replied that the Germans would not allow her near the place, or give information on any of the inmates. She was looking forward to seeing him in October.

Manny returned to school, but things weren't the same. Everything looked different, felt different, and there was a decision to be made. Should he stay on these last few months, take the entrance exam and go to university as he had originally planned, or what? Work with his uncle and become a baker?

He had been through hell and back these last few months, but the decision might be out of his hands for news reports on the radio were pretty grim. Hitler had closed the borders with Poland, demanding the return of Germany's colonies. With Britain and France reaffirming their pledge to assist Poland against any attack by Germany, it seemed that after twenty years of peace, the world might be at war again.

Manny was doing his homework, the radio playing softly in the background, when the programme was interrupted.

'This is a special announcement. At 11am today, September 3rd 1939, Britain declared war on Germany. The King will speak to the Commonwealth tonight.'

Manny stared at the radio, pen poised in mid-air, and thought of his father, Daniel Krantz, and others like them, who fought in the First World War, a war that was supposed to end all wars.

Walking home from school, he stopped for a moment to watch some workmen erecting an air-raid shelter; this was happening all over London.

*

As September drew to an end, newspapers and radio reports were about Poland now lying shattered under Germany's onslaught. Refugees who had managed to escape the Nazis arrived in London by ship and train, while Londoners stumbled home through blacked-out streets, with air-raid wardens yelling, 'Put that light out!'

Manny was worried. He hadn't heard from Joan since her last letter on 30 August. She was supposed to be home in October, and it was now the first week in November. He telephoned the Foreign Office, but they wouldn't divulge any information to him over the telephone.

Instead of going to school, he took the bus to the Strand, walking the short distance to the Foreign Office.

After a two-hour wait, something he'd grown used to, a clerk told him that as he wasn't immediate family, they were unable to give him any information about Miss Withers.

'All I want to know,' pleaded Manny, 'is has she left Austria and safe? Could you at least tell me that much?'

'I'm sorry, sir, but as I've already stated, I cannot divulge any information regarding Miss Withers to anyone other than her immediate family.'

Without another word the clerk turned and walked away, leaving Manny feeling furious. He was also angry with himself, because he hadn't once asked Joan for her parents' address. All he knew was that they lived in Leeds.

Dejected, but not undaunted, he took the bus back to school. Tomorrow he would phone Directory Enquiries; perhaps Joan's parents had a telephone.

The next morning the directory operator gave him two numbers, which he telephoned, but they didn't know a Joan

Withers. He then tried to get through to the British Embassy in Vienna, but there was no reply. In frustration he telephoned the Embassy in Zürich, hoping to speak with Mrs Reece-Davis, but the lines were constantly busy.

There was nothing left to do but write to her and ask if she knew of Joan's whereabouts.

Chapter 9

Friday, 10 November 1939

M ANNY was getting dressed for Shabbat when there was a knock at the front door. Aunt Doris shouted, 'I'll go.'

Running a comb through his hair, Manny took no notice of the voices downstairs until Aunt Doris called, 'Manny, there's someone here to see you.'

He frowned, wondering who would want to see him on a Friday night and walked out of the bedroom onto the landing, leaned over the banister looking down into the hallway below. There was a woman standing next to Aunt Doris, who turned and looked up at him.

'Joan,' he yelled, leaping at breakneck speed down the stairs, she moved forward to meet him. They embraced and kissed, a lingering, loving, longing kiss, oblivious to the amused stares of Aunt Doris, Uncle Mark, and the children looking down from the landing above.

Joan glanced sideways at Manny's aunt and uncle, and tapped him on the back to get his attention. He looked into her eyes following her gaze, slowly removing his lips from hers, but still holding her close.

'Ahmm; I'm sorry for being so rude. Aunt Doris, Uncle Mark, meet Miss Joan Withers.' He pointed to his siblings and cousin who were now on the bottom of the step, 'Joshua, Hannah and Samuel.'

Manny had told them all about Joan – well, not everything, just the part where she helped him to return to England. Aunt Doris smiled as they shook hands, saying, 'We're just about to sit down for Sabbath dinner, would you care to join us?'

Joan returned the smile. 'If I'm not intruding, I'd love to, thank you.'

During the meal, Joan described how the Embassy personnel were under constant threat. 'Our Austrian staff left as, like us, they were subjected to incessant abuse by the Nazis. We lived in constant fear for our lives. The Ambassador decided it best to evacuate everyone and their families. One night we gathered at the Embassy, and assisted by the Grenadier guards escaped into Switzerland. I returned to London three days ago, was given a new job and moved into my flat. I haven't unpacked yet.'

'I'll help you,' Manny said eagerly.

Joan smiled, her eyes showing her happiness at being with him. 'Thanks, that'll be nice.'

'Where is this flat?' Aunt Doris asked.

'Not far from here, Fieldgate Street, Whitechapel.'

Uncle Mark waved a toothpick in Joan's direction. 'Surely the Foreign Office could have given you somewhere better than Whitechapel and nearer Whitehall?'

Joan's eyes sparkled as she looked across the table at Manny, not noticing Aunt Doris, after looking from one to the other, give a slight nod as she realised that there was more than just friendship between her nephew and Joan.

'It's the only flat available, so I took it. As I'm so close to you, I thought I'd look Manny up to see if he was OK.'

Aunt Doris patted her arm. 'That's very nice of you dear. Hannah, help me clear the dinner things away and then I'll serve dessert.'

Hannah made a face, but obediently left her seat.

'I'll help,' said Joan getting up from her chair.

Aunt Doris smiled. 'Thank you dear, but you're a guest.'

'It's the least I could do after such a wonderful meal.'

'Thanks, I'm glad you enjoyed it.'

Manny stood. 'I'll help too.'

'No stay,' Aunt Doris said it more like an order. 'Joan and I can have a chat. It'll be nice having another woman to talk too.'

Manny groaned inwardly, knowing his aunt would in her charming way obtain Joan's life story. She would be no match for his aunt when it comes to extracting secrets, and it was inevitable that she would know all about him and Joan within five minutes. He should have told them before now about Joan, but hadn't. But most important of all was how was he going to explain that to Joan?

Fifteen minutes later, the two women entered the dining room carrying in the desserts, smiling and chatting to each other. Manny looked from one to the other, wishing he'd been a fly on the kitchen wall and wondering with a knot in his stomach what they had said to each other.

Joan placed the dessert on the table, looked at Manny, pursing her lips slightly in a kiss and winked. Alarmed he glanced around at the others, but they were too busy ogling the dessert to notice.

Later, as they walked hand in hand towards the bus stop, Joan said, 'I had a wonderful evening. Your family were exactly as you described them, and I love your Aunt Doris.'

'What did the two of you talk about?' he asked tentatively.

'Oh! Just this and that, women's talk mostly.' She turned and smiled at him as they reached the bus stop. 'Why don't you ask your aunt?'

He could see she was teasing him, wanting him to ask her outright what had been said, but he wasn't going to play that game – not now, maybe another time. Placing an arm around her waist he drew her closer.

'I've been worried sick about you, wondering if you're OK and where you were. The Foreign Office wouldn't help me because I wasn't next-of-kin, and like a fool I never had your parents' address. I tried getting through to Vienna, but couldn't. Yesterday I sent a letter to Mrs Reece-Davis, hoping she would know where you were, and suddenly you're here.' They kissed.

'I've been dying to do that all night,' Joan said, leaning her head against his shoulder.

'Me too.' He kissed the top of her head. 'I hope you're not angry with me for not telling my aunt and uncle about us.'

'No, I'm not angry, I'm sure that after this evening they'll know anyway.'

'What made you say that?'

'Oh! Nothing really; just call it woman's intuition.' Her bus approached the bus stop.

'I have to go to the synagogue tomorrow,' Manny said. 'I'll come over when Sabbath is over and help with your unpacking.'

They kissed and Joan boarded the bus. As it pulled away she blew him a kiss. 'See you tomorrow.'

That night, for the first time since his return, the nightmares of Mauthausen did not keep him awake.

Chapter 10

For the first time since 1914, Britain faced food rationing and the coldest winter since 1888. Manny, Joan and the family took the opportunity to skate on the River Thames, which was frozen over.

Their noses and cheeks red from the cold, Manny and Joan walked arm in arm towards her flat singing, 'Somewhere Over the Rainbow'.

'I'll put the kettle on,' said Joan as they entered the flat. Manny took her coat and hung it with his on a hook behind the door, crossed the room to stand behind her, wrapped his arms around Joan's slim waist and kissed the nape of her neck.

She turned to face him, giving him a peck on the lips and said, 'Aunt Doris invited me over for Shabbat dinner this Friday, in fact I'm going to light the candles.'

His arms dropped to his side and he took a step back – 'What?'– with a look of astonishment on his face, he made a gesture with his hands as if to say something, but the kettle came to the boil, interrupting whatever he was about to say.

Joan turned, poured the boiling water into a teapot and placed the cups and saucers onto a tray. 'I said that I'm—'

'I understood what you said – it's what you haven't said. Something's going on here. Protestants don't light Shabbat candles – well, Jewish ones anyway.' He followed her across the kitchen as she carried the tray over to the table. Dropping onto a chair beside it, she looked up at her, waiting for a reply as she poured the tea into the cups.

As she returned the teapot onto the tray, without looking up, she said, 'I'm converting to Judaism.'

'You're what? No, never mind I heard you,' he said quickly.

She knelt in front of him, arms on his knees, looking up at him. 'You remember the first day I came to your aunt and uncle's house, and you asked me what Aunt Doris and I talked about in the kitchen.'

He nodded.

'It was about my love for you. I told her that all the time we were apart I couldn't think of anything else but you. I wanted to marry you, and would convert to Judaism to do so.' She took his hand and carried on. 'Aunt Doris asked me lots of questions. How I felt about God, and my own religion, and how would my family feel about me converting. I haven't seen my family since I ran away from my father's beatings when I was sixteen.'

'You never told me about that.' He frowned. 'If I recall, whenever I asked you about your family, you always changed the subject.'

'Now you know why. Please let me continue.'

He stroked her face, bent to kiss her on the lips, but she moved her head away.

'Since that time in the kitchen your aunt and uncle have been helping me with my Hebrew, Jewish law, kosher foods, and how to cook.' She anticipated his next question. 'Yes, I've been to see the rabbi, and he's helping me as well.' She was silent for a moment. 'You haven't said anything.'

'I'm amazed, stunned and speechless, that my own family, rabbi and girlfriend should conspire to this—'

'Will you marry me?' Joan asked softly, interrupting him.

Manny was surprised by the proposal. The thought of marriage hadn't... well, not yet, not until ... He looked at her, seeing the love in her eyes and sighed. 'I love you, you know that, but what about our age difference? And I'm—'

'It hadn't bothered us before.'

'I'm going to university this year. How am I going to support you?'

Knowing in his heart it was a lame excuse, he smiled, lifting her to her feet and did an about-turn, pushing her gently onto the chair. 'Anyway, it should be me asking you, not the other way round.' Going down on one knee he took her right hand in his, he looked into her eyes and said seriously, 'Joan, I love you very much, will you please marry me?'

She leaned forward to kiss him, overbalanced and fell on top of him, saying happily between kissing his lips, eyes and cheeks, 'Yes, yes, yes.'

Aunt Doris smiled and nodded her head in approval as Joan recited the prayer for lighting the Shabbat candles. There was the usual chatter around the table as the platters of food were passed around.

Manny stood and clinked a spoon against his wine glass. There was silence as everyone turned to look at him. He hesitated for a moment and then, taking a deep breath, looked at his aunt and uncle as he said, 'I've asked Joan to marry me. I know you would say I'm too young, and a million other reasons, but,' he looked down at Joan, 'I love her, and I know she loves me. Tonight, as she lit the Shabbat candles I realised how much.'

There were shouts of 'mazeltov'. Aunt Doris kissed Joan and Manny. Mark, smiling, shook Manny's hand and hugged Joan, while his sister, brother and cousin ran around the table singing, 'We're going to a wedding, we're going to a wedding, a lovely, lovely wedding.'

'Oh! Shut up,' Manny, red-faced, said in good humour as one by one they gave Joan, who they already adored, a hug and a kiss.

'It seems,' said Manny, 'that you all approve.'

Chapter 11

1 July 1940

AT THE OUTBREAK of the war, there were approximately 75,000 Austrians and Germans living in Britain. Some had resided in the country for many years, having arrived in the early 1920s, fleeing from either political or religious oppression.

On 10 May 1940, fearing enemy spies infiltrating the country following Germany's invasion of the Netherlands and the Allied retreat at Dunkirk, Parliament passed a bill for the internment of all Austrian and German nationals between the ages of 16 and 50.

Two policemen arrived at the house, handing Manny an official document, informing him that he was to be interned in Ochan, on the Isle of Man.

There was dismay on his face and in his voice as he said, 'What, I've to go now? I'm going to Cambridge University next month.'

'I'm very sorry, sir, but that's the law,' the taller of the two officers said, adding, 'The university may have information about an appeal.'

'We'll collect you at 6.30 tomorrow morning, so you can pack and notify Cambridge,' the shorter of the two policemen joined in sympathetically.

'Thank you, I'll do that.'

Manny telephoned Cambridge to notify them of his internment, and was told that he wasn't the only one.

'What about an appeal?'

'Others have tried. It seems there's no appeal,' was the reply.

Manny couldn't believe it; having escaped from one internment camp, he was now being sent to another, even though they weren't the same.

Joan was naturally very upset. She had spoken to her boss, but there was nothing he could do to help; and as they weren't married, there was no way she could go with him.

'I'm sure they'll release me once they know I'm not a threat to them. They aren't interning my aunt, uncle, Sam, Hannah or Joshua, so the family would still be here for you to visit, and you could come over on weekends and in the holidays.'

He took her hand, 'The government was more anxious than ever about sabotage, and what better way to infiltrate this country than posing as an Austrian or German refugee – you know that, because you work for the Government.'

'Yes, I know, but it doesn't mean I have to like you going away.'

For the first time since Joan returned from Vienna, she stayed the night with Manny. His aunt and uncle knew about their liaison, so didn't object.

*

The next morning, Manny and Joan sat on the settee, arms around each other, his suitcase by the front door waiting for the police to arrive.

Aunt Doris handed him a bag. 'You'll be hungry. I've made some sandwiches, and there are pieces of chicken in a lunch box and a thermos of coffee.'

Manny laughed. 'You mustn't worry, I'll be—'

He was interrupted by a knock at the front door. Manny and Joan walked into the hallway just as Uncle Mark opened it.

'Good morning.' The two policemen from the day before said in unison. The taller of the two looked past Mark at Manny. 'Ready?'

Manny nodded, gave Joan a kiss, hugged his sister, brother and cousin, shook his uncle's hand and kissed a tearful Aunt Doris, picked up his bags, and with policemen either side walked towards an army lorry parked at the kerbside. A soldier with a rifle stood by the tailgate. Manny followed his suitcase and bags aboard and sat on the wooden bench running along the inside of the lorry.

The soldier followed Manny into the interior, pulled up the tailgate, banged his rifle butt on the floor, and they moved off with Manny waving goodbye to his family, who stood arms around each other, waving back.

Manny looked into the dim interior to see four other internees, their luggage at their feet, looking at him; they nodded silently and then faced the front.

Manny placed a foot on the tailgate and suddenly his stomach tightened, swallowing nervously, feeling sick as a feeling of *déjà vu* swept over him. He turned to look at the soldier who moved his rifle into a more comfortable position.

'Where are we going?' Manny whispered, hearing Saul's voice asking the same thing on their way to Mauthausen

'Euston Station, but on the way we have to pick up some more internees.'

The lorry came to a halt outside a building with a stone-carved sign above the door saying Islington Police Station. Four men boarded the lorry. One, a tall, broad-shouldered man with thick brown hair, sat next to Manny, who gave him a welcoming smile.

Dark green eyes smiled back, the teeth white against the black stubble, holding out his hand to introduce himself.

'Isaac Steinberger,' he said in a soft voice, which didn't go with his build.

Manny, from habit, glanced at the soldier before taking the offered hand, 'Manny Grenfeldt.'

The lorry moved off once again, stopping ten minutes later at King's Cross Police Station. A suitcase and a musical instrument-case were placed beside Manny's feet, followed by a man, who leapt aboard dropping onto the seat opposite Manny, placing the suitcase between his feet and the music-case onto his lap, and then looked around the lorry as it moved away.

Coal-black eyes come to rest on Isaac, who smiled holding out his hand, 'Isaac Steinberger.'

The man shook the offered hand. 'David Wasserman,' he said, in a deep, baritone, slightly accented voice that seemed out of place in a man of such slight stature. He then offered his hand to Manny, who said, 'Manny Grenfeldt,' taking the offered long, slim-fingered hand, expecting a limp grip, but it was strong.

David took off his wide-brimmed hat to reveal black, curly hair that hung over his ears and down the velvet collar of his overcoat.

There was a noisy sound of steam, whistles and people as the lorry came to a halt inside Euston Station. Their guard jumped down, lowering the tailgate, ordering them out. As Manny and the others got down from the lorry they were surrounded by soldiers.

A sergeant stepped forward. 'Please don't be alarmed, we're your escort till you embark at Liverpool Docks for the Isle of Man. Please bring your luggage and follow me.' He smartly about turned and marched away with Manny and the others following, with their escort marching either side.

The four front carriages of the train were for the internees, many having arrived earlier from other parts of London.

Manny, Isaac and David found some empty seats, placing their suitcases on the rack above their heads. Ten minutes into their journey, they were given cheese sandwiches, that must have been standing on the tray all morning, and watery tea.

Manny took the bag Aunt Doris had given him from the rack, offering his cheese sandwich to Isaac and David, who said they didn't want to take the food out of Manny's mouth. But when he opened the bag Aunt Doris had given him and saw the mound of freshly wrapped sandwiches, their eyes widened.

Manny placed the lunch box on the seat beside him, opening it to reveal pieces of cooked chicken, the aroma filling the carriage.

Isaac, mouth watering, said, 'There's enough food there to feed an army.'

Manny looked at his new-found friends with a wry smile. 'My aunt tends to do that. Would you both care to join me?'

Taking a large red handkerchief from his pocket, David spread it across his lap. 'Whatever you can spare, old friend, will be gratefully accepted.'

'Ditto,' said Isaac, placing his suitcase on his lap and licking his lips in anticipation.

Manny shared out the chicken and sandwiches, and the three new friends tucked into the food with relish, leaving some for later in case they didn't receive anything to eat until they get to their destination.

Manny folded his arms, stretched out his legs and looked out of the window. The green countryside sped past. David and Isaac were asleep. Gradually, with the side-to-side motion of the train and the rattling wheels on the track, Manny's eyes began to close and his chin slowly dropped onto his chest as he fell into a smiling, dreamy sleep.

Manny was rudely awoken to the shout of '*Rous, rous.*' For a split second thinking he was in Mauthausen, he stood to attention, eyes on the ground. 'Liverpool in ten minutes, get ready,' yelled the voice in German.

Manny looked up to see a British army captain walking along the carriage aisle, yelling the same thing as he entered the next carriage.

'Anyone would think we were German prisoners,' said Isaac.

'There's some aboard this train,' a man at the other end of the carriage informed them.

'Just keep them away from me,' said another. 'I won't be responsible for my actions.'

Soldiers, rifles at the ready, lined the platform as the train entered Liverpool's Lime Street Station, coming to a gradual stop.

The train's armed guards opened the doors, allowing the alien internees to get off first, ordering them to stand in a line beside the train.

The German prisoners, who were mostly sailors and a few airmen, were then allowed to leave the train. When they did, they were kept well apart from Manny and his group.

Manny couldn't understand why they needed so many soldiers to guard them – it seemed a little excessive. An officer, a major with a sergeant in tow, walked along the line counting them; he nodded, agreeing with the count and moved to the centre of the road.

He looked silently at them for a moment and then said in fluent German, 'You'll march from here to the docks, where you'll board a boat that will take you across to the Isle of Man. There will be no talking, and anyone—' He moved across to stand in front of the German prisoners as he continued '—and I mean anyone, trying to escape will be shot.' He turned to the sergeant, 'Carry on, Sergeant.'

The sergeant saluted the officer then faced the internees and prisoners and yelled, 'Right turn.' The line turned. 'Quick march.'

They moved off, the major leading the way, their escort strung in a line either side of them, rifles at the ready.

At Pier Head, the internees boarded the ferry, moving to the rail, watching the German prisoners march up to the ship.

A German sailor in the lead, a naval non-commissioned officer, looked up as he stepped onto the gangway to see the internees watching them. He pointed at them, '*Juden* bastards,' he shouted, along with other obscenities. The other sailors followed his lead, yelling and making rude gestures at the internees.

'It's like a broken record,' said David, pointing his music case at them as they move onto the gangway. The lead sailor, thinking it was a gun stepped back, losing his footing and fell onto those behind him, who tumbled in a heap at the bottom of the gangway amid laughter and jeering from the internee's lining the rail.

'I'm going to join the British army and fight those Nazi bastards,' said David vehemently. 'I'm not going to spend my time interned on an island while others fight my battles.' He shook his fist at the Germans, who were now shame-faced, picking themselves up. 'I owe those Nazi scum a lot of pain.'

Manny's eyes were full of hate and anger for the way the German sailors had verbally abused them; the sailors faced the men lining the rail, expressions of loathing on their faces as they walked up the gangway.

As the naval non-commissioned officer walked onto the deck, Manny stuck out a foot. The sailor tripped over it and, regaining his balance, turning quickly, fist clenched, face red with anger and leapt at Manny who calmly sidestepped to the left. The ship's rail stopped the German's momentum; he turned to be met with a kick in the groin and as he doubled over, Manny threw an uppercut to the jaw.

The dazed, glazed-eyed Nazi dropped to the deck and was unable to stop Manny from stomping on his right leg just below the knee. He screamed in agony as the bone snapped and his kneecap shattered.

Manny grabbed his hair, lifting the defeated man's head and whispered, 'What master race?' and let go.

The sailor's already bloody face hit the deck. Manny, breathing a little heavily, stepped back and a feeling of calm satisfaction swept over him.

While he had been fighting the German sailor, Manny was unaware of what had been going on around him.

The sailor behind the non-commissioned officer ran onto the ferry, intending to join in the fight against Manny, but was met by the six foot one Isaac, who grabbed him by the neck just under the chin, lifting him off his feet. The sailor's eyes bulged as he tried to hit Isaac but soon realised he couldn't reach him, so he grabbed Isaac's hands, trying to prise them from his throat as Isaac said, 'How does it feel, Nazi scum, to be helpless?'

While all this was happening, the soldiers on the dock were try to get up the gangway blocked by the German sailors, while those aboard the ferry were held back by the internees, but were in no hurry to intervene.

Isaac lifted the sailor above his head, walked to the side of the boat and was about to throw him on to the dock when a voice said quietly, 'Don't do it, otherwise you'll be no better than they were. You've proved to those morons that in the future we'll never again go blindly into cattle trucks.'

Isaac turned, the sailor still held aloft to see who the speaker was. Green eyes looked at Isaac, a slight smile on the chubby-cheeked face, as he said, 'I would dearly love for you to kill him, but you're an intelligent man, what would it prove? He's just one amongst millions.'

Isaac nodded. Holding the sailor by his legs, he lowered him to the ground. As the German's arms bent on the deck, Isaac stomped on them, breaking both arm bones, and then let go the sailor's legs. The German screamed in agony as he dropped onto the deck. Isaac squatted down beside him, saying into the sailor's ear, 'You should thank that man for your life.'

The British soldiers had at last reached the top of the gangway and the internees allowed the others through. The sergeant yelled, 'Step back, it's time for the ship to sail.'

The major arrived standing between the Germans and internees. He pointed to the wounded men, and then at the other sailors. 'Carry those men to the stern of the ship; the doctor will dress their wounds.' The two German sailors screamed in pain as their shipmates picked them up and under guard carried them to the stern.

The major turned to face the internees, a slight smile on his lips. 'I'll now have to fill in an accident report.' He hesitated, turning his head away, trying hard not to laugh, and then turned back facing them. 'I think we all witnessed the poor German sailor slipping on the gangway and falling on top of two shipmates.' He turned to his sergeant standing not too far away. 'Do you agree with that, Sergeant?'

The sergeant stood to attention, with just a hint of a smile on his lips, 'Yes, sir.'

The major looked at the sea of faces in front of him. 'But I must warn you—' he waved a hand. 'Oh forget it, Sergeant, make sure these men are fed.'

Before the sergeant could answer the major disappeared into his cabin. The mooring lines were released and the ferry moved away from the dock. The sea was calm with circling, squawking, seagulls following them throughout the journey.

*

On landing, the German prisoners disembarked first; carrying their wounded comrades, marching away under heavy escort. Some looked back at the internees lining the rail waiting to disembark and shook their fists at them, but were silent.

A tired Manny and the others boarded a coach waiting at the jetty and were driven to Onchan. As luck had it, Manny and his new friends were dropped off at the same house.

'I'm afraid you three will have to share a room,' said the owner of the boarding house, a short, stout woman with blonde curly hair tied away from her red-cheeked face, one hand in the pocket of her clean apron.

'That's fine,' replied Isaac. 'Lead the way, madam.'

*

Onchan camp consisted of sixty Victorian and Edwardian houses strung out along the seafront beyond the northern end of Douglas Promenade on a headland overlooking the sea. The site dominated the small electric railway terminal that looked down on Derby Castle. A barbed-wired fence enclosed part of the road which had magnificent views over Douglas Bay.

In Manny's house there were five bedrooms and fifteen internees, a mixture of German and Austrian Jews; all refugees from Nazi oppression.

Ochan camp had a lecture scheme, known as *The Popular University*. The university was staffed with people who had been lecturers and tutors at universities throughout the western world.

There were courses in chemistry, science, literature, theology, philosophy, music, languages, and many other subjects, giving the student the opportunity to listen and learn from some of the greatest minds in Europe free of charge.

Concerts and exhibitions were held, plays in different languages, a camp newspaper and other leisurely activities, plus a canteen where people could meet and enjoy each other's company.

On warm summer afternoons in Hutchinson Square the internees knelt or sat on the lawn, while officers and their ladies sat on chairs in front of them as the sentimental strains of a Strauss waltz was being played by the two great Austrian pianists Rawicz and Landauer, drifting across the sea.

The three friends continued their studies, knowing they would never get a better opportunity to be taught by such great and renowned tutors. Manny persuaded David to teach him to play the saxophone.

A week didn't go by without Manny and his two friends sending applications to join the British Army. In the eyes of British law, they were enemies, but in their hearts and souls they were allies. They, like many on Ochan, listened to the war news every day coming from the radio in their room, leaping for joy as the newscaster said, 'British bombers bombed Berlin last night.'

Night after night they heard the drone of enemy aircraft above, seeing the searchlights over Liverpool seeking enemy bombers. The skyline was alight with fires set off by German incendiaries. German prisoners of war arrived; mostly airmen who had been shot down, and now and again a U-boat crew who were amongst the staunchest Nazis. Luckily they were kept well away from the internees.

Manny read a censored letter from Joan. She was unable to obtain permission to visit him, but hadn't given up hope of trying. The unmistakable voice of Winston Churchill made the memorable speech about the Battle of Britain fighter pilots: *'Never has so much been owed by so many to so few.'*

With 1941 only a month old, the three friends stepped up their relentless bombardment on the Commandant, requesting to enlist in the British armed forces and fight.

'I agree with you,' the Commandant said, 'but my hands are tied by Act of Parliament.'

Chapter 12

12 May 1941

MANNY would never forget this day. He was practising the saxophone under David's tutelage, when he received a message that the Commandant would like to see him. The others went with him, thinking that at last their persistence had won and that they were going to be sent to an army unit.

They waited outside as Manny knocked on the Commandant's door, opening it on hearing, 'Enter.'

The Commandant stood as Manny entered the office, picking up a folded typewritten sheet from his desk as he walked around it. 'I've just received a communiqué, which I have been instructed to give to you.'

Manny, a worried look on his face and a feeling of apprehension, stared at it for a moment, before taking it from the outstretched hand, unfolded the communiqué and began to read.

```
Dear Manny,

I am sorry to inform you, that in last
night's bombing raid Joan was killed. She
was as usual helping others when it
happened. I've taken care of the funeral
arrangement, with the help of your family,
who are now in mourning for their beloved
niece and sister.

In her will, Joan said that she wanted to
be cremated, because she doesn't want you
to grieve for too long.

Please accept my deepest sympathy for your
loss. I know how much she loved you, and
you her.

Yours truly,
```

Mrs Reece-Davis

'Is there anything I can do for you?' the Commandant asked sympathetically.

Manny's eyes, wet with tears, hardened. The Nazis had killed the people he loved most in the world and he wanted revenge.

'Yes sir, there is,' he spoke harshly. 'You can transfer me to an army fighting unit, and the sooner the better.'

His fists clenched by his side, Manny wanted more than anything to take his feelings out on someone or something, and in spite of the intense shock and grief he was feeling at this moment, when the one woman he had ever loved had been so cruelly taken away from him, he somehow summoned up out of all the pain and sadness within him, a bitter, burning and lethal anger, not towards the German pilots whose bombings had killed Joan, but the monstrous Nazi regime, which he knew was ultimately responsible for everything that was happening.

'What you, and the British Government don't seem to realise,' he added vehemently, 'is that we're on your side. You've no idea what some of your alien internees have been through to get to this country and help her in the fight against Hitler and his Nazi army. We, the Jews of Germany and Austria, have been humiliated, beaten, kicked and spat on.'

His body shook with emotion. 'Our families and everything we own, even our dignity, taken from us.' He stopped; breathing heavily from his outburst, he wiped the tears of frustration from his cheeks and then continued with a voice filled with emotion. 'Hundreds, including whole families, have been thrown into concentration camps and murdered, many the recipients of the most sadistic torture ever devised by a depraved Nazi mind.'

He stopped, aware of his outpouring, and then added quietly, 'So you see, sir, we need to avenge those that cannot avenge themselves.'

'I understand, Mr Grenfeldt, you may not think so, but I do, and I'll try my damnedest to help you and your fellow internees. Once again accept my deepest sympathy at your loss.'

The others were waiting for Manny as he left the office. He told them about Joan and his conversation with the commandant. Three days later Manny received another letter from Mrs Reece-Davis.

```
Dear Manny,

Joan gave me this envelope a short while
ago with instructions that if anything
should happen to her I was to give it to
you. If I can do anything for you, please
do not hesitate to contact me

Yours sincerely,

Mrs Reece-Davis.
```

For two days the letter from Joan lay unopened in Manny's pocket. Isaac and David knew that until he opened the letter he would never be able to let Joan go and carry on with his life.

The three friends were in their room studying, when David said, 'Manny, you can tell me to mind my own business, but I think it's time you opened Joan's letter.'

Isaac looked up from the book he was reading, adding, 'I agree. We're your friends, more than friends, brothers, but until you open that letter and read what she's written, you won't be able to get on with your life.'

Manny looked from one to the other, nodding grimly in agreement; he reached for his jacket that hung on the back of the chair, took the letter from the inside pocket, stared at it for a moment, then lifted it to his nose, eyes closed, smelling the slight aroma of her perfume and then tore open the envelope. His two friends walked silently out of the room, David squeezing Manny's shoulder as he passed. The door closed and he began to read.

My dearest darling Manny,

I know that if you're reading this letter something dreadful has happened. In these terrible times no one is sure what the future holds. What I want you to do for me is to carry on with your life, discover all the wonders it has to offer, and find someone to share it with. Please Manny, do not grieve too long, as you can see, life is too short.

I loved you the very first time I saw you, and when you asked me to send the package for you, I decided then and there that I was not going to let you go, no matter what it took.

I never in my wildest dreams thought that you felt the same as me, but when you told me you loved me, I was the happiest girl in the world.

I don't regret one moment of our time together, just that it wasn't long enough. When you asked me to marry you, even though I was doing the pushing, I was over the moon.

You have a wonderful family, who welcomed me into their home. Aunt Doris had been like a mother to me, in fact better than my own. And Uncle Mark was always there to help me with my Hebrew, and give me little snippets about you.

I love you so much my heart is fit to burst. I only regret that these last few months we've been apart. My arms ache to hold you, and my body longs for yours to be close to it, but now that's not to be. Just keep me in the hindmost parts of your memory, like an old book on the shelf that you bring out now and again to look at and caress.

But most of all my darling, please, please carry on. I'm sure someone else will come along who will love you the way I do, and I know you'll love her back.

God bless you Manny and keep you safe.

Your ever-loving fiancée

Joan xxxxxx

Tears rolled down Manny's face. He let out a scream of anguish, hurling the cup of tea on his desk across the room. Isaac and David entered the room, going quickly over to Manny, hugging him to them as his racking sobs echoed around the house.

*

His friends and Joan are right; life must go on. Manny resumed his studies, but was still unsure of the direction to take regarding a career.

The sun was shining in a cloudless sky as he walked beside the sea-wall on his way to class and stopped to listen to a professor of economics talking to half a dozen young students as he leaned his back against the wall. Manny recognised him as the man who stopped Isaac from throwing the German sailor overboard.

The professor's green eyes looked intently at each of the students as he brushed a lock of curly brown hair away from his forehead, saying, 'It's times like these that industrialist make money – how much?' He shrugged his shoulders. 'It's all according to how long a war goes on. In times of war, raw materials such as steel, iron, wood, oil, and textiles are badly needed. Ships, tanks, planes, guns, uniforms, and even small items like buttons, ball-bearings, bullets, gunpowder and a thousand other things are needed to keep a country at war going.

'Industrialists, although patriotic, still want to earn money to pay their workers, but most important of all, they are answerable to their shareholders.' He wagged a finger at the class. 'Some people were greedier than others, but make no mistake, all's fair in love and war is still true, even today.'

Manny listened intently to the professor until the class was over, and then approached him.

'Excuse me, sir.'

'Yes, young man, what can I do for you?'

Manny held out his hand. 'I'm Manny Grenfeldt.'

The professor took the offered hand. 'Abraham Rosenblatt.'

'Professor, I—'

'Abe,' Rosenblatt smiled and let go the hand.

Manny returned the smile. 'I overheard what you said about raw materials and wonder if it's still possible to buy shares, even though we're interned here.'

'Firstly', said Abe, 'yes, it's possible to get hold of shares from here. The problem was being able to get hold of the shares you want, and if they're worth buying. Wars don't last forever, and you have to know the market – when to sell and when to buy. If you have spare cash and want to dabble, I'm sure there's some for sale somewhere.'

'I don't want to just dabble, I want to make money.'

'Aha, well in that case, you and I must have a serious talk.'

'What do you mean?'

'Have you ever bought shares before?'

'No.'

'Do you know anything about steel, coal, diamonds, or any other commodities?'

'No.'

'Well, Manny my boy, you're going to need an advisor, and I know just the man.' Abe placed an arm around Manny's shoulders. 'Come with me, I need to know more about you, and to enlighten you on what shares to buy.'

Manny told Abe that he had an account at the Bank of America. His money was safe there, and if need be could obtain money from the Midland Bank in East London.

Abe explained in great detail about buying and selling stocks and shares, and how at any moment it could all come crashing down.

'Do you own any shares?' Manny asked.

'I did, in Germany, but they were taken from me. Let's put it this way, it's either sign my shares and other assets over to a certain Gestapo major and escape, or be taken forcibly to a concentration camp, so here I am.'

Manny nodded understandingly, glanced at his watch, gasping in surprise: time had flown – it was nearly time for lights out and they had missed their evening meal. 'Let's meet up in the morning. I need to think more about what you've told me. How much do you charge for your services?'

'Four per cent,' was the quick reply.

'Manny gave a glimpse of a smile. 'One.'

'Three,' Abe came back.

'Two,' Manny said quickly.

Abe nodded.

Manny smiled eyes sparkling holding out his hand. 'You've got yourself a deal. I'll see you in the morning.'

News reached internees that Marshal Pétain, the leader of Vichy France, had ordered the arrest of 12,000 Jews accused of plotting to hinder Franco-German cooperation.

Manny and his friends sent a strongly worded letter to *The Times*, asking for help in attaining their release from Ochan to fight, but as usual didn't receive a reply.

The entire country was using the 'V' for Victory sign, started by the BBC, who played the opening notes of Beethoven's Fifth Symphony when broadcasting to occupied Europe. The letter was the same as used in Morse code for Victory.

The radio was playing in the background as Manny, in Abe's room, discussed what shares he should try to obtain. Suddenly the music stopped and for a second there was silence.

Both men frowned turning to look at the radio, when a voice announced, 'Here is a bulletin for the 8th of December 1941,' said the newscaster. 'Japan has attacked the American fleet at Pearl Harbor. This fateful message was received by the Associated Press today. The Imperial Headquarters in Tokyo announced tonight that it was at war with the United States of America and Britain.'

There was silence for a second as the newscaster let the news sink in to his listeners, and then continued. 'Some hours ago 360 Japanese warplanes made a surprise attack on the US Pacific Fleet at its home base at Pearl Harbor in Hawaii. In two hours they sank, or seriously damaged five battleships and some smaller ships, destroyed 200 aircraft, killing 2,400 people. They also attacked bases in the Philippines, Guam and Wake Island.'

Manny and Abe looked at each other with a stunned expression of disbelief on their faces. The door suddenly burst open, Isaac, David, and other internees entered the room.

'Have you heard the news?' David asked.

Manny and Abe just nodded in reply.

Three days later Germany and Italy declared war on the USA. The world was now truly at war.

On 28 December, Manny, with his two friends and other internees, received orders to report on 5 January 1942 to the British Army's Pioneer Corps Depot in Ilfracombe for training.

Chapter 13

AFTER twelve weeks of marching and drilling, Manny, with the rest of the company were sent to the Kent coast to build defensive positions, tank traps, bunkers, pillboxes and lay barbed-wire fences.

The Pioneers were considered to be the dogs'-bodies of the British army, and were facetiously called, the King's Own Loyal Enemy Aliens (Koleas). It was said that the Koleas were treated like Chinese coolies. They chopped down trees to produce timber for building camps and an endless number of huts; installing electricity, drainage systems, and water-towers.

Manny was used to this physical labour; compared to Mauthausen it was easy. He and his fellow Koleas shuttled tons of bricks and bags of cement to make concrete defences; loaded and unloaded, packed and unpacked a mammoth of stores and materials needed by various army fractions.

At night, he and David, with other musicians, entertained the townsfolk and troops by playing jazz, or the new boogie woogie brought over from America.

In the meantime Manny and Abe ventured into the stock market; and at last the Pioneers to Manny's satisfaction, received regular firearms training.

Now armed, Manny was more determined than ever to have a go at the Germans, volunteering for the newly formed Parachute Regiment, or the Commandos.

While building tank traps, Manny's thoughts turned to his friend Hans, and wondered if he was one of Rommel's Panzers fighting the British Eight Army in the desert.

*

As 1942 came to an end, Manny realised that there was a slight change in the war as news reached them that the US fleet had won a fierce battle around Midway Island in the Pacific, forcing the Japanese fleet to withdraw. At the same time British troops halted the Germans advance at El Alamein. Every week Manny bombarded his commanding officer, requesting combat duty, especially when he and his fellow Pioneers received news and pictures, showing atrocities against Jews in the Warsaw Ghetto.

This at last stirred certain members of Parliament into action. Led by Anthony Eden, they condemned the Nazis, for their policy of exterminating Jews in Europe, and in no uncertain words, said that those responsible would not escape retribution. This also changed the British Government's attitude in allowing alien refugees to join combat units.

Manny, Isaac and David, with twenty other pioneers, received orders to report on 24 May 1943 to Airborne Forces Depot, Hardwick Hall, for selection into the Parachute Regiment. Abe stayed with the Pioneers.

*

Hardwick Hall was a cheerless place, with red-brick huts and barbed wire fences. Manny wondered if the fences were there to keep the volunteers in or the enemy out.

Regardless of rank, all volunteers for the Parachute Regiment must undergo a selection course lasting two weeks. Those found to be medically unfit were sent back to their units.

A captain from the Intelligence Corps stood in front of Manny and the other Jewish volunteers and said, 'All Jewish volunteers, in case of capture by the enemy, must choose an English name and different religion. I'll give you thirty minutes to decide on an alias. Write the name of your choice on the piece of paper in front of you and I'll see if you can pronounce it so it doesn't give away your foreign origins.'

Manny wanted to keep his initials. With the end of the pencil in his mouth, he tilted the chair back looking up at the ceiling for inspiration. He let the chair drop back and wrote, Michael Green, Atheist. David showed his friends the name he had chosen, keeping his first name, David Wilson, Isaac smiled holding his up, Tom Williams. The officer returned to the room, asking each in turn to say the name they had chosen. One tried to pronounce the name Braithwaite; causing hysterical laughter from everyone, including the Captain, and in the end changed it to Benson.

The Captain walked around the room handing out a document. 'This is an official declaration. Read it very carefully then sign your new name and birth name.'

The declaration read, 'I HEREBY CERTIFY THAT I UNDERSTAND THE RISKS TO WHICH I AND MY RELATIVES MAY BE EXPOSED BY MY EMPLOYMENT IN THE BRITISH ARMY OUTSIDE THE UNITED KINGDOM. NOT WITHSTANDING THIS, I CERTIFY THAT I AM WILLLING TO BE EMPLOYED IN ANY THEATRE OF WAR.'

Manny signed his name, with a smile on his lips and an icy glint of vengeance in his eyes.

The three friends managed to stay together. Although unprepared for the relentless scrutiny and shouting by the instructors, with everything being done at the double, they were prepared to do anything to get into combat.

David found it hard-going, especially the two-mile run, which they had to do in sixteen minutes in full battle order.

'Come on, David,' Manny, running beside him, urged his friend on.

Isaac was just behind him, encouraging him too. 'We've only a little way to go. Come on, you can do it.'

Manny glanced at his watch, calculating how long at this pace it would take them. Their biggest fear was the dreaded letters, RTU, meaning, Return to Unit, but as far as he was concerned, that was never going to happen to him.

Manny looked at his friend, who was gasping for air, sweat pouring down his face. 'David, we are going to step up the pace, otherwise we aren't going to make it. You once said you wanted to fight Germans, have you still got that desire?'

With those last few words, a grim look of determination came over David's face and he increased his pace, for a moment leaving Manny and Isaac behind. The three friends crossed the line together. Manny looked at his watch and smiled. 'We did it,' he yelled, looking round for David, who was on his knees, gasping for air.

A few days later, the three friends and a small group of men were on their way to Ringway in Manchester for a two-week parachute training

On a platform, twenty feet from the ground, Manny waited for Isaac, who was scared of heights, to jump. Isaac looked down, gripping the harness so tightly his knuckles were white. The instructor on the ground yelled for him to hurry up.

Manny leaned towards him and whispered in his ear, 'You're so big, your parachute won't be able to carry your weight, and you'll land on some fat Nazi.' Isaac launched himself from the platform with a roar of laughter.

*

Two days later, in a cage suspended 700 feet in the air from a balloon, the three friends waited for the instructor to order them to jump. Manny's enjoying himself and grinned at Isaac, who winked his fear of heights gone. David stood by the entrance to the cage, gave the thumbs up and stepped into space.

Manny looked down from the platform, took a deep breath and stepped from the cage; for a second his heart skipped a beat and then a big grin lit up his face at the sheer exhilaration of a 120 foot of freefall before the parachute opened. His laughter could be heard by those below, but he's brought back to reality when the instructor yelled through his megaphone, 'Keep your fucking feet together.'

The second week of parachute training was the real thing. Manny, his legs dangling into space, the cold wind whipping against his body from the slipstream of the aircraft, looked down at the ground below and then, letting out a yell of sheer delight dropped into space.

There was a queasy, exciting feeling in the pit of his stomach before pulling the ripcord, he was jerked upward as the canopy unfurled. He looked up, the blue skies covered by the white silk of the open chute as he floated slowly towards the ground, then suddenly, quickly, far too quickly, the ground came up to meet him; he rolled over and rose to his feet, at the same time punching the harness release, leaping into the air and shouting, 'Yes, yes,' blue eyes sparkling from the sheer thrill of the jump.

*

At the end of the week, having completed his seven descents, Manny was given his parachute wings.

However, there was little time for him and the others to rest on their laurels as they now faced battle training on the wild moors of the Derwent Valley. If he and his friends thought selection training was tough, they were in for a shock as a sergeant explained what he demanded of them.

'I expect one hundred and one per cent commitment from you all.' He paced up and down in front of them, stopping suddenly and pointing his swagger stick at them. 'Anyone that doesn't meet my standards, or cannot keep up, will be RTU immediately; there'll be no second chances.'

He began pacing again. 'I and my corporals are going to push you to your limits.' He stopped in mid-stride, turning to face them. 'I don't like whiners or skivers, and if any of you fit that category you can leave now. OK, get some rest, we start first thing in the morning.'

Manny was tired. Exercises took place by day and night, with and without live ammunition, and mostly with very little sleep, but he was in his element, revelling in the assault course, unarmed combat, and exercises over bleak, wild, treeless heather-clad moorland that rose to 2000 feet, with small streams of cold, clear water running through them. Although it wasn't the same as the snow-clad mountains and peaks of Austria, he was happy in that environment.

*

Their training over, Manny, and those few that were left, received the coveted red beret and Pegasus badge. Before joining their unit the men are given a week's leave.

David was going to Aylesbury to stay with his mother and brother, but Isaac was alone, and was going to stay in camp.

'Isaac you can come with me?' Manny said.

'Are you sure? I think you'd better ask your aunt first.'

Manny telephoned his aunt and uncle. Aunt Doris answered the phone: 'Mile End 3362.'

'Aunty.' Before he could say another word there was a scream of delight from her. 'Aunty, I have a week's leave. Is it OK if I bring a friend?'

'Of course you can. When are you arriving?'

'I'm not sure, either late tonight, or tomorrow morning. It's all according to how the trains are running.' This would be the first time he had been home since his internment, and Joan's death.

PART III

Chapter 14

20 September 1943

ST PANCRAS Station was crowded with servicemen and women as Manny and Isaac's train pulled in. Some, like themselves, were on leave, while others were catching trains to various destinations. Men and women leaned out of open carriage windows, holding hands with loved ones, saying their goodbyes, not knowing whether they would ever see them again. Some were crying while others held back the tears, showing a brave face.

A train pulled slowly out of the station, the women running alongside clinging to the hands of husbands, lovers, sweethearts, not wanting to let go, till at last they had to, waving despairingly as the train disappeared, and now letting the tears of parting roll down their faces.

Staring out of the taxi window, Manny was appalled at the devastation London's East End had suffered from the bombing. Streets, where once stood houses and shops, were just a pile of rubble. But here and there amidst it all, one house stood in defiance of the carnage around it.

They made a detour as fire engines and ambulances blocked the road, their crews hunting in the rubble for survivors from last night's air raid.

Before Manny could place the key in the lock, Aunt Doris opened the door throwing her arms around his neck, standing on tiptoe to hug and kiss him, eventually letting go, her eyes slightly moist.

'Auntie, this is my friend, Isaac.'

Isaac held out his hand, but Aunt Doris moved forward, kissing him on both cheeks. 'Welcome to our home Isaac, please come in.'

Isaac murmured, 'Thank you,' and then followed Manny into the house.

'Perhaps you'd like to unpack and freshen up.' She looked at Manny. 'I've put a campbed in your room you two could share. Uncle Mark should be home shortly. He's in the Civil Defence, you know. He went out early this morning to help clear the rubble away from a row of houses in Cannon Street Road that were hit by bombs last night. Hannah said she hoped to be home in time for dinner. When you're ready please come downstairs and I'll make a cuppa.'

'Is Sam coming?' asked Manny.

'I'm not sure, he said he would try. He's in...' she hesitated, 'Well, you'll see, when and if he gets here.' She turned and headed for the kitchen. 'I'd better get dinner going, it won't cook itself.'

Isaac followed Manny to his room. 'I'll empty this drawer and you can put your things in there. There's room in the wardrobe to hang your clothes.'

'I appreciate your aunt and uncle letting me stay,' Isaac said. 'You sure I'm not intruding?'

'Don't be silly, they're only too pleased to have you. The more the merrier. Just relax, think of this as your own home.'

Manny and Isaac were in the kitchen having a cup of tea with Aunt Doris when the front door opened and a raised voice said, 'I'm home.' Aunt Doris leapt from her chair and ran towards her husband, giving him a hug and a lingering kiss.

Manny greeted his uncle, who was covered in dust. 'I'd love to give you a big hug, but you'll be covered in this.' They shook hands. 'You look good.'

Manny gestured to Isaac. 'This is my friend, Isaac.'

The two men shook hands. 'It's good to have you both here. I apologise for my appearance; if you'll excuse me, I'll have a bath and change.'

'Did anyone get out alive?' Manny asked quietly.

'Just one little six-year-old boy. I'm afraid the rest of his family were dead.'

Manny was surprised to see how tall his brother Joshua was, but then it had been over two years since he had last seen him. He had their father's light-brown hair and hazel eyes.

Isaac was helping Aunt Doris lay the table when Hannah walked in with another woman, both in nurse's uniform. Hannah ran across the room, leaping into Manny's arms, planting a kiss on both his cheeks.

Manny gently pulled her away, holding Hannah at arm's length. Her fair hair curled down to her shoulders, the light-blue eyes sparkling with happiness, the nurse's uniform not hiding the curves of her body.

'My,' he whispered, 'you're beautiful.' She giggled with pleasure as he grabbed Isaac's arm, pulling him towards them. Isaac hadn't taken his eyes off her since she arrived. 'Hannah, this is my friend, Isaac; Isaac, Hannah.'

Isaac took Hannah's hand, bowed and kissed it. 'Manny had told me so much about you, but he never told me how beautiful you were.'

Hannah laughed, her face red with embarrassment. 'Thank you.'

Isaac reluctantly let go her hand as she turned to stand beside the other nurse, placing an arm around her shoulders. 'Manny, Isaac, this is my friend, Rita.'

Rita's raven-black hair was tied back from her face. Emerald-green eyes stared into Manny's as they shook hands. Isaac nodded on being introduced, but had eyes only for Hannah.

'We're going to freshen up and change, see you in a while,' Hannah said, taking Rita's hand.

They had just sat down for dinner when Sam entered, wearing the uniform of a captain in the Commandos.

'Hello everyone, sorry I'm late.' He hugged his parents and gave each girl a peck on the cheek. Manny stood to greet his cousin with a hug. 'A Para? You should have enlisted in the Commandos.'

Manny laughed. 'I tried, but the Paras needed me more than your lot.' Manny introduced Isaac to him and Aunt Doris looked proudly at the young men and women around her as they took their seats.

Uncle Mark stood. 'Before we eat this scrumptious meal—' Aunt Doris had used two of her precious chickens '—I would like to say how proud Doris and I are in having the family here, including Rita and Isaac. It's been a long time since we've all sat at the dinner table together. I pray that there will be many, many more times.'

Isaac sat opposite Hannah, and couldn't stop gazing from her as Manny told the family about their internment, especially the bit on the ferry. Hannah kept glancing from time to time at Isaac, who looked away when he caught her eyes on him, she doing the same when he looked at her.

The talk turned to the war. Uncle Mark told them about his duties as a warden and how lucky they had been so far to survive the bombing. 'As you see, there's just a little damage to the front windows. Mr and Mrs Goldstein lost everything last week.'

'She's staying with her sister in Ilford,' Aunt Doris chimed in. 'She worked with me at the hospital serving food and helping the patients.' She gestured towards Joshua, who like Isaac, wanted to be a doctor. 'Joshua helped the ambulance crews on weekends, but he...' she hesitated looked across the table at Joshua who turned to his brother.

'What Auntie is trying to say is that now the British Government is allowing Jews to fight I've enlisted in the RAF. I report for flying training in two days.'

Manny smiled, looked at his brother's hair. 'Now I know what that smell was, Brylcreem.'

Everyone laughed as Joshua took a comb from his pocket, running it through his hair.

Sam looked at the fork he was twirling on the empty plate in front of him, and then at his cousin asking quietly, 'Manny, how many languages do you speak?'

'Why?'

Sam rimmed his wine glass with the index finger of the other hand. 'Mm, call it curiosity.'

'German, French, Italian and Yiddish, English, and a little bit of Swiss.'

'Fluently?' Sam enquired.

'It's all according to what you call fluent.'

Sam didn't answer but looked across the table at Isaac, who said without being asked, 'French, German and Italian,' he smiled, 'and naturally Yiddish, but with an American accent.'

The others burst into laughter at this. 'No, it's not a joke. I do speak it with an American accent.'

'OK, say something in Yiddish,' Hannah said, laughter in her voice.

Isaac looked into Hannah's eyes. 'Would you go to the cinema with me tomorrow?'

Laughter erupted around the table, all agreeing that he did speak with an American accent. 'How come you speak Yiddish that way?' asked Uncle Mark.

'I used to watch American films spoken in Yiddish with my father,' Isaac replied, still looking at Hannah, raising his eyebrows questioningly.

'Anyone for dessert?' asked Aunt Doris.

'We have dessert?' Mark said in surprise.

Doris beamed at her husband. 'This dinner wouldn't be complete without it.'

Everyone looked towards Aunt Doris, except for Hannah and Isaac, who had eyes only for each other. 'Well, what is it, woman? Don't keep us waiting,' Mark smiled at his wife, his eyes showing his love for her.

'Stewed apples and Carnation cream.' They all clapped as Aunt Doris added, 'Hannah, Rita, let's clear the table.'

'I'll help,' Isaac offered, jumping up to walk beside Hannah as they headed towards the kitchen. 'You haven't answered my question.'

'I'm free after five. Pick me up outside the nurses' home of the London Hospital at six.'

Isaac grinned like a Cheshire cat. 'Great.'

'Bring Manny; we'll make a foursome with Rita.'

Isaac's face dropped; he would have preferred it to be just the two of them, but nodded understandingly. Manny hadn't taken a girl out since Joan's death.

Manny didn't really want to go, but felt obliged too so as not to spoil his sister's first date with Isaac.

*

Rita was a pleasant companion, but Manny really wasn't interested in having a relationship. She knew all about Joan from Hannah. Walking home from the cinema she asked quietly, 'What was Joan like?'

Manny's eyes took on a faraway look, and in a voice soft with love, told about their first meeting at the British Embassy in Vienna. The way he had told Rita about Joan, it was as though she was still alive, and gone somewhere.

*

After that first night, Manny never spoke about Joan again. He didn't have to – she was in that special place where he could bring her to life whenever he wanted.

On their second 'date', Rita tried to kiss him. He held her gently at arm's length and said, 'Rita, I'm flattered, but I don't want another relationship. Not now, not while there's a war on. I'll be going into combat soon, and anything could happen, it wouldn't be fair on you or me.'

'I hope this doesn't mean we will stop seeing each other?' She didn't wait for a reply, as with tears in her eyes she turned and entered the nurses' quarters.

Manny and Isaac met the girls every day, even if it was just for a short time after work.

On the last day of their leave, the two men waited for the girls to appear. When they did, Rita took Manny's arm, steering him away from Isaac and his sister. 'Where are we going?'

'You're taking me to lunch at the café in Victoria Park, and then you can row me around the lake.'

Manny turned to ask Isaac and Hannah if they would like to do the same, but they were disappearing around the corner. 'Shouldn't we ask them if they want to come too?'

'No, I think that you and I and they should be alone today.'

Manny stepped in front of Rita, who had a slight dimpled smile on her face. 'OK, what's going on?'

'Nothing.'

He leaned towards her, hands on hips feigning anger. 'Look here, Rita, I can see when something was going on, why all the secrets? Is there something I should know?'

His face was now inches from hers. She moved forward and kissed him. It was their first kiss. Manny slipped an arm around her waist pulling her closer. There was a hunger in his kiss, and she responded, but he suddenly pulled away. 'I'm sorry, I'm really sorry, but I shouldn't do this.'

'Do what?' She was angry and disappointed, and it showed on her face and in her voice. 'What? Have a kiss to comfort one another in times of need, have a little happiness, when around us there's destruction and misery?'

Manny knew she was right, but that gut feeling of not wanting to hurt Rita was still there as she jabbed her fingers into his chest.

'You mustn't think that because Joan and Saul died it's your fault, that you're a sort of jinx on them and the people around you. If you think like that, why have friends, why come home on leave to see your family?'

She moved closer, their bodies an inch apart as she continued. 'I know that in the very short time I've known you, I love you.' There were tears forming in the corner of her eyes as she continued. 'I'm not asking you to stop loving Joan, but if you don't let go, then the rest of your life will be a miserable one.'

She stopped for a moment to wipe the tears from her eyes with a finger, and then said softly, her hand on his arm. 'I'm not asking you to love me, if it happened, great, but I'm here now, and I'll be here when you get back from wherever you're going, or would be doing.'

Manny was full of mixed emotions, wanting to run away from Rita, who was opening her heart to him, but also to hold, kiss and make love to her.

She touched his face, her fingers sending tingling sensations up his spine, as she said tenderly, 'I'll be here for you to have someone to talk too, a shoulder to cry on, and love if necessary. I'm not asking for a commitment, that would be foolish, but as I said, I'm here.' Her voice changed to one of gaiety. 'Now let's go and have that meal, then you can sing to me like a gondolier in Venice while you row me around the lake.'

Manny gave a throaty laugh. 'I'm afraid the singing is out of the question. It would even frighten Hitler, but the meal and a row around the lake you shall have.' He bent, kissing her on the lips. 'Thank you.' She put her arm through his and as they walked towards the bus stop he said, 'You still haven't answered my question.'

'Isaac's taking Hannah to Hatton Garden to buy her an engagement ring.'

Rita nearly fell over as Manny came to an abrupt halt. 'Why the crafty bugger, he never said anything to me, and I'm his friend.'

Everyone was smiling when Manny and Rita entered the house. Isaac and Hannah walked over to them. 'We became engaged today,' Isaac said. Hannah showed Rita her ring, made from a diamond her mother had bequeathed her, as Isaac continued, 'I hope you don't mind, Manny, but I asked your aunt and uncle.'

Manny grabbed Isaac giving him a bearhug. 'Do I mind? Don't be silly.' He frowned. 'You know there's a war on and we—'

'We know that,' Hannah interrupted. 'I know I love him and he loves me. We talked it over, we knew that you wouldn't approve, so we spoke to Aunt Doris and Uncle Mark about it. They said we should find happiness whenever we can.'

Manny wrapped his arms around his sister, kissing her on both cheeks, 'Wouldn't approve, my dear Hannah? I'm very happy; you couldn't have chosen a finer man. Our aunt and uncle are right, is there a bottle of champagne somewhere?'

'I have one, black market bottle of plonk,' Mark said, popping the cork to everyone's delight. The only person missing was Sam.

Rita turned to Manny. 'I wonder if you realised what you just said.'

He was about to say something in reply, but she asked Hannah, 'When do you plan to get married?'

'As soon as I can arrange another leave,' replied Isaac, his arm around Hannah's waist.

At St Pancras, Hannah clung to Isaac's neck as he stooped from the train window to kiss her. The guard blew his whistle and the train began to move. Hannah didn't want to let go of Isaac's hand, but had to as the train gathered speed. He blew her a kiss and she yelled, 'I love you.'

Manny leaned out of another window to see Rita waving; he returned the wave and then closed the window.

*

Manny didn't take any notice of the rumours circulating the camp, on their return, about the forthcoming invasion, but something must be happening as training intensified with day and night exercises. Most of their jumps were done at night, followed by a thirty-mile or more cross-country route march, a mock attack and consolidation of the objective, always led by their CO. Only after target practice were the men allowed to return to their billets, clean their kit and get some sleep.

Sweating heavily, although it was bitterly cold, Manny, now a corporal led his platoon towards their objective on the outskirts of Shepton Mallet. He turned to Isaac, whose striding step-for-step beside him. 'By this time next week you'll be a married man.'

Isaac grunted in reply.

'Not getting cold feet are you?'

'No, but my feet are killing me right now.' Isaac turned to David behind him. 'Are you sure the band will turn up?'

'No problem, don't worry, everything's arranged, they'll be there,' David replied with a confident smile.

Turning about to face his men, Manny yelled, 'Let's pick up the pace.'

*

Later, he and the men lay against their packs eating rations waiting for their transport back to camp.

Lieutenant Briggs, second-in-command of Manny's company, strode purposefully towards them. Manny rose to his feet, stood to attention and saluted.

'Corporal, you've ten minutes left for chow and then we march back to Netheravon.'

'Yes, sir, but I thought we're being transported back to camp.'

The lieutenant gave a wry smile. 'Believe me, Corporal, it's not my idea. Make your complaint to the CO, it's his orders.'

Naturally, the men complained, but took it well, got to their feet helping each other with their packs. Once they were ready, Manny ordered, 'Quick march.'

Someone began to sing 'The White Cliffs of Dover' and the rest of the platoon joined in, stepping out to the rhythm of the tune, wanting to get back to barracks as quickly as possible for a hot bath and bed.

*

Manny was best man and Rita the only bridesmaid at Hannah and Isaac's wedding. Aunt Doris and Uncle Mark acted in place of Hannah's parents.

Isaac broke the traditional glass underfoot, with the guests yelling happily 'Mazeltov'.

The rabbi smiled saying, 'You may kiss the bride.'

Isaac and Hannah kissed to the cheers of the guests.

There were tears of joy and sadness as Aunt Doris hugged her niece. 'You're so beautiful, like your mother.'

As a wedding present, Aunt Doris and Uncle Mark hired the Bouverie Ballrooms for the newly married couple's reception, but how they obtained the abundance of food and drink was a mystery to all, and they would not divulge their source to anyone.

As promised, David produced a band that kept everyone dancing even as the air-raid sirens sounded; no one left the hall and the band outplayed the noise of ack-ack guns and the crash of exploding bombs. The Germans weren't going to spoil this wedding.

The lights were low, just a silver ball turning lazily in the middle of the ceiling, its beam lighting the dancers on the ballroom-floor with sparkling stars.

Manny and Rita danced cheek to cheek to the sweet sound of 'Moonlight Serenade'. Her skin silky to his touch, the freshness of her perfume filled his nostrils. Taking his cheek from hers he looked down at her upturned face and was struck by her beauty.

Green eyes stared back into his with a slight glint of amusement. 'What?' she asked.

'I was just thinking how beautiful you were and what would everyone say if I kissed you?'

She smiled. 'You'll only know the answer to that question if you do.'

His lips moved towards hers, and for a split second he wondered if she was teasing and would pull back, but she didn't.

Chapter 15

IT WAS a cold but sunny morning when the three friends received orders to report to the orderly room.

'You three report at Reading Station on Monday morning. There's also a weekend pass,' said the staff-sergeant handing them a sealed envelope. 'Inside the envelope are your travel documentation and orders. If you don't arrive at your destination by 1300hrs, you'll be reported as being AWOL.' His dark brown eyes stared at each of them in turn. 'Is that clear?'

'Yes, Staff-Sergeant,' they chorused in unison. Standing to attention, smartly about-turned and left, marching quickly to their barrack. Locking the door, Manny opened the envelope, withdrawing three rail tickets and instructions to wear civilian clothes. They would be met at Reading Station under the clock by platform nine.

'I wonder what this is all about,' Isaac said, rubbing his chin thoughtfully.

'Whatever it is, we're rid of this place for a while,' said David, grinning broadly. 'I must make a phone call. There's someone I'm dying to see. I hope she's in.'

Manny grabbed David's arm, pulling him to a standstill. 'You never said a word about this. Who is she? Where did you meet her?'

'What's this, an interrogation?' David shrugged off the hand, turning to walk away, but Isaac moved in front of him, placing a hand on his chest. 'Whoa there, pal, friend, you aren't going anywhere until you tell us the full story.'

Manny moved beside Isaac. 'I second that.'

David chuckled. 'OK, OK. I met her on our first leave. I was playing the sax with friends at a club in Stamford Hill. She was dancing by the stage, our eyes met, and I was smitten. Her name is Eve Bronstein and she works in a munitions factory. I walked her home, and knew straight away that I was in love. I've seen her twice since then, and speak to her on the phone most days, when I'm able to get through.'

'So, when were we going to meet this love of your life?' Manny asked.

'Well, I er … I um…'

'I know there's a dance at the Lyceum in the Strand on Saturday night, if the girls aren't working let's all go there,' suggested Manny.

'Good idea,' added Isaac. 'Come on, we have some phone calls to make.'

*

After a very enjoyable weekend, the three friends arrived at Reading Station, and were surprised to see Manny's cousin Sam under the clock, also in civilian clothes.

'Hallo, Sam, you ordered here too?' asked Manny as they shook hands.

Sam smiled. 'No, I'm the person meeting you. Follow me, I've a car outside.'

Ten minutes after leaving the station they turned off the main road onto a country lane.

Manny couldn't help noticing that Sam kept glancing into the rearview mirror, but didn't make any comment about it. They turned right into a wide drive. Twenty yards in front of them were wrought-iron gates, which opened as they approached, closing once they passed through. The car's tyres crunched on a curved gravel drive bordered by bushes and trees that gradually thinned out as ahead of them appeared a red-bricked stately mansion with plush lawns, oak, maple, and plane trees dotted here and there.

Sam stopped the car between white stone fluted vases on plinths that stood either side of stone steps, which led up to an oak door with the coat of arms of the Rothschild family above it.

The three friends followed Sam through the door where they were met by two men in civilian clothes with Sten guns slung across their shoulders and pistols at their sides, who searched them. Sam looked on, an amused smile on his face. The two men turned to Sam and nodded.

'Follow me, I'll show you to your room,' said Sam.

They trailed behind him, across a black and white squared marble floor, climbing maroon-carpeted stairs curving slightly to the left; they turned right on the first floor into a corridor, stopping at the first door on the left. Sam opened the door and stepped to one side, allowing them to enter.

'Wow, you could sleep a platoon in here,' said Isaac enthusiastically as he stepped into the bedroom. Its walls were lined with plain pastel fawn-coloured wallpaper and a crystal chandelier hung from the ceiling. Glass patio doors led onto a balcony overlooking the gardens. Three beds lined one side of the room, with wardrobes at the far end, and in the left-hand corner an open door.

Sam pointed to it. 'The bathroom's through there. Have a wash and change, then come downstairs to the dining room. One of the guards will show you where to go.' Sam turned, and without another word left closing the door behind him.

Isaac was about to say something to the others, but Manny placed a finger to his lips and strode over to his brother-in-law, whispering in his ear, 'This room could have listening devices.'

Isaac drew back, a look of surprise on his face. 'You're mad,' he said aloud, walking across to the open bathroom door. 'Sam wouldn't do that to us,' adding 'bathroom and toilet large enough to live in,' and turned to see Manny undressing.

'Are there any towels in there?'

Isaac poked his head back into the bathroom. 'Yes.'

'Well, let's get washed and changed. The sooner we go downstairs, the sooner we find out what this cloak and dagger stuff's all about.'

*

An hour later the three Paras were shown into the dining room. Its walls were a pastel shade of green with paintings of mountains, waterfalls, running streams and other countryside scenes hung between Baroque plasterwork; above them hung a Waterford crystal chandelier.

In the centre of the room on a Persian carpet, seated at an eighteenth-century dining table, was Sam and three men who were as different from each other as chalk and cheese.

Sam stood, wiping his mouth with a napkin and rose to his feet. 'Ah, there you are.' He gestured towards the man on his immediate left. 'May I introduce Mr White?'

Mr White was an enormous man, completely bald with deep-set brown eyes; he stood and bowed, but was silent.

Manny guessed he must be nearly six foot tall and weigh about twenty stone. Mr White sat gently back onto his chair for such a big man pouring a glass of red wine from a bottle in front of him.

Sam motioned to the middle of the three men, 'Mr Black.'

Mr Black stood. He was slightly taller than Manny, broad-shouldered and muscular with a slight tan, thick black hair a tad too long and penetrating grey eyes under long lashes that stared at each of them in turn. He nodded silently and sat down.

Sam looked towards the third man. 'Mr Amber.'

Mr Amber nodded his shaggy, grey, hairy head. His beard, the same colour as his hair, covered his face and chest like a napkin that moved like wheat in the wind as he smiled; the green eyes under bushy eyebrows had a glint of mischievousness in them. He raised his wine glass in greeting, and like the others didn't say a word, but took a sip of wine, then replaced the glass on the table and sat down.

'Take a seat, dinner will be here in a moment,' said Sam.

No sooner had they sat down when a waiter, a pistol at his hip, entered with their meal. Manny's eyes widened as he looked down at the plate covered with a steak, new potatoes and peas. He hadn't seen a steak for more than two years.

'Not the sort of meal you usually have, Herr Grenfeldt?' said Mr White in German.

Manny looked up, his fork poised in mid-air, a piece of meat on the end, showing no surprise, replying nonchalantly in English. 'I'm sorry; you must have the wrong man, my name's Michael Green.'

'Reply in German,' Sam said harshly in that language.

Manny turned to his cousin, whose cold stare communicated his meaning. Manny nodded, this time repeating what he'd said previously in German.

Mr Amber took a sip of wine, his bushy eyebrows rose slightly as he looked across the table at Isaac. 'I understand, Monsieur Steinberger, that you were recently married?' he said in French.

Isaac looked across at Sam, who nodded. 'Yes, sir, that's correct, but like my friend you must have me mixed up with someone else.' He grinned at Mr Amber. 'My name's Tom Williams,' Isaac replied in fluent French.

David placed his knife and fork on the edge of the empty plate, poured himself a glass of wine, raised it to the men opposite; his dark eyes staring unafraid at Mr Black. 'To the death of Hitler and the Third Reich,' he said in German. The three men raised their glasses, as do the others.

'Do you hate the Nazis that much, Mr Wasserman?' Mr Black asked in Italian.

'Firstly, Mr Black,' David replied in Italian, 'my name is David Wilson, and secondly, if I could kill every Nazi with my bare hands I would, but before doing that I would torture them till they cried for mercy, does that answer your question?'

There was silence between them for a moment, then Manny turned to Sam. 'What's this cloak and dagger stuff all about, Sam?'

'The three of you are good friends, and have been together since your internment on the Isle of Man. You speak fluent German, as that's your mother tongue, including French and Italian. These men just wanted to talk to you, and regarding the cloak and dagger stuff – well, let's see what happens.'

Sam stood. 'I'll have the waiter bring in dessert.' He looked across at the three men on his left. 'Time is short, gentlemen, you have one hour and then I'll return.' He turned and left the room.

Nothing more was said as they finished their meal and the waiter brought the dessert.

Over dessert and coffee, the three friends chatted to the three men opposite in Italian, German and French, about the countries and various cities they had visited.

On the hour Sam returned, interrupting their conversations. 'Well?' he asked.

'We have our men,' Mr Black replied.

'Thank you.' Sam walked across the room, drawing the drapes and then turned to face them. 'There's a special mission that needs men who speak fluent German and French, and have parachute and combat training. You three fit those categories. It's a dangerous mission, and I couldn't order you to go, but must ask if you would volunteer.' He turned to Isaac. 'No disrespects to you, Isaac, but you have a wife and may want to think twice.'

'I don't have to think about it. If it meant having a go at the Nazi scum, I'm in,' he replied emphatically.

Sam nodded and walked over to the far wall, sliding a large painting of snow-capped mountains in Scotland to one side, revealing a small cinema screen. 'OK.' The lights dim and a picture of a German general appeared.

Mr Black strode across the room standing to the right of the screen. 'This is Generaloberst Claus Von Schweck. He is, or was, the commander of an Infantry Brigade in Russia.' There was a click and another photo appeared. 'Oberst Johann Shtick commanded a Luftwaffe Squadron, also in Russia. The German army had lost one and half million men, killed, wounded or missing – and lost an untold amount of military equipment during their Russian campaign. We, the British Government, received a message from the General that needed a reply.'

The two pictures were now side by side as Mr Black pointed a finger in their direction. 'These two men, with other high-ranking officers, are fed up with the way Hitler has been running the war, and are calling for a coup against him, forming an anti-Hitler movement. Our job is to contact these men who are convalescing in France, and give them a message from the British and American governments and their allies; that we're willing to offer an immediate ceasefire once they have either handed Hitler over to us, or killed him. They must also hand over to the Allies for trial, all those who have taken part in atrocities against Jews and other nationalities.'

'Apart from Manny, we look like Jews,' David said, 'Surely we would jeopardise the mission.'

'Firstly,' Mr Black intervened, 'the General might be insulted that we are Jews, but that's his problem, not ours. The powers to be need a message taken to the General and his fellow conspirators, and the answer brought back to England. But for us, this is not all we're going to do. Once we've made contact, given our message and received a reply, we will then carry out another mission.'

The screen changed to a map of France.

Mr Black pointed to the map with a long pointer, 'Here—'

'Excuse me,' Manny interrupted, all eyes turning in his direction. 'You tell us that we're going to France, to meet these anti-Hitler people, and then carry out another mission.

You want us to parachute into France wearing our red berets, walk through the German army, meet those generals and walk out again. And exactly who is "we"?'

Mr Black smiled, replying in German, 'If you wait a while and don't jump the gun, I will reveal all.' He moved away from the map, looking at the three men, the smile now replaced by one of belligerence.

'From now on you speak only German, or French when necessary. In a little while we're going to another location, and when I mean we, that's you—' he pointed to the three friends. 'Sam and me, we're going to parachute into enemy territory wearing German officers' uniforms of the 1st SS Panzer division Leiberstandant Adolf Hitler, who are veterans of the Russian campaign. You've one week to acclimatise yourself with their campaigns, and in the use of German and Russian weaponry, and learn to sing SS songs, especially their marching song, *"Let death be our battle companion we are the black band."* He looked at Manny. 'Does that answer your question?'

Manny nodded in reply, a slight smile on his face.

'If you're caught – well, I need not go into that.' His face set in a grim mask adding, 'By the way, my name is Zachary Bergman, and for your information I hadn't changed my name, and would not change it, because – I want – the – Germans – to know – who I am.' The words although quiet were spat out like bullets from a gun. 'I assure you of one other thing, they would not get me alive,' he added icily.

Isaac shivered with Bergman's words. David wrapped his arms around his body, but Manny wanted to stand up and let out a howl of delight. This was a man after his own heart.

Bergman turned back to the map. 'Our General, the Oberst and other members of the anti-Hitler movement are resting at a château in the town of Vernon. I believe, Isaac, you've been there?'

'Yes, it's a lovely place with Parisian architecture, situated on the bank of the Seine.'

'Do you know the Château de Leon?'

'Yes.'

'Good, then we should have no problem getting there.'

'What about this other mission?' David enquired.

Bergman turned back to the map, pointing to an area some fifty miles from Vernon. 'We have been told by the French Resistance, that just here there is a petrol depot supplying fuel for aircraft, tanks and other transport in that sector. We're going to blow it up. From there we move quickly across country to Grandcamp-Maisy on the coast just north of Bayeux, where hopefully a motor-torpedo boat will pick us up. OK, let's get this show on the road. Sam, is transport waiting?'

'Yes.' Sam rose to his feet.

'What about our gear?' asked Isaac.

'Don't worry about that, follow me,' replied Sam, leading them down into the wine cellar, walking to the far wall and pushing one of the bricks. The wall swung open revealing a well-lit tunnel. He gestured for them to enter, closed the entrance behind him, with Bergman leading the way. They emerge to find a lorry waiting and climbed aboard; Sam pulled down the tarpaulin and banged on the floor.

As the lorry moved off, Manny said, 'That was a very nice meal, Sam.' He smiled. 'It was the sort of meal condemned men got before being led to their execution.'

Sam smiled back. 'That was not my intention. It was meant as bait for you to agree to the mission.'

'I would have come, even if you had given me baked beans on toast; not that I didn't appreciate the gesture.'

'I'll remember that next time, baked beans it is.'

Chapter 16

France, 16 February 1944

THE five men, their breath evaporating into clouds of vapour, strode confidently in step along the road. The early morning dew clung to their camouflaged combat jackets that showed no insignia. Their unshaven faces were dirt- and sweat-streaked under their helmets, with snow goggles above the brim.

Just before daybreak, they parachuted into a field some twenty miles from Vernon, buried the chutes, arriving in the early hours on the outskirts of the town.

Apart from Schmeisser machine pistols strapped across the front of their chests ready for action, all carried backpacks and an assortment of weapons.

Bergman, the leader of the operation was wearing sunglasses and, on his left hip, his father's Russian officer's sword strapped to the webbing belt.

Manny strode step-for-step beside him; a Russian PS1141 hung from a strap on his right shoulder, ready to be brought into action. It was a lethal weapon with a 30-round magazine that had been modified to take the German 9mm bullet.

Behind them, Sam, with Isaac and David either side of him, had a wrapped sniper's rifle tied to his backpack. Isaac had become lethal in throwing the three stiletto knives, the hilts protruding behind his neck from holders strapped across his back. Sam had a smile fixed on his face, a hatchet in a specially made holder on his left hip.

An Oberfeldwebel of the Wehrmacht stood feet astride between two half-tracks set in a V-formation, blocking the entrance to town. The butt of his machine pistol rested on his hip; hard brown eyes stared unflinchingly at the five men coming towards him.

The Oberfeldwebel raised the muzzle of his weapon, pointing it at Bergman, finger on the trigger, raising his left hand palm up for them to stop, looked them up and down, and snapped his fingers impatiently. 'Papers.'

Three soldiers appeared from behind the half-tracks, their weapons aimed at the five men, who moved apart, standing in a line with Bergman in the middle. Bergman's mouth widened in a smile, but not the eyes behind the sunglasses, which stared angrily at the German as he unbuttoned the top pocket of the combat jacket with his left hand, the right resting on his Schmiesser as he handed the papers to the Oberfeldwebel, who leaned towards him and yelled, 'Take those stupid glasses off.'

Manny moved menacingly towards the German, combat knife half out of its sheath. Bergman grabbed his arm and shook his head.

The Oberfedlwebel looked down at Bergman's papers; the thick-lipped mouth moved like a fish in water as he looked at Bergman. 'I, I'm ss-sorry Sir, bb-but you weren't wearing any insignia.'

In a harsh whisper, Bergman said, 'It seemed you've never been to the Russian front. If you had, you would know that the lifespan of any officer showing insignia was exactly three minutes, if he's lucky. Perhaps you'd like a transfer to that part of the world; it might teach you a thing or two, if you survive.'

The Oberfeldweber, with shaking hand and without another word, handed Bergman his papers.

'Do you want to see these gentlemen's papers?'

'That won't be necessary, sir.' The Oberfeldwebel clicked his heels to attention, saluted and moved to one side, allowing them through. Manny shouldered him to one side as they passed, the Oberfeldwebel's face showing the fear of being sent to the Russian front.

Bergman moved beside Isaac. 'Where's this hotel?'

'Turn right at the next turning; it's about twenty yards on the left.'

Bergman nodded, taking the lead once more.

They turned right into Avenue le Foche entering the Grande Hotel, dropping their backpacks on the floor and strode over to the reception desk.

'Can I help you, gentlemen?' the elderly clerk asked with a fixed smile.

'We want adjoining rooms for two nights, maybe more,' Manny demanded.

'I've two adjoining rooms on the second floor. I can arrange for another bed to be put into one of them.'

Manny nodded and slipped the man some francs. 'Thank you, we'll take them.'

The receptionist picked up a phone, spoke into it for a second, replaced the receiver, and turned the register around for them to sign, at the same time reaching for two keys that hung on a board behind him, handing them to Manny, who smiled his thanks.

Isaac looked up after signing the register; his and the receptionist's eyes met. The elderly man's brow puckered in thought, as though trying to remember where he'd seen him before. Isaac turned quickly away, picked up his backpack and followed the others towards the lift.

The five men stowed their gear, their weapons near at hand. Manny picked up the phone, pressing the button for the concierge, who answered immediately. 'I'd like a table for five at the Club Etiénne for tonight, please.'

'I'll see what I can do, sir. You do know it's for officers only.'

'Yes, yes,' Manny said impatiently.

'I'll do my best, sir.'

'Make sure you do,' Manny demanded, adding, 'Send someone up immediately; we need our uniforms cleaned and pressed.'

Within minutes the telephone rung. Manny picked up the receiver. 'Yes.'

'Sir, this is Henry, the concierge. I've made reservations for ten o'clock.'

'Ten o'clock?' Manny questioned.

'I can assure you, that it was the best time to arrive, sir.'

'Thank you, Henry.'

There was a knock at the door and David opened it. The two maids curtseyed; the shorter of the two said. 'We've come to pick up your uniforms, sir.'

David stepped aside. 'They're on the bed.'

*

There was a mixture of laughter and low, murmured conversation that stopped as Manny and the others entered the Club Etiénne. Iron crosses and battle medals adorned their dress uniforms as the five of them stood proudly for a moment inside the doorway, contemptuously surveying the room.

The maître d' approached with a fixed smile on his face showing no emotion, giving a slight bow, 'Welcome gentlemen, you have reservations?'

'Yes,' replied Manny, 'in the name of SS-Hauptsturmführer (Captain) Bergman.'

Bergman looked towards the other diners, who quickly turned back to their meal and conversations.

The maître d' opened the folder that was tucked under his arm and glanced at it. 'Ah! Yes, please follow me.' He showed them to a table with a reserved sign on it. As they took their seats, he handed each of them a menu.

Having given them enough time to read the menu, a waiter moved over to their table, bowing slightly. 'Good evening, gentlemen, are you ready to order?'

'Yes,' Bergman replied.

Once they had ordered their meal and drinks, Bergman asked the waiter, 'Do you know if General Von Schweck would be here tonight?'

'I'm sorry, sir, I don't, but I'll ask the maître d'.'

A pretty waitress brought their drinks. Bergman placed a tip on the tray. The waitress smiled at him, showing even, white teeth. 'Thank you very much, sir. Is there anything else? Perhaps some company?'

Bergman smiled back. 'Not at the moment, thank you. Perhaps later.'

The maître d' sidled over to Bergman, giving a slight cough, to make sure Bergman noticed him. 'Excuse me, sir, you enquired about General Von Schweck?'

'Yes, I did.'

'The General will not be in tonight, but he's booked his usual private room for tomorrow evening. I could ask his aide-de-camp if it's possible for you to join him.'

'Yes please; I'm SS-Hauptsurmführer Bergman, 1st Panzer Division, on leave from the Russian front.' He gestured to the men at the table. 'And these are my officers. We're staying at the Grande Hotel, room 202.' Bergman slipped the man some money.

Finishing their meal, they left the club and returned to the hotel for a good night's sleep. On entering the hotel the concierge handed Bergman a message. It was from General Von Schweck's aide-de-camp, telling them that the general requested their company at nine sharp the following evening.

*

On the stroke of nine, having rested throughout the day, Manny and the others entered the club, and were shown to Von Schweck's private room. There was a warm atmosphere about the place; the smoke from the cigars and cigarettes of the officers standing in twos and threes talking amongst themselves swirled upward. The officers glanced at the new arrivals, then ignored them, which suited Bergman and the others. A waiter with a tray approached offering some canapés, while another was serving fluted glasses of champagne.

A Wehrmacht Oberst, with blond cropped hair, his tailored uniform immaculately pressed, walked over to them, stopping in front of Bergman.

The two men were the same height, but where Bergman was broad-shouldered and muscular, the Oberst was slim and narrow-shouldered. The Oberst clicked his heels, giving a slight bow from the waist and then looked into Bergman's eyes, glanced down at the medal ribbons on his chest and then back to Bergman's eyes.

'No matter how many bravery awards you have,' his voice was courteous and arrogant, 'it is not appropriate for officers, even those of the Waffen-SS, not to show their insignia. Don't let it happen again. Do you understand me, Hauptsturmführer?'

Bergman was silent for a second, staring unflinchingly back at the German officer, then clicked his heels and bowed slightly. 'SS-Hauptsurmführer Bergman,' he said slowly, eyes resting for a moment on the one campaign medal and then back to eye contact. 'I assume, sir, you were referring to the incident at the checkpoint.'

The Oberst nodded.

'We,' Bergman turned to his officers and then back to the man in front of him, 'have just returned from six months on the Russian front.' He leaned closer, his face like thunder, prodding a finger into the officer's chest. 'Firstly, don't speak to me without introducing yourself, speak down, or try intimidating my men or me,' he said, adding with venom, 'Secondly, if you want to take it further, I'll be happy to accommodate you, or you could run to the General for protection.'

The Oberst looked from Bergman to the four men, taking a step back, eyes showing fear on seeing the stern-faced men around him. In an act of bravado the Oberst spoke in a slightly higher octave, 'Are you threatening me, Bergman?'

Bergman gave a sinister grin, turning to his men. 'Did you hear me threaten this officer?'

'No, sir,' they replied in unison.

'See, Herr Oberst, no one heard me threaten you,' Bergman said quietly.

The officer stepped away from them, his face pale and without another word walked away, just as the General entered the room. All the officers clicked their heels to attention and saluted.

'Sorry for being late, gentlemen, too many forms to sign.' The General walked across the room, noticing Bergman and the others, and made a beeline for them, coming to a stop in front of Bergman.

'I haven't seen you here before.' He gestured towards the decorations on Bergman's chest and the badge of a diving eagle in a wreath of oak and laurel leaves. 'It seems you and your men are specialists, and have been very busy people.'

'It's the Ruskies, sir; they're like ants from a nest.'

The General's features changed to one of surprise. 'Yes, ants could be a bit of a problem, until you get rid of their queen.'

'We do our best, General. Sometimes it needs a little help from some friends.'

The General's eyes slit slightly at the mention of ants from the nest, as it was a recognition code.

'I'm very impressed, gentlemen, by your valour.' The General shook hands with each of them and then turned to the officer who had confronted Bergman earlier. 'Gratz,' the General beckoned to the Oberst, who moved quickly to the General's side.

'Yes sir.'

'Make sure these officers sit next to me, and after dinner drive them to my château.'

Gratz gave Manny and the others a withering look. 'Yes sir.'

During the meal the General talked passionately about the Russian campaign, tears in his eyes at the loss of so many of his men.

On arrival at the château, Manny and the others were shown into the library, where, apart from the General, there were five other officers in the room. The General didn't introduce them as he took a cigar from a silver box on a table beside a leather-bound armchair, lifted the cigar to his nose, inhaling its fragrance before cutting off the end. Gratz, as quick as a flash, was beside Von Schweck with a light.

'That will be all, Gratz. You can take the rest of the night off.'

Gratz looked a little hurt at the dismissal, but the Oberst saluted – 'Heil Hitler' – turned and left the room. One of the other officers followed him out, returning minutes later nodding at the General, who lowered himself onto the armchair, crossed his legs, blowing smoke across the room, and then turned to Bergman.

'Herr…' he waved the cigar in a circle.

'Major Zachary Bergman.'

'You are a…'

'Jew, yes Herr General. But that's irrelevant at the moment. I have a message – you might call it an offer – from the British and American government, and their allies regarding the wishes of … um, your surreptitious organisation.'

On hearing that Bergman and his men were Jews, the General's demeanour changed, his face showing disgust. 'I find it abhorrent that you and your men were dressed in the uniform of such an illustrious regiment.' Von Schweck took an angry puff at the cigar.

'To tell you the truth, General, I find it nauseating to wear it, as do my men.'

Before Von Schweck could reply, Manny stepped close to the General, saying quietly so only the General could hear, 'If it were up to me, I'd kill every man in this room, but it's not, so please give the major your answer and let's be on our way.'

The General, stared unafraid into Manny eyes, then leaned slightly forward in the armchair, asking Bergman with a hint of caution in his voice. 'What's the offer?'

'When, and if, you capture or kill Adolf Hitler, you must also hand over all those that have committed atrocities against humanity, and then we'll offer a just and fair surrender.'

Bergman took an envelope from his tunic pocket, handing it to the General, who tore it open, taking out a typewritten letter. He quickly read the contents, raised an eyebrow at the signatures and gestured to a Luftwaffe Oberst, whom Manny recognised from the photo as Joehann Schtick. The General handed him the letter, puffed on his cigar, exhaling the smoke towards the ceiling as the letter was passed from one officer to another, until it was back in the General's hand. He placed it in the ashtray and set it alight with the end of the cigar, watching it burn until it was only black ash, and then looked at Bergman.

'We accept the terms. I hope to God we can carry it off, otherwise there will be reprisals, and the brutality carried out on those arrested doesn't bear thinking about.'

Von Schweck took headed notepaper from a rack on the table beside him and began to write. For the next few minutes there was silence in the room until he blotted the notepaper, placed it in an envelope, handing it to Bergman. 'Give this to you-know-who; we accept the terms.'

Returning to the hotel, Isaac said to Manny, 'You surprised me talking to the General that way. It seems that the loving caring Manny has turned into a hard, mean man.'

Manny smiled grimly. 'I really wanted to kill them, and in any other situation I would have.'

'We all feel the same way,' said Bergman, 'but the mission comes first.'

They entered their room to find two knapsacks on Bergman's bed. 'Great, I was worried that I wouldn't get those in time.'

'What's in them?' Manny asked, walking over to the bed.

'Explosives, already primed,' replied Bergman. 'All we do is set the timers. OK, let's get changed and on our way.'

Chapter 17

20 February 1944

THE group settled down between a copse of trees overlooking the petrol depot, which was hidden in a valley between two hills. A single road ran from the north into the depot continuing out towards the south.

Surveying the area through binoculars, David asked, 'Any ideas?'

'It wasn't going to be easy,' Bergman muttered under his breath. 'Anyway, whoever said it was, was crazy.'

'Anyone count the guards?' Sam asked.

'We couldn't cut through the fence, those guard dogs would smell us a mile away,' Manny commented.

'Very clever,' Isaac joined in, moving his binoculars slowly from right to left adding, 'You drive through the gates and come out the other end. Keeps the traffic moving, but—'

A faint rumbling sound interrupted him, becoming louder by the second. The dimmed headlights of a convoy of trucks and tanks appeared around the bend. 'Mmm, now we know why there wasn't much traffic during the day. They move everything at night,' Isaac said.

'Apart from lobbing a few mortar bombs into the compound, I couldn't see our way past the guards,' said Sam.

A siren sounded and the gates opened, allowing the convoy through, closing once the last vehicle had passed. This went on all night, with convoys entering and leaving, until dawn began to streak the sky. The group were no nearer to solving the problem of getting into the depot than when they arrived.

Manny, his back against a tree, stared down into the compound, knowing that like all puzzles, given time, this one could be solved, but they hadn't got the luxury of time.

The guard system was ingenious. At no time was there a part of the perimeter left unguarded even for a minute. The guards were not the only problem – it was the dogs. Even though he and the others were in German uniform, they couldn't just walk up to the depot and ask if they could blow up the place. Manny turned to look back along the road as a Tiger tank approached. By the sound of the engine it was nearly out of fuel.

As the gates closed behind it the engine spluttered and died. Two crew members leapt from the tank, grabbed an oil drum and rolled it towards the tank, bringing the drum to a stop next to another crewman who unwrapped a hose from around his waist, uncapped the drum, plunged the hose into the open hole, placing the other end into his mouth, sucked for a second, then quickly took the hose from his mouth, placing it into the tank's fuel pipe.

'What?' Manny whispered. He gave a silent whistle, taking the binoculars from his eyes and blinked a couple of times before replacing them, whispering, 'There's the answer to our puzzle.'

A couple of minutes later he awoke the others.

'What's going on?' Bergman asked, immediately awake as Manny's touched his arm, not replying to his question until he had aroused the others.

'Question,' said Manny. 'How does all that oil and petrol get there? We hadn't seen a convoy of fuel tankers, except for those that refuel the tanks in battle, and we couldn't see a sign of any oil pipes. I think I have the answer to our problem.'

'If you've something to tell us, get to the point,' Bergman said impatiently. 'This isn't a debating society, or a quiz.'

'We never noticed it before, because it was hidden by a stack of oil drums. If you look into the compound at about ten o'clock, there's railway buffers and a rail track leading into the hill. The fuel comes in by rail. All we had to do was find the track which was probably on the other side of the hill. But what I want to know is, why weren't we told about the railway tracks by the Resistance?'

'Blow me down with a feather, he's right,' said David quietly, looking through his binoculars.

The moon slipped in and out of the clouds, giving the ground mist an eerie glow. Manny led the group silently around the hill, where they found a single railway track that disappeared into the hillside.

They slid down the embankment, moving either side of the tunnel. Manny was surprised there were no guards as he peered into the black hole, tilted his head to one side listening for the slightest sound and sniffed the air for any smell of cigarette smoke as someone might be having a sneaky smoke. He looked across at Bergman who nodded.

In a crouched position, the safety-catch of his Schmeisser off, Manny entered the tunnel, dropping to all fours at a bend, crawling cautiously forward until he was able to see the end of the tunnel. There was a slight glow along the wall, and the sound of men working, but still no guards.

He returned to Bergman and the others who gathered around him as he said quietly, 'I don't know why, but there doesn't seem to be anyone guarding the other end, which seems strange considering the amount of guards around the perimeter of the compound. I think they probably patrol the tunnel at intervals.'

'Sam and I will go on the left side of the track,' said Bergman, pointing to the others. 'You three on the right side. Once we get to the compound, because we're wearing German uniforms, we would be able to walk around without any problem and lay the charges.'

'What about blowing the tunnel when we leave?' Isaac remarked.

'Let's cross that bridge when we come to it. The dump's our main target,' replied Bergman, distributing the explosives. 'OK, let's go.'

They reached the bend in the tunnel without incident, and were about to proceed further, when they heard voices. A beam from a torch cut through the darkness, waving up and down like a small searchlight.

Bergman came across the track. 'We've nowhere to hide, and we can't get into a gun battle. This must be done silently. I'll take David across with me; you two distract them while we get behind them.'

Bergman and David disappeared on the other side of the track as the beam of light came closer, cutting through the darkness just in front of Manny, who could now hear what the soldiers were saying.

'I tell you, it took all my willpower to return here. Forty-eight hours' leave wasn't enough; Paris was a fun city, and the women – I get horny just thinking about them.'

Another beam followed the first and then stopped. There was the sound of a match being lit, and a sigh of someone who had been longing for a cigarette. The smell of exhaled smoke drifted towards Manny and Isaac.

The beam of light moved forward as another voice said, 'I agree, Paris was all they say it was, and more.'

Approaching a bend, Manny calmly unsheathed a commando knife holding it with the blade upside down along his forearm. Isaac withdrew a stiletto from the sheath on his back, the two men moving side by side into the middle of the track.

Three soldiers appeared around the bend as Manny said, 'I second that.'

There was the sound of rifle bolts sliding a bullet into the chamber as two beams of light revealed Manny and Isaac.

'Who are you?'

Manny recognised the voice of the soldier who had just returned from Paris, his and Isaac's hands over their eyes shielding them from the light. 'Are we glad to see you.' Manny moved forward and to one side of the track, letting the hand drop. As Isaac stepped onto the other side, a corporal and two privates of the Wehrmacht, their rifles pointing at them, moved closer.

'Our tank broke down, must be a blockage in the fuel pipe. We managed to pull onto the side of the road.' He pointed at Isaac. 'My gunner and I left the rest of the crew by the tank, while we came to fetch some help. I thought it would be quicker this way.'

While Manny was speaking, Bergman, Sam and David crept slowly and silently behind the three men.

'What's your unit? You could have radioed for help.' The corporal leaned forward. 'Where's your insignia?' There was suspicion in his voice.

'Shit, how stupid could one be, I never thought of that.'

'What's your unit, where are you based?' The voice an octave higher.

Manny could see in the beams from the torches, the Germans were getting edgy and suspicious. The tank story wasn't that good. He saw Bergman and the others getting closer; he must keep the soldier's attention on him and Isaac for just another couple of seconds.

'Where did you stay in...' Manny hesitated as one of the soldiers raised his rifle and pointed it at Isaac.

'We asked you a question; if you don't answer I'm going to shoot you.'

Raising his left hand Manny said, 'Whoa there, what's your problem? Let's not get too hasty, we're in the same army.'

The corporal must have heard a sound, or felt something. He started to turn; in one fluid movement Manny's right arm jerked forward, the commando knife flew across the gap between them. The corporal dropped his rifle, clawing at the hilt of the knife embedded in his throat, a wide-eyed look of surprise on his face as he fell slowly to the ground; he tried to say something to his two companions, one looking down at the hilt of a stiletto embedded in his chest, while the third had no chance as Sam clamped a hand over his mouth, running the commando knife across his throat.

Laying the three dead men against the wall, they moved off along the tunnel. Manny, without emotion, pulled his knife from the soldier's throat as he passed, wiping it clean on the German's tunic before following the others along the tunnel.

Near the end of the tunnel they dropped to the ground snaking towards the entrance, peering cautiously into the compound which was a hive of activity as another convoy had just arrived

'Take a row each and set the charges for thirty minutes,' Bergman ordered. 'Meet back here—' he looked down at his watch '—in twenty minutes, that should give us enough time to get out of here.'

Leaving the rest of their gear except for their Schmiesser inside the tunnel, they stood and moved cautiously out into the compound.

There was a feeling of nervous excitement inside Manny as he walked nonchalantly towards a large oil tank, glancing quickly around. No one was taking a blind bit of notice of him. He moved to the rear of the tank and with a steady hand laid the charges. Twenty minutes later he rejoined the rest of the group who picked up their gear and headed quickly back along the tunnel, laying their last remaining explosives against the wall close to the three dead soldiers.

The railway track started to hum and vibrate. 'Train coming,' warned Isaac.

'Let's get out of here fast,' yelled Manny and Sam in unison as they ran towards the end of the tunnel, followed by the others. Emerging into the open they quickly clambered up the embankment, diving behind some bushes as a locomotive came around the bend its headlight lighting up the track and entering the tunnel.

Manny knew they needed to get as far away from the compound as possible. 'There's a lorry coming, let's stop it,' he yelled, getting to his feet and running into the middle of the road, holding up his hands for the vehicle to stop. The others joined him to straddle the road, guns pointing at the lorry as it came to a halt in front of them.

The driver leaned out of his window. 'What's going on?'

Quick as a flash, Manny was at the driver's door, wrenching it open, pulling the surprised man from the cab. His mate reached for a weapon, but Bergman was too quick for him. Opening the door, he threw him to the ground. 'Stand up, and keep your hands where I can see them,' Bergman ordered harshly.

While this was going on, the other three ran around the rear of the lorry, guns ready in case there were soldiers there, but it was loaded with oil drums.

Suddenly, night turned into day; the sound of the explosion reached them seconds later. The driver reached for his pistol. Manny shot him as his mate leapt at Bergman, who side-stepped to the left, slammed the butt of his weapon against the German's head, then shot him.

Manny leapt behind the wheel. 'Jump aboard,' he yelled above the noise of explosions from the depot.

The others climbed quickly into the back of the lorry, Bergman moving onto the seat beside Manny, who put his foot hard down on the accelerator. The ground under the lorry's wheels shuddered; flames erupted from the mouth of the tunnel like a giant flamethrower.

Bringing the lorry to a stop, Manny and Bergman opened their doors, standing on the running board looking back at their handywork with satisfaction. Tongues of flame lit up the night, followed by flying debris as explosion followed explosion, mixed with the sound of fire bells.

The two men got back into the vehicle. Manny put it into gear and they moved quickly away. Bergman pulled a map and small torch from his pocket while, in the back of the lorry, Sam and the others pushed the oil drums out, watching them roll along the road, spilling oil as there caps burst open.

Bergman looked at Manny. 'Take the next left,' he ordered. Manny did so, turning into a small country road as behind them they left exploding oil drums and devastation.

'Turn left stay on this road till you reach Ussy...' He hesitated for a moment looking down at the map with his finger on the road they were taking. '... At the end of the town turn right and keep your foot down; we must cross the River Orme by daybreak.'

Manny glanced sideways at Bergman. 'What do you think I'm doing? Any harder on the accelerator I'll be through the floorboards.'

Bergman looked at Manny. 'Have you ever driven one of these before?'

Manny smiled, gritting his teeth as they skidded around a bend. 'No, I don't think I have.'

'Forget I said anything.' Bergman closed his eyes, pushing his hand against the dashboard in front of him. 'Just make sure you stay on the road,' he yelled, as the lorry skidded around another bend, its rear wheels racing on the grass verge, splattering grass and earth behind them before the tyres gripped on the road and they sped onward.

Bergman opened his eyes. 'I'd rather die fighting the Germans than sit beside you while you're driving.'

Manny glanced across at Bergman and smiled broadly, 'Isn't this fun?'

'Keep your bloody eyes on the road.' Bergman burst out laughing. 'You're an idiot, turn next right.' They drove through Ussy, turning at the end of the town where the road narrowed into a country lane that skirted high hedges as it twisted and turned. 'Pull in here for a moment,' he said.

Manny pulled off the road, letting the engine tick over as he and the others got down from the lorry to stretch their legs, munch on dry biscuits and drink from their water bottles.

Bergman spread the map on the bonnet of the lorry and the others moved either side of him as he pointed to a spot on the map. 'We're approaching a bridge over the River Orme. There'll probably be a checkpoint there. Leave the talking to me.' He looked up at the sky, which was now turning a light grey. 'We want to be at least twenty miles from the river before full light; OK, let's go.'

Two miles before the river they came across a squadron of Tiger tanks parked by the roadside, and were stopped by military police. Two combination motor bikes stood on the side of the road, the riders astride their bikes, the side-car passengers sitting behind machine guns aimed in their direction, while two heavily armed policemen checked the back of the lorry.

Manny and Bergman handed their papers to a sergeant, while an Oberleutnant looked on, smoking a cigarette.

Moving his Schmeisser across his knee, Manny slipped off the safety catch, at the same time placing his Tommy-gun beside him.

Bergman looked across at the German officer, slowly easing his pistol from its holster as the officer walked across the road, having one last drag of his cigarette before flicking it away, taking the papers from the sergeant, who whispered something to him, glancing in their direction and walked slowly towards them.

Bergman hid the pistol behind his back as the officer saluted, and jumped onto the running board. 'Why aren't you showing your insignia?' He spotted the Russian Tommy-gun on the seat beside Manny, and then at their unshaven faces, nodded understandingly, returning the papers to Bergman, '1st Division?'

Bergman looked him straight in the eyes and whispered, 'Yes.'

The Oberleutnant stepped off the running board. 'I understand, sir, I was there in November. Please follow the side-car.' He clicked his heels together, saluted and yelled, 'Gunther, let them through.'

One of the motorbike combinations pulled out in front of Manny who breathed a sigh of relief flicking off the safety catch of his Schmiesser following the motorbike, its side-car passenger bent forward against the slipstream.

The motorbike pulled to the side of the road as the guard lifted the barrier allowing the lorry through: Bergman returned the military policeman's salute as they passed.

*

It was nearly daylight when, fifteen miles past the river, they turned onto a dirt track looking for a place to hole up for the day. Manny pulled the lorry between clumps of trees and camouflaged it with branches and loose grass. Throughout the day each of them took turns on guard duty while the others slept.

The light began to fade as Manny, munching on a biscuit, took a swig from his water bottle before waking the others.

Bergman said, 'We can take a chance with the lorry, or cut across country. If we travel fast with a bit of luck we should be able to reach Caumont l'Evente before daybreak.'

'And if we take the lorry?' David asked.

'We'll travel faster, but have the added worry of road blocks, all it needs is a suspicious Nazi and—'

'We leave the lorry and foot-slog it on the road,' Manny interrupted. 'This way if we come across anything suspicious, we could go around it.'

The others agreed with him.

'OK,' said Bergman, 'the road it is, just take your weapons, ammunition and water. We'll find food along the way.'

By daybreak they were resting on the outskirts of a farm some forty miles from Grancamp-Maisy. Manny and Isaac stole bread and cheese from the farmhouse, whilst the woman of the house was hanging out the washing. There didn't seem to be any men around.

Throughout the morning they were kept awake by the constant sound of ME 110s taking off and landing from an airfield close by.

'The airfield was just across that road,' David pointed in the direction, adding, 'Do you think we should...' He hesitated.

'We should what?' Isaac prompted.

'Blow up some of the planes.' He looked at each of his companions in turn, plucking a piece of grass from the ground. 'Well ... what I mean was, we're here.' He pointed across the field. 'And they're there. It seemed a shame to just walk on by.'

'And if we decide to do what you suggest, what are we going to blow them up with?' Manny asked

'I never thought of that.'

'There's a way,' declared Isaac. 'Molotov cocktails.' The others waited silently for him to continue. 'I saw some crates of bottles in the barn. We could siphon off some petrol from the tractor over there and use pieces from a shirt as a taper, and *voilà!*'

'Good idea.' Bergman broke off a piece of grass, twirling it around his fingers. 'But you've forgotten one thing.'

'What's that?' Isaac looked up.

'When the first aircraft blows up, all hell would be let loose, and while we're running along the line of aircraft throwing our Molotov cocktails, the whole airfield would be on our tail. How do you propose we get out of that?' He and the others dropped closer to the ground as two military police combination motorcycles drove through the farm gates, stopping outside the barn.

The policemen dismounted, talked amongst themselves for a moment, took off their helmets and leather jackets, placing them in the sidecars and entered the barn.

Within seconds a girl ran out of the barn screaming, with two policemen chasing her. They quickly caught her and threw her to the ground.

While one sat astride the girl's body, the other ripped open her blouse. She tried to beat him with her fists, but the German just laughed, pulled up her bra, releasing her breasts and then grabbed her hands while the other slid down to sit on her legs, pulling up her skirt.

She screamed, struggling as he unbuttoned his fly, revealing his erection. Pushing her legs apart, he lay on top of her sucking her breast and trying to enter her, while his friend goaded him on saying that his dick was too small, and to hurry, otherwise he would have to show him how it was done.

Manny looked at Isaac, then at David, they both nodded, reading what was in each other's minds. The three men unsheathed their knives and snaked quickly along the grass. Bergman slid the sword from its sheath as he and Sam followed the others.

The second soldier had taken off his trousers, ready to take over from his mate, who clamped his hand over the young girl's mouth to stop her from screaming and mounted her, while his friend yelled encouragement, unaware that there might be anyone behind him.

Bergman caught up with Manny, who had never seen him so angry. Without a word, Bergman stood and thrust the blade of his sword into the soldier's back, stopping his goading in mid-sentence as he fell to the ground.

Manny was behind the German, lying on top of the girl, wrapped his arms around his throat pulling him from her.

'What the fuck?'

Manny slid the blade of his commando knife across the German's throat and the dead man fell to the ground.

Isaac grabbed the soldier's jacket, handing it to the girl, who was pulling down her skirt, telling her in French who they were. There was a scream from the barn.

'My mother,' said the girl; anguish on her face and in her voice.

'Stay here and keep quiet,' Bergman ordered as he and the others raced across to the barn. Manny gestured with his fingers crawling. The others nodded, and he led the way into the barn, unseen by the two military policemen, who were busy with the young girl's mother. One was on top of her, while the other unbuttoned his fly, trying to place his penis into her mouth saying with a smirk on his face, 'This should stop you screaming.'

Manny made a circular motion to Isaac and Sam, who nodded, crawling around the crates of bottles and milk churns. When they were in position, Manny and Bergman got to their feet.

'Can I join you?' Bergman asked.

The two Germans looked up. 'Who the fuck are you? And no, go find your own bit,' said the one on top of the woman, turning to look up at Bergman and the sword in his hand.

His companion reached for his gun lying close by, but Sam chopped down with his hatchet and the man leapt screaming to his feet, blood pouring from the severed artery. Bergman turned to face him and the German ran blindly onto the point of the sword, his momentum knocking Bergman off his feet who let go of the sword, rolling to one side before the Garman could fall on top of him.

Manny pulled the other soldier off the woman.

'OK, OK, you can have her,' the soldier gasped. 'The daughter's outside, you can have her too.'

Isaac moved in front of him, tapping the end of the German's penis with the tip of his knife. 'Bit small, isn't it?' He looked at the woman as Manny wrapped a coat around her nakedness.

'Thank you,' she said, holding the coat tightly across her body as Manny whispered something in her ear.

Surprise showed on her face, breaking into a beaming smile, looking from one to the other asking. 'Is that true, you're—'

'Yes, madam,' David nodded.

The German, not understanding what was being said, looked at the people around him asking, 'What are you saying, why was she smiling?' his voice high-pitched in fright.

'Your daughter is safe,' said Bergman just as Sam entered the barn with the young woman.

'How can we ever thank you?' said the mother.

'We don't need any thanks,' replied Manny, pointing to the German soldier, 'What are we going to do with him?'

'What are you saying? Please can I put my clothes on?' The naked man was shivering with fright.

Manny and the others laughed, and the daughter asked them what the German had said.

'He wants to put his clothes on,' David translated.

'He's quick to take them off,' the mother retorted, adding, 'no, let him stand there, doesn't he look pathetic with such a small one.'

'What are we going to do with him?' Manny asked, turning to look at the German, adding, 'Or what would you—'

The woman run forward, thrusting a dagger she had taken unnoticed by them from the German's belt, and plunged it into his chest.

Manny, and the others stared at the woman and the soldier, as like a slow motion film she stepped back, her eyes following the soldier, a look of horror on his face as he slowly crumpled to the ground.

They hid the military policemen's bikes in the barn and buried their bodies at the end of the field, making sure to leave no blood traces. The mother, whose name was Georgette, and her daughter, Odette, insisted they stay the rest of the day, offering their beds so they could get some sleep.

Manny was suddenly awake, a smile on his face. He had thought of a plan to attack the airfield, and shook Bergman, who was instantly awake. Manny outlined the plan to him.

Bergman smiled. 'Why didn't I think of that, but can you ride one of those things?'

'Can you?'

'Without a sidecar probably, but—'

'Let's wake the others.'

'The problem is,' said Manny to the others, 'have any of you ridden a motorbike, or one with a sidecar before?'

They all shook their heads.

'I assume it's like riding a bike with a motor,' David muttered, checking the magazine of his weapon.

'I don't think it's as easy as that,' Isaac said disconsolately, then looked at Manny. 'The plan ... mm ... brilliant, but we've not the time, or place to practise without being noticed, so let's pack up and be on our way.'

'Hey, that's not like you to give up without a fight,' Manny said. 'For the first time in a long while I feel alive, because I'm here doing what—' he pointed to Isaac and David '—we said we wanted to do when we were at Ochan. I feel loath to leave without doing something. If we could put some of those planes out of action for only a short time, it would save the lives of some of our bomber crews.'

'I agree,' piped up David. 'Manny's right, I know I'd feel guilty, knowing that someone was going to die because I couldn't ride a motorbike.'

'I'll drive the thing. Who'll take a chance and be my sidecar passenger?' asked Bergman.

'I will,' David offered.

'I'll drive the other one,' Manny uttered.

'I can do with a bit of action. I'm getting bored sitting here,' said Isaac as he rose to his feet and strode towards the door. 'Let's start by making the cocktails.'

'What about me?' Sam asked.

'You can be my pillion passenger,' said Manny with a grin.

Odette asked, 'What are you doing with the milk bottles?'

'We're making Molotov cocktails.' Manny replied.

'Why?'

'We're going to attempt, with the help of the motorbikes, to ride into the airbase and destroy as many German aircraft as we can.'

'The only problem we have,' Isaac pointed out, 'is we don't know the layout of the airfield, and—'

'Neither of us have driven a motorbike before,' Sam piped up in a cheery voice.

'I know the layout of the airfield,' Odette said. 'We deliver poultry, milk to the kitchens there.'

'That's wonderful,' said Manny. 'Can you draw a sketch for us?'

Odette nodded and sat at the kitchen table, drawing a layout of the airbase and showing where the aircraft were dispersed. She answered their questions about guards, and any gun emplacements that she'd seen, while her mother cooked them a meal.

The light was fading, the sky a light grey and cloudy, the moon appearing now and again, as the five men said their goodbyes to the two women.

In the sidecars, Isaac and David have a crate of Molotov cocktails between their feet. Sam's on the pillion behind Manny.

They start up the bikes and move off, waving to the women as they drove through the farm gates. Manny's heart skipped a beat as he turned out of the gates too sharply, nearly tipping them over.

The two motorcycle combinations turned into the entrance of the airfield, the guards without hesitation raising the barrier. They drove along the road, peeling off to the right, following Odette's instructions and stopping in the shadows of some trees and then switching off their engines. As arranged earlier, Manny and Bergman left the others to reconnoitre the area.

There was a slight smell of oil and petrol in the air as they approached the runway to find Messerschmitt 110s and 109s lining one side. The sound of mechanics working on aircraft echoed from a hangar to their left. Bergman grabbed Manny's arm, pulling him into the shadows as two guards appeared from behind one of the aircraft and walked along the line, disappearing into some bushes, probably to have a smoke.

Bergman tapped Manny on the shoulder, jerking his head for him to follow, rejoining the others. Bergman outlined the plan of attack. 'We'll drive along the line of aircraft with David and Isaac throwing their Molotov cocktails at alternate aircraft.'

They all nodded in agreement and started up the bikes.

With Bergman in the lead, they sped onto the runway. David lit the petrol soaked rag protruding from the top of the bottle with a cigarette clamped between his teeth, throwing the Molotov cocktail at the first aircraft in the line. The petrol-filled bottle shattered as it landed on the canopy of the first Messerschmitt, spilling petrol down the fuselage, and within seconds the aircraft was a ball of fire.

Sam, facing backward on the pillion, was tied to Manny with a webbing belt, a Schmiesser in each hand. Isaac picked up a bottle from the box between his feet, lit the taper and tossed it at the second aircraft in line. It landed underneath the Messerschmitt; the broken bottle spilling petrol which ignited, engulfing the aircraft in flames.

One by one the Messerschmitts were set alight. Manny, a grin of exhilaration on his face, adrenalin pumping through his veins, took no notice of the crack and whine of igniting ammunition as they roared along the line of aircraft.

Soldiers and airmen ran towards them, firing their weapons. Sam returned fire until his magazines were empty, and then expertly reloaded.

Reaching the end of the row of burning aircraft, they turned back, throttles open, bodies bent low, racing alongside the hangars. Isaac and David tossed their last remaining Molotov cocktails into them, while Sam added to the confusion and the noise of exploding ammunition by firing a whole magazine into the hangars, the mechanics diving for safety.

Bullets whizzed around them, some pinging off the side of the bikes and sidecars, but miraculously none of them was hit. The soldiers in front of them dived for cover. A hail of bullets from David and Isaac's mounted machine guns meeting those not quick enough, and then they were past and heading for the gates.

Sam grunted as a bullet struck him above the left shoulder blade. The Schmeisser fell from his left hand, but was held against his body by a sling across his shoulders; he carried on firing the weapon in his right hand, face set in a grimace of pain.

Two guards knelt in front of the gate firing at them, but stood little chance against the firepower from the two sidecars.

David jumped out of the still moving bike, raising the barrier, then leapt on behind Bergman. They turned onto the road and sped away. Sam, slumped forward, held onto the bike by the webbing attached to Manny, blood spreading across the back of his camouflaged jacket.

Manny yelled at Isaac to look at Sam, whose body was pulling him backward. Isaac grabbed Sam's jacket, pulling him upright, at the same time yelling through the wind of the slipstream, 'Sam's been hit, but I can't see how badly.'

Manny dared not stop as he followed Bergman's tail-light. They sped past a convoy going through a checkpoint; no one fired at them. Ten minutes later Bergman turned into an opening between some trees, stopping as soon as they were hidden from the road.

Isaac was out of his sidecar before they had come to a stop, untying Sam from Manny, lowering him carefully to the ground.

'I'm OK, it's my shoulder.' Sam whispered, but his face showed the pain.

Isaac unzipped Sam's camouflaged jacket, cutting the blood-soaked shirt from the wound with his commando knife, his face apprehensive as he cleansed the wound. 'We need to get the bullet out.'

'If we do that, I don't think he would be fit to travel,' stated Bergman.

'If we don't, it could get worse.'

Bergman squatted beside Sam, looking at the wound then stood with a thoughtful look on his face. 'What if we clean the wound and give him some morphine for the pain then—'

'Hey, talk to me, I'm still conscious.' Sam pushed Isaac away, grabbing the front of David's jacket, hauling himself to his feet and facing Bergman. 'How far have we got to go before we reach our rendezvous?'

'About forty kilometres, but you're in no fit state to walk that far,' said Bergman.

'Where are we now?' Manny asked, looking over his shoulder at the map.

Shining a torch onto his map, Bergman pointed. 'We're about two kilometres past Balleroy.

Manny looked at the map for a moment then pointed a finger along a road. 'What if we use the bikes to cut across to the coast road, and then abandon them at—' his finger stopped at St Pierre-du-Mont. 'That'll leave us about eight kilometres from our rendezvous point. If need be we could carry Sam between us.'

'You're not carrying me anywhere. I'll be OK,' snorted Sam indignantly, but his face was pale, teeth clenched against the pain.

'There are patrols along the coast road,' stated Bergman.

Manny glanced up from the map, saying firmly, 'I'm willing to take that chance, plus we need to get the reply from the General back.'

'We could do it.' David added. 'We came to create a little havoc; we've done that, so let's get ourselves home.'

The others murmured their agreement.

Bergman smiled grimly. 'OK it's a unanimous vote. Isaac, clean up the wound and give him as much morphine as you're able.'

'Isaac, you ride pillion,' said Manny, helping Sam into the sidecar.

They reached St Pierre-du-Monte without any more mishaps, booby-trapped the bikes, and placed Sam on a makeshift stretcher and then moved off. It was still dark when they reached Grandcamp-Maisy, passing quickly through the sleeping village, advancing carefully down to the beach, where Bergman directed them to some bushes.

They lay the stretcher on the sand and Bergman pulled the bushes aside to reveal an opening in the rocks and crawled inside with Isaac and David dragging the semi-conscious Sam close behind him. Manny brushed their footprints from the sand, then pulled the bushes back over the entrance. Inside they found food, spare ammunition, British uniforms, and a dinghy.

Night turned into day, and the noisy squawking of gulls looking for their breakfast broke the silence. Manny moved across to look at Sam, whose face was the colour of chalk, and then at Isaac. 'How's he doing?'

'Not too good. We need to get the bullet out, otherwise it might turn gangrenous.'

Bergman stood beside Manny and looked down at Sam. He turned to the others. 'We have to wait till nightfall, and then hopefully the motor-torpedo boat will arrive.'

'It's too long to wait,' Isaac said, as he knelt beside Sam, wiping the sweat from his brow. 'He's burning up. If we don't do something now he could die.'

'OK. David you stand guard,' ordered Bergman. 'Let us know if anyone comes near this place.'

David nodded, picked up two Schmeissers and headed for the cave's entrance.

Manny knelt beside Sam and shook him awake. 'Sam, we have to take the bullet out, but you mustn't make a sound. Isaac will give you as much painkiller as he can.

Bite on this' He gave Sam a piece of wood with a cloth wrapped around it.

Sam tried to smile, but was too weak from loss of blood and high temperature. 'OK, Manny, I understand,' he replied weakly

Manny placed the wood into his cousin's mouth, nodding at Isaac, who gives Sam a morphine injection.

'Ready?' Isaac asked, picking up a knife. Sam winked and nodded.

Isaac slowly pushed the point of the knife into the wound until he felt it touch the bullet. Sam's body stiffened; his faced screwed up in pain, but he didn't make a sound as Isaac carefully prised the bullet back through the entry hole, showing it Sam, who, sweating with the pain, gave a weak smile. Isaac cleansed the wound, placing a sterile pack over it and giving Sam another shot of morphine.

While Sam fell into a drugged sleep, Manny and the others changed into British uniforms, burying the German ones.

Sam awoke, his temperature now back to normal. Manny helped him into his uniform as they waited patiently for darkness, moving the dinghy towards the entrance.

Bergman looked at his watch. It was time. He moved towards the cave's entrance, pushing the bushes cautiously away looking around, head to one side listening. 'Won't be a minute,' he said, walking a few paces onto the beach, aiming his torch out to sea and flashed a signal, which was answered immediately.

'Right, let's go,' he ordered the others.

Carrying the dingy with Sam inside to the water's edge, they got aboard and rowed out to the motor-torpedo boat. No sooner were they aboard, than the engines roared into life. Suddenly the sea was alight with beams of searchlights moving across the waves searching for them, but the boat was too fast and within seconds was hidden in the darkness.

*

An ambulance and car were waiting for them as the boat docked at Newhaven. Sam was taken away in the ambulance, while Manny and the others were whisked off to Reading, to be met by Mr White.

'Well done, follow me, I'll show you to your rooms. If there's anything you want to eat or drink, just pick up the phone. Get cleaned up; there's fresh clothes in your rooms, debriefing is in the morning.'

'What about Sam?' Manny asked just before entering his room.

'He's being well cared for. I'll keep you informed of his progress.'

Manny nodded and entering the room he closed the door behind him, shredding clothes as he walked slowly into the bathroom. Refreshed after a hot shower, he sat on the edge of the bed, picked up the phone and ordered tea and toast.

He didn't hear the knock at the door, or it being opened. The orderly smiled and quietly closed the door without leaving the tray as he'd been ordered to do.

Manny awoke with a start, not realising at first where he was. Stretching his body on the queen-size bed and smiling on seeing the plush surroundings, he glanced at his watch. Seven o'clock. *Is it morning or evening?* he asked himself, shrugged his shoulders saying, *Anyway who cares.* He got out of bed and pulled back the drapes: it was dark outside.

Turning from the window, he noticed for the first time the hangar-stand with his dress uniform, shirt and tie neatly pressed; polished shoes, the socks inside them.

He whistled 'This Is The Army, Mr Jones', he headed for the bathroom, emerging some twenty minutes later, shaved, showered and very hungry and made his way to the dining room, finding Mr White, Mr Amber and Bergman already there.

'Manny, please join us. I bet you're starving. I'll ring for the orderly,' said Mr Amber.

'Is it morning or evening?' Manny asked, moving across the room.

'Evening,' Mr Amber replied.

'Well then, I think I'll have a steak medium rare with greens and baked potato, followed by chocolate ice cream.'

Bergman burst out laughing. 'I'm afraid the best we can do is roast chicken with boiled potatoes and mushy peas, this isn't SS headquarters.'

'It was worth the try.' Manny grinned, pointing to the pot of tea in front of them. 'Is that hot?'

'Just been made,' replied Mr Amber, turning to face the door as it opened and David with Isaac entered the room.

'I'm starving,' said David.

'Don't ask for steak,' Manny said, lifting the cup of tea to his lips.

For the next two days Mr Amber and Mr White debriefed them. Did they notice unit insignia, how many tanks, and what units? Manny was surprised how much he'd remembered.

On the second day, Sam, looking a little pale, arm in a sling, joined them. He walked over to Isaac. 'The doctor said that if you wouldn't have removed the bullet, I would have died.' He held out his hand, the two men shook and Sam said, 'Thanks.'

'Don't be silly, you would have done the same for me, anyway were family.'

*

After a week's recuperation at the mansion, Manny, Isaac and David rejoined their unit at Larkhill Camp on the edge of Salisbury Plain. Manny was pleasantly surprised when he was promoted to sergeant and put in charge of a platoon of new recruits with David and Isaac as his corporals. It seemed someone had pulled some strings to keep them together.

Manny was puzzled by his men. They never seemed to interact with each other when in barracks, or to grumble, even though training intensified.

In training his men were seriously aggressive, learning very quickly what was needed of them. But they seemed to hold back as though they didn't fully trust him.

It suddenly dawned on him that none of them attended church services. Two of the men, Martin O'Brien and Trevor Fry, seemed familiar to him. But no matter how he racked his brain to know why, he couldn't come up with an answer. He asked David and Isaac if they had noticed anything strange about the men.

'If I didn't know better, I'd say they were Jewish, but to have a Jewish section in the British army was—'

'Impossible,' Isaac interrupted, 'and they do look, well…'

'Jewish.' Manny finished. 'There's another thing,' he added. 'None of them ever attend church services, two or three are down as atheist, the others as C of E or Catholic.'

'That doesn't mean a thing, we're down as atheists and we're Jews.'

'I haven't seen them at Friday evening services.' Isaac pointed out.

Manny shook his head. 'There had to be a reason for this, but what?'

'We thought we'd be split up when we reported back here,' David said, 'but instead were promoted and you're given a platoon and—'

'We rarely see an officer, except for inspection.' Isaac interrupted again.

Manny rubbed a hand thoughtfully across his chin, brow creased in thought. 'The thing is, what to do about it? He looked from one to the other. 'We're down for a week's leave on the 21st. I'll wait till we return, then I'll have a little talk with them.'

'Good idea,' Isaac and David said in unison.

Chapter 18

MANNY and Isaac opened the front door of the house to be greeted with hugs and kisses by Aunt Doris, who had a big happy grin on her face. Manny held her at arm's length, knowing by her silence and facial expression that something was going on.

Isaac broke the silence. 'Auntie, where's Hannah?'

'She's in the kitchen.'

'Thanks.' He moved past the pair, Manny's eyes slitting looking intently at his aunt and said, 'What?'

'I never said anything.'

'It's what you haven't said.' He leaned slightly towards her. 'OK, why the beaming smile? It seems you're dying to tell me something – you're pregnant,' he said jokingly.

She slapped him playfully on the arm. 'Don't be stupid.' Still smiling, 'Come.' She took his hand leading him into the lounge where to his surprise Sam was sitting on the settee beside a pretty young woman with shoulder-length auburn hair. Sam stood, smiled at the woman, helping her to her feet.

'Manny, may I introduce my fiancée, Sarah.'

Manny had that silly, wide-eyed, surprised look on his face as he looked from one to the other, and then to his aunt and back to Sam. 'When did this happen? You never— I'm sorry Sarah, how rude of me.' Manny took her hand to shake, then changed his mind, kissing her on both cheeks. 'Congratulations, it's nice to meet you.'

Her green eyes sparkled as she said with just a tinge of accent. 'It's nice to meet you at last. Sam has told me so much about you. I can now put the face to the name. You're not how I imagined.'

Manny was about to ask in which way, but she anticipated him.

'You don't want to know,' she giggled.

'Would you like some tea?' Aunt Doris asked, adding, 'Mark should be up in a moment, he's down in the cellar looking for the champagne he saved for a special occasion.'

Just then Uncle Mark entered the room, a bottle of champagne in either hand, followed by Isaac, who was also surprised to see Sam.

'Who's this pretty little thing holding on to your hand, Sam?'

'Isaac, meet my fiancée, Sarah. Isaac is Hannah's husband,' he explained.

Isaac's mouth opened in surprise, looking quickly across at Manny, who shrugged his shoulders, and then back to Sam. 'You devious, secretive—'

'My sentiments exactly,' Manny interrupted.

As Isaac shook Sarah's hand he said, 'Hannah told me to come into the lounge as I would be pleasantly surprised. That's an understatement. I'm very pleased to meet you.' He then shook Sam's hand. 'Congratulations to you both.'

'Thank you,' Sam and Sarah said in unison.

'Well, I'd better get back into the kitchen and help Hannah.' Isaac left the room with Aunt Doris trailing behind.

'I might as well get the glasses ready,' said Uncle Mark. 'David and Eve will be over later.' He waved the two bottles. 'Then we'll open the champers. Oh! And Joshua phoned. He'll try and get away.'

Manny was tempted to follow Isaac and see Rita, but instead turned to Sam. 'Well, you're a secretive one. How long have you two been together? Where did you meet? Or is it top secret?'

Sam looked at Sarah, who nodded.

'I was attending a meeting with—'

'We saw each other across a crowded room.' Sarah interrupted, looking with loving eyes at Sam. 'There was an explosion—'

'A bomb from a raid the night before. It was probably a delayed fuse,' Sam added. 'We both dived under the table and—'

Sarah laughed, taking over from Sam. 'I landed on top of him.' Sam raised Sarah's hand to his lips and kissed it. 'He asked me if I'd like a drink after the meeting. I said yes—'

'I knew the minute I saw Sarah, I was in love with her,' Sam unintentionally interrupted again.

'He asked me to marry him the day after he got back from – well, you know where.'

Manny raised an eyebrow. 'You know about that?'

'Sarah's a member of Mr White and Amber's staff,' Sam disclosed.

'How's the shoulder?'

'It's as good as new.' I started training and—' He was interrupted by a knock at the front door.

'I'll go.' Manny stood and strode quickly to the front door, stepping back in surprise on seeing Bergman.

'Great, we're at the right address.' Bergman had an arm around the waist of a beautiful, dark-skinned woman with long, jet-black hair. The ebony eyes smiled at Manny as Bergman introduced them, 'Manny, meet my wife Dominique.'

Manny leaned forward, kissing her on either cheek. 'It's nice to meet you, please come in.' Moving aside, allowing them to enter, he was about to close the door when there was a shout.

'Hang on, don't close the door.' David and Eve held hands, as they ran up the front steps. Eve gave him a peck on the cheek as she passed. 'Where are the others?'

'Well, most of them are in the kitchen, but there's a surprise in the lounge.'

Dominique and Sarah greeted each other like old friends. Uncle Mark and Isaac carried in trays with glasses of champagne.

Bergman asked Manny to do the introductions, just as Joshua comes into the room with another bottle of bubbly wearing RAF uniform, a pilot officer's band on his sleeve and pilot's wings prominent on his left breast.

'Ladies and gentlemen,' Aunt Doris called out, 'could you please make your way to the dining room, where dinner will be served.'

Uncle Mark had placed two tables together, borrowed some chairs from their next-door neighbour, Mrs Rothstein, and raided his coveted wine cellar.

Aunt Doris, Rita, Hannah and Eve came into the room, carrying platters of hot food. Aunt Doris and the girls had been busy roasting three of Aunt Doris's precious chickens, and from her vegetable garden, roast potatoes, peas and cabbage.

There was happy banter around the table, the young men and women smiling, talking and eating; all praising Aunt Doris with each mouthful. Uncle Mark stood, chinked a glass with a knife, and there was immediate silence, all eyes turned in his direction.

He looked around the table for a moment and then said, 'Doris and I are very proud to announce the engagement of our son Sam to Sarah.' He raised his glass towards Sarah. 'We welcome you to our home and hearts.'

There were loud cheers and banging of cutlery on the tables.

'Please join Doris and me in a toast—' he moved his glass in a circle '—to Sarah and Sam.'

Everyone stood, directing their glasses in the direction of the happy couple, repeating the toast, 'Sarah and Sam.'

Once the washing up was done, and Mrs Rothstein's chairs returned, Aunt Doris and Uncle Mark, tired but happy, went to bed, leaving the youngsters, as she called them, to talk amongst themselves.

Sarah explained why her parents weren't there. 'Two years ago the ship bringing them to England was torpedoed. They were rescued by another ship, which was on its way to Canada with children and refugees.' There were tears in the corner of her eyes as she added, 'My parents had been unable to get passage back here and were still in Canada. I've been in contact with them, and they're very happy about my engagement.'

Candles gave a warm glow to the room as dance music played softly from the radio. Sam, with Sarah nestled in the crook of his arm, sat on the settee kissing. Opposite, David and Eve were in an armchair chatting quietly, happy to be with each other, while Isaac, Hannah, Zach and Dominique danced cheek-to-cheek in the middle of the room. Joshua had returned to his squadron.

Manny sat quietly in the other armchair, a glass of brandy in his hand, thinking how different things would have been if Joan were alive. He felt an arm around his shoulder and looked up. It was Rita smiling down at him.

'Is something bothering you? You've hardly said a word to me the whole evening.'

'We've been training very hard lately. I'm trying to get my platoon into shape. I'm sure the invasion—'

She slipped onto his lap placing both arms around his neck.

He hesitated for a moment then continued. 'And we're going to be part of it and I've a—'

'Are you sure that's what it is?' she interrupted, her eyes staring intently into his.

He didn't say anything for a moment, brushing a lock of hair away from her forehead. 'Are you sure that's all it is?' she repeated.

He looked away, his eyes moving around the room at the other couples and then back to Rita. 'Very soon, I'm going to be fighting a war. I don't know what's going to happen to me, I could die. If I'm thinking what you are thinking, then I'm still not ready for—'

'All you do is make the same old lame excuses and hide your head in the sand. Just for once be truthful to yourself and what you really feel. All I need to know is that you love me. If you do, then that's great.'

Joan, he knew, was in the past. He never thought he could love anyone else, but he was wrong. Rita was always in his thoughts: her smile; her emerald-green eyes; the way she pouted when things went wrong or she didn't get her own way; and naturally her infectious laugh. Yes, he loved her, but didn't want to commit himself. He was scared – scared that something would happen to her. He couldn't stand the loss of another person he loved so deeply.

'I do love you, more than you probably realise, and to be truthful, I couldn't stand it if something were to happen to you.' He took her hand, looking pleadingly into her eyes. 'So can we stay as we—'

'If that's true,' she interrupted, 'then we should go a stage further, and I promise faithfully that nothing will happen to me.' She gave him a peck on the lips. 'I know I need you, and I'm sure that deep down you need me; so let's stop pussy footing around.'

He was about to say something, but she placed a finger to his lips. 'Don't you think that we owe it to ourselves to be happy? No one can predict what's going to happen, but I want to know that if something did happen to you or me, we would have had each other even for a short span of time.' She smiled, 'You could make all the excuses you like, but in your heart you know I am right.' She swept an arm around the room as she continued, 'Just look around you.'

'My goodness, you do go on, woman. Can you just shut up for a moment so I can kiss you?'

Later, Manny and Rita, his arm around her waist, stood by the front door saying their goodbyes to Bergman and Dominique.

Bergman leaned forward and whispered in Manny's ear, 'Get to know your men. You haven't tried yet. Do so.' He moved away. 'I'll be seeing you soon, thanks for a wonderful evening.'

Rita and Dominique hugged, promising to meet with the other girls for lunch. Bergman leaned towards Rita, kissing her on both cheeks, and then turned to Manny, a mischievous glint in his eye.

'Marry this beauty or I'll find someone who will.' Before Manny could say a word he turned and walked away, placing one arm around Dominique's slim waist, waving goodbye with his other.

*

On the way back to camp, Manny told Isaac and David what Bergman had said. 'I think that Bergman and the others made a deal with someone over the General Von Schweck caper, and that he and his friends might have something planned for us and the men. When we get back I think we'll have a serious chat with them.'

The following morning, Manny ordered David and Isaac to get the men lined up. 'No backpacks, weapons only.' As the men lined up, Manny's eyes moved along the line, lingering for a second on Martin O'Brien and Trevor Fry.

'Stand at ease,' he shouted, and paced up and down saying, 'This week, as usual, we're going to do night jumps and route marches. The bad news is: all leave was cancelled.'

He stopped pacing and was silent for a moment, glancing quickly once more at each man, and then continued. 'We're now going for a little run.' He turned to David and Isaac. 'Bring up the rear, make sure there's no stragglers.'

Manny set a fast pace, the men following him. They had covered a good six miles when Manny ran into an empty field hidden from the road by high hedges and trees. Manny halted under a clump of trees, he and the men breathing heavily, but not strained. 'Everyone gather around,' he ordered, beckoning for David and Isaac to stand beside him.

'Sit if you want.' Manny waited for them to settle down, stepping away from the tree. Turning to his left, he walked forward a couple of paces, and then turned quickly, yelling in German, 'Get to your feet, stand to attention.' A smile creased his face as the men obey the order.

'OK, you can sit down again,' he ordered quietly in English, turning with a raised eyebrow to Isaac and David, who stared at the men in open-mouthed amazement.

With Isaac and David either side of him, he said, 'I and my two corporals had noticed certain things about you.' He looked silently for a second at the men in front of him. 'Firstly, you don't attend a church service, which was OK with let's say five or six of you, but an entire platoon, no way. You don't come to the services my two companions and I attend on Friday evenings in the church hall a couple of miles from the camp. You train well, giving me a hundred per cent, but there's this keep-away sign you all seem to have around your necks, and it puzzled us.'

He looked at David and Isaac. 'We had come to the conclusion, with the help of an acquaintance and my little trick that you, like us, are Jewish of German or Austrian descent.' Manny paced up and down in front of the men.

'I'm sure there's a reason for that, because up till now the British government in their stupidity, had gone out of their way to ensure we don't have an all Jewish fighting unit and—'

'We think that we,' Isaac interrupted his brother-in-law, 'at some time in the future would be used as a specialised unit for operations behind enemy lines.'

'Thanks, I never thought of that,' Manny said sarcastically, looking at Isaac in a manner that said 'don't interrupt again', then turned back to the men. 'So let's cut out the crap, because if I'm not mistaken the invasion of Europe was not too far away, and we're going to need each other, and I'm going to need you to trust us, and we you.'

His blue eyes slit as he looked at O'Brien and Fry. 'So, let's start with you two. Where have we met before?'

'My real name is Moshe Schere, we—'

'Same Hebrew classes,' Manny interrupted, turning to Fry, snapping his fingers, remembering, 'Saul Friedlander.'

Trevor nodded. One by one the men told them their true names, country and city of origin.

Manny took a notebook and pencil from his pocket, waving it at the men. 'I'm going to pass this around. Inside is your English name. I want you to write your birth name beside it. You know me as Michael Green, but my real name is Manny Grenfeldt.'

He pointed to the two corporals, 'David Wasserman and Isaac Steinberger. It's taken a long time for Jews to be accepted into a fighting unit so we could fight the Nazis.' He pointed to himself, David and Isaac. 'We, like you, had family and friends still in Austria and Germany, and I for one intend to find them.'

His face hardened, 'I know at first hand about concentration camps, but I'm not going into that now. I want revenge for all those innocent men, women and children who have been tortured and killed so brutally.' He slammed a fist into the palm of his hand to emphasise his words, then pointed a finger at them. 'Do you?'

There was a yell from the men, 'Yes sergeant.'

Feet astride hands on hips Manny said, 'OK, no more secrets, we're going to be the best platoon, and we,' he pointed to himself, Isaac and David, 'are going to make sure you are.' There was a new spring to the men's step as they ran back to the camp.

Chapter 19

30 April 1944

BRITAIN had now become a huge armed camp as plans for the Allied invasion of Europe were completed. Large-scale military exercises took place in different parts of Southern England, as thousands of British, American and Commonwealth troops moved to their assembly points.

Rivulets of sweat run down Manny's mud-splattered, smiling face, as he crawled under barbed wire, strung across the assault course; his men in close pursuit, trying their hardest to beat him as live machine-gun bullets flew above their heads and mortar shells threw up mounds of earth around them.

Clearing the barbed wire, Manny rose to his feet yelling: 'Come on you lazy lot.'

He leapt onto the third rung of a ladder; hauled himself to the top, running along a narrow walkway; leapt across a gap; crawled along two ropes strung side-by-side; abseiled down a rope at the other end, reaching the ground on the run just ahead of Isaac; leapt a ditch in one stride; climbed the last obstacle, a wall, and sprinted to the end of the course, coming to an abrupt halt, a surprised look on his face.

'What are you doing here?' he asked a little breathlessly.

'Is that how you greet a friend and superior officer?' Bergman replied.

Manny saluted. 'Excuse me, sir, I won't be a minute.' Turning, he encouraged the men as they raced for the finishing line, ordering each one to get showered and changed, except for Isaac and David, who were also surprised to see Bergman, a worried frown on his face.

'What's going on, Bergman? By the look on your face it's something serious. Sam OK?' asked Manny.

Bergman nodded, taking a piece of paper from his pocket and handing it to Manny. 'Here are your orders.'

Manny waved the orders away. 'Forget the orders. What's this all about?'

'I can't tell you now, except I need you and your men's help SAP. I've transport waiting outside your barracks. Get showered and changed, and make sure your men keep their mouths shut, speak to no one.' He looked at his watch. 'You've thirty minutes.'

Manny and his men had been travelling for some time, and day had turned into night. Manny hadn't a clue as to where they were. Bergman, who was driving, turned the lorry onto a narrow bumpy country lane full of potholes.

'I didn't know you could drive a lorry.' Manny broke the silence.

Bergman glanced over at Manny, a smile on his face. 'After our last meeting, I thought I could drive anything.' He held up a hand before Manny could ask an awkward question; returning the hand quickly onto the steering wheel as the lorry hit another pothole. 'All would be revealed when we reach our destination.'

Manny pointed a thumb to the rear. 'My men are having a rough ride.'

'Be there in a second.' They turned right between wild overgrown bushes and trees. Bergman flashed the headlights without slowing down, and two trees blocking their path moved aside, the lorry just scraping past.

The trees thinned out, and ahead of them on either side of the road were two armoured cars, guns pointing in their direction. A few feet further on was a wooden barrier, the barrels of machine guns protruding over sandbagged gun emplacements either side of it. They came to a gradual halt at the barrier.

A sergeant and two privates moved from behind a gun emplacement. The sergeant walked to Bergman's side of the vehicle; the two soldiers stood a couple of yards from the vehicle weapons, ready for action.

The sergeant saluted. 'Papers please, sir.'

Bergman returned the salute, handing him his papers.

The sergeant looked at the papers, and then at Manny. Without a word he walked to the rear of the vehicle, looked inside, and then walked back, returning the papers to Bergman and saluted. 'I'll notify the sergeant major that you're on your way, sir.'

Bergman returned the salute. 'Thank you, Sergeant, could you notify the mess to get some hot food ready for the men.' He pushed the gearstick into first as the sergeant turned to the men at the barrier, making a lifting motion with his right hand, and they drove through the open barrier.

Within a few yards the muddy track became a concrete road, with trees forming a roof above them hiding the moon as they twisted and turned through a series of bends. The road straightened and widened, and then suddenly in the darkness a compound of camouflaged buildings appeared.

Bergman pulled up beside the door of one of them. No sooner had he switched off the engine than the door opened and a sergeant major appeared. His uniform immaculately pressed; toecaps of his boots shining like glass, back ramrod-straight, a swagger stick under his arm as he marched towards them. He banged on the side of the vehicle.

'Everyone out,' he yelled in a parade-ground voice. The men jumped from the vehicle. 'Line up!' he yelled again.

'Quietly, Sergeant-Major, we're not at Aldershot now,' said Bergman as he stepped from the vehicle.

The sergeant major saluted, 'Yes, sir.'

'Take the men to the barracks to stow their gear. Then take them over to the mess.'

The sergeant major saluted smartly and about-turned, facing the men. 'OK, gather your gear and line up,' he ordered quietly.

Bergman said to Manny. 'You, Isaac and David, follow me.'

Manny's men marched away as the three friends followed Bergman into the building, where they were met by Mr Amber, who shook their hands. 'Good to see you again.'

Manny now knew there was something happening, otherwise why did they need his men?

'What's up?' asked Isaac.

Mr Amber ignored the question. 'I'm sure you could do with some refreshments, follow me.' He turned and they followed him into a room with a trestle table and chairs. There were no curtains, the two windows painted black.

'What would you like to eat and drink?' asked Bergman.

'Something hot, and a cuppa,' Manny replied, dropping on to a chair; the other two nodding in agreement.

Bergman picked up a phone on a table by the wall, and ordered their food and drink.

Manny unbuckled his webbing belt, placing it on the floor beside him, his sten-gun next to it, and leaned slightly forward, arms crossed on the table. 'OK, what's this all about?'

Mr Amber said seriously, 'Four days ago an American Army Air Force Colonel, Jeffrey Bellamy, a member of General Eisenhower's planning staff; decided to go on a bombing mission over Bremerhaven.' Mr Amber held up his right hand, stopping anyone from commenting. 'The problem was—' He was interrupted by a knock at the door.

Bergman opened it and two privates entered. One turned to Bergman. 'I'm sorry, sir, but the cook said that all he had was sandwiches.'

Bergman looked peeved. 'OK, put the trays on the table over there,' he ordered, pointing where he wanted the trays to be placed. The privates did as they had been ordered and left.

'I'm sorry about this,' Bergman apologised.

Mr Amber waited while they reached for a sandwich taking a mug of tea. Once they had settled back into their seats he continued, face red above the bushy beard, fists clenched tightly, saying in a tight-lipped voice, 'Our colonel.' He raised his voice in anger. 'The irresponsible bastard, this stupid idiot got himself shot down.' Mr Amber walked over to the table and picked up a mug of tea.

'What's that got to do with us?' David questioned.

Mr Amber, the anger still on his face, turned and looked across at Bergman. 'Could you?'

Bergman nodded, carrying on from Mr Amber. 'Colonel Bellamy escaped the crash, but was captured and taken to Bremen police station. The idiot knows our plans for the invasion of Europe. We had received information that he was going to be interrogated by the Gestapo. If they get wind of—'

'Does this mean they knew who he was?' Manny asked, reaching for another sandwich.

'If you had asked me two days ago, I would have said no. It's not unusual for the SS or Gestapo to interrogate such a high-ranking officer. But we couldn't take that chance, so two days ago we sent in an agent to rescue the colonel, but we, or should I say the agent, had a stroke of bad luck. Someone recognised her and she was captured.'

'Why a woman?' asked Manny.

'She knew the area, and was the only one we could send at such short notice. Anyway, she volunteered.'

Mr Amber, the mug of tea in his hand, walked over to stand beside Bergman, pursing his lips and then explained. 'The thing was that over the last few months, British and American deception experts had sought to give the Germans the impression that the invasion was going to take place somewhere other than where it actually is.

'We know for certain that the deception had worked, but now it's taken a different turn. Bellamy and our agent are being transferred to Gestapo headquarters situated in a prison some twenty miles from Bremen. We believe the

Germans still don't know who Bellamy was, but if they torture him and the agent, which was a certainty, they'll definitely find out where and when the invasion will take place.' He hesitated, glancing from one to the other, and then continued, 'I'm sure you know what would happen then.'

'Where do we fit into all this?' Manny enquired.

'We need to get the colonel out of the Germans clutches,' Bergman answered.

'What about the young—'

'Yes, her as well,' Bergman interrupted.

'We, what do you mean *us*?' Manny looked at Mr Amber and then across at Bergman, who was standing by the door, hands in his pockets.

'You three, your men, Sam and me,' he said in a matter-of-fact voice.

'Where's Sam?' Manny enquired quietly.

'He was making preparations for the trip – that's if you agree to go.'

'Do you have a plan?' Isaac asked as he stood walking across the room.

'More or less,' Mr Amber replied hesitantly.

There was silence for a second. 'What do you mean—' The door opened, interrupting Manny, as Sam strode into the room.

Manny was shocked by his cousin's appearance. His face was drawn, eyes bloodshot, as though he hadn't slept for days. Sam looked at Bergman. 'Have they agreed to go?'

'Well, no, not yet. I was waiting for you to arrive. I haven't told them about Sarah.'

Shock of what had just been said showed on the three Paras' faces, and they asked in unison, 'Sarah, what about Sarah?'

'She's the agent that went to rescue the colonel.'

'What!' Manny stared at his cousin, a worried expression on his face; now knowing why Sam looked the way he did. He must be worried sick.

'How long has she been an agent?' Manny asked, just above a whisper.

'For some time; before we met.'

'I know now what you meant when you said she worked for Mr White and Mr Amber.'

'I couldn't tell you, could I?'

'You can count me in,' said Manny. The others nodded their agreement.

'Thanks,' Sam sighed. 'Yes I have a plan—'

'I'll tell the sergeant major to bring your men over,' Bergman interrupted.

Sam moved towards the door. 'We're waiting for Mr White to arrive before going over the plan. Let's go down to the cellar.'

In the centre of the cellar was a table covered by a sheet. Manny's men looked at it as they had filed into the room just as the phone rang. Bergman picked up the receiver, spoke quietly into the mouthpiece, nodded and replaced the receiver back onto its cradle saying, 'Mr White's arrived.'

The cellar door opened and closed. Manny and the others turned to see Mr White taking off his overcoat as the person behind him moved to one side.

'Joshua, what are you doing here?' There was surprise on Manny face and in his voice.

'I was passing and thought I'd drop in to see what my big brother's up to.' The two hugged. Manny turned to Sam. 'Where does he come into this?'

'I'll explain it in a moment.' Sam walked over to the table, taking off the sheet, revealing a model of a town. 'Bremen,' he said, picking up a pointing stick. 'We haven't much time.'

Chapter 20

IT WAS late afternoon, the sky a dull grey, when a Luftwaffe staff car followed by two half-tracks came to a halt by a one-pole barrier ten yards in front of the iron gates of Bremen prison. Two privates of the Waffen-SS stood behind the barrier rifles pointing at the car.

An SS-sergeant emerged from a wooden guard hut situated just before and to the right of the barrier, walking slowly towards the driver's side of the car, left hand on the Schmeisser hung from a strap across his chest and snapped his fingers.

'Papers,' he ordered in a rasping voice, not looking at the driver, who was Isaac in the uniform of a Luftwaffe corporal, or the rear of the vehicle where Bergman, a Luftwaffe group-captain sat, back ramrod straight, with Manny next to him, a Luftwaffe major.

Bergman opened the rear door of the car as the SS-sergeant turned his back on them; and in one fluid movement Bergman was out of the car and smacking a swagger stick across the SS-sergeant's back.

'What's your name, you insolent pig; don't they teach you to salute officers in the SS?'

The sergeant turned, pain showing on his face, body bent slightly, unable to stand erect from the pain as he saluted. 'I'm sorry, sir. I didn't see you sitting there.'

'Are you blind, ignorant or just plain stupid? You never saw me! Stand up when I'm talking to you.'

The sergeant stood facing Bergman, hatred in his eyes.

'Lift the barrier and open the gate. I'm here to pick up the American aviator.'

'I'm sorry, sir, I can't do that.'

Bergman took a step forward, menace in his voice. 'What, are you disobeying my order?'

'Excuse me, sir, but I'll have to speak to the duty officer.' The sergeant saluted, about-turned, walking painfully back to the hut.

Bergman could see him talking on the phone, rubbing his back glancing from time to time in his direction.

Manny got out of the car to stand beside Bergman, a briefcase in his right hand. The sergeant replaced the receiver, returning at a brisk but painful pace to Bergman, stood to attention and saluted. 'SS-Second Lieutenant Fleck should be here in a moment, sir.'

Bergman nodded, as a small door fitted into the huge prison gates opened, and an officer marched quickly over and saluted, saying in a clipped tone, 'SS-Second Lieutenant Fleck, could I see your papers please, sir.'

Bergman handed him his papers, Manny doing the same without being asked. While Fleck checked them, Manny took a sheath of paper from his briefcase, handing it to Bergman.

Fleck looked up, his mouth widened in a smile, but not his eyes as he handed the papers back to the two officers. 'How could I be of assistance, Herr Group Captain?'

Bergman stared straight into the German's blue eyes. 'I'm here to see the American Air Force officer, and escort him to my prison of war camp.' Bergman handed him the paper Manny gave him. 'Here are the orders for his release.'

Fleck looked at the paper in Bergman's hand, not taking it from him. 'I'm sorry, sir, but I cannot help you. He's awaiting interrogation by SS-Captain Koltz.'

'You've had him here for five days, he's mine now.' Bergman pointed to the wings on his uniform, leaning towards Fleck. The Knight's Cross around his neck swayed. 'He's an aviator, as I am,' Bergman said angrily, thrusting the papers towards the unhappy Fleck. 'Here are the orders transferring him into my care, signed by Generalleutnant Hartmann. You do know who he is, I presume?'

'Y-yes, s-sir, I'm sorry, sir, but you'll have to speak to the officer in charge. He would be the only one who could authorise the Americans release. If you'll excuse me, sir, I'll try and get hold of him.' Fleck saluted, moving quickly to the hut.

Bergman whispered to Isaac, 'Be ready to drive into the prison.' He turned his back to the hut, saying to Manny, 'Get the men out of the half-tracks; tell Sam that we might have to go to plan B. Wait for my signal; if you and I are able to get into the prison, then we'll carry on with plan A.'

Manny strolled over to the two half-tracks. 'Get down and stretch your legs,' he ordered the men.

Sam slid from the front seat of the half-track, straightened his uniform with the insignia of a lieutenant. Manny stood in front of him, gesturing as though giving him an order, telling him word for word Bergman's instructions. Sam nodded and saluted.

Manny returned to Bergman's side just as Fleck came out of the hut and marched over to them. 'I'm very sorry sir, but I couldn't contact SS-Captain Koltz.'

'Well, Fleck, in that case, as I can't wait all day, I'm ordering you to take me to the prisoner at once.' Bergman's eyes narrowed. 'He is here, I presume,' his stance and the hidden threat in his voice, intimidating.

'Y-yes, s-sir,' Fleck stammered.

Manny and Bergman breathed a silent sigh of relief. 'Take us to him.' Bergman moved his right hand, holding the swagger stick.

Fleck noticed the movement, and hesitated.

Bergman smacked the swagger stick into the palm of his left hand. 'Did you hear me?'

Fleck nodded. 'If you'll please follow me, sir, I'll take you to him.'

'Not on foot I'm not.'

'I'm sorry, sir, but only the SS and Gestapo are able to drive through the gates.'

'If you think for one moment that I'm walking the prisoner out to here, you've another think coming,' Bergman said angrily, pointing to the half-tracks. 'I'm taking no chances of the prisoner escaping. Open those gates, and that's an order, or do I have to phone the Air Vice Marshall?'

There was a look of dismay on Fleck's face; they could see he was in a quandary at what to do, trying to figure how best to deal with Bergman. 'I'll allow just your car, sir, with your aide and driver; the half-tracks could wait here.'

Bergman smacked the swagger stick against his boot. 'OK, open the gates.' He turned and gestured for Manny to get into the car.

The gates opened and they drove into a cobbled courtyard. The formidable grey stone walls showed no windows. Four stone steps led to a metal-studded oak door with a guard either side. Fleck flicked his hand, and one of the guards opened the door.

Manny patted Isaac on the shoulder as he got out of the car. 'Deal quietly with the guards and let the others in.'

Isaac nodded.

Manny ran up the stairs joining Fleck and Bergman as they entered the prison, their jackboots echoing on the stone floor as they marched stride for stride along the corridor.

On the right was a staircase and a sign on the wall with an arrow: COMMANDANT'S OFFICE. Just past the stairs a notice on a closed door told them it was the Mess Hall. Opposite through an open door, beds and lockers lined both sides of the guards' sleeping quarters. Manny slowed his step, glancing inside to make sure none of the guards was there, breathing a sigh of relief on seeing it was empty.

Ahead, from wall to wall, and floor to ceiling were steel bars. Fleck came to a halt in front of a guard, his machine pistol aimed in their direction.

'Brock, open the gate.' Without a word the guard did as ordered with a key attached to a chain clipped to his belt, relocking the gate once they were through.

Thirty yards further on, Fleck came to a halt inside an enclosed courtyard. Manny and Bergman stood either side of him. Stairs led up to a steel-grated landing that went around the courtyard. The doors of the cells were open, which meant there were no prisoners there. Under the landing on ground level were more cells. Fleck moved a couple of paces to his left towards a closed door with a guard outside, who came to attention as they approached.

'Open the door!' There was a muffled scream from behind a door opposite.

'Is the American being interrogated?' Bergman moved quickly across the corridor to the other side.

Fleck stepped in front of him, swallowed nervously; face white, licking his lips. 'I wouldn't go in there if I were you, sir.'

Bergman eyes turned hard, saying loudly, 'Are you telling me what to do again?' He turned to Manny, 'Shultz,' pointing to the cell where the scream had come from.

Manny nodded at Bergman, who took hold of Fleck's arm. 'Take me to the American.' The second lieutenant tried to pull away from Bergman, but his grip was too strong. 'If you don't do as I say, I promise you will regret it.'

Fleck looked into Bergman's eyes, stopped struggling and nodded. Bergman released his grip. Fleck, angry at being thus treated by this Air Force officer, straightened his uniform jacket and crossed the corridor to the other cell. 'Glebe, open the door,' he ordered.

The guard opened the door and Bergman followed them into the cell.

Manny moved quickly to where the scream had come from, at the same time drawing a dagger from its sheath, holding the blade along his forearm and opened the door, closing it quickly behind him.

Two men in sweat-soaked shirts turned to see who's entered.

'This cell was out of bounds to you fly boy,' sneered one of them, his bald head dripping sweat like a tap.

Manny was silent, taking in the scene. His lips drew tightly together, jaw set, eyes angry at seeing Sarah tied naked to a chair, head down on her chest, eyes closed, hair hanging loose and damp, body bent forward against the restraints across her midriff and hands tied to the arms of a chair stopping her from falling. There were red welts across her back, burn and teeth marks on the right breasts and nipple; blood dripped onto the ground from her nose.

Bald Head waved his arm, stepping towards Manny. 'Get out; fuck off, before—'

Manny moved close to the man yelling back. 'Who do you think you're talking to? Stand to attention when you speak to me.'

The second man moved beside his partner, a cigarette dangling from the corner of his mouth, eyes squinting from the smoke, the braces of his trousers hanging down his side. 'You were told to fuck off fly-boy; this is none of your business. I'm Gestapo Agent Goth, so be on your way before I have you shot.'

Manny smiled, not with his eyes, just the mouth. Suddenly, in one movement, he took a step towards Goth; the Nazi looked down at his chest in astonishment to see the hilt of a knife protruding from it and slowly dropped to his knees.

Before Bald Head could move, Manny's right hand grabbed his throat, pushing him back against the wall, the point of a gun jammed into his side. 'Make no noise, do exactly as I ask, and you'll live,' he whispered harshly in his ear. 'If not I'll kill you too.'

The man tried to struggle, but Manny's fingers tightened around his Adam's apple in a grip of steel. 'If you think I won't shoot because of the noise, forget it: the gun has a silencer.' He bit the Gestapo agent's ear, the scream muffled as Manny's tightened the grip around his throat.

'This is what we're going to do,' Manny ordered. 'Walk over to the American's cell. If you try anything silly, I'll shoot you, and believe me I'm not scared of dying, because you'll die before me. Let's go.'

Manny took his arm away from the man's throat, sliding it down to the back of his braces, gripping them tightly and jamming the gun into his side. They walked across the corridor into the American's cell where Bergman was helping Colonel Bellamy into a Luftwaffe lieutenant's uniform; the guard and Fleck lay dead at his feet.

The Gestapo agent turned to run. Manny fired twice, saying to Bergman. 'Sarah's in a bad way, she's in no fit state to walk out of here.'

'Colonel, I'm going to lock you in again. Don't worry we'll be back,' Bergman said as he moved out of the cell, locking the door and crossing the corridor to Sarah's cell, where Manny's untying her hands. Bergman's face hardened on seeing what the Gestapo had done to Sarah; and in anger kicked the lifeless body of Goth. Taking the Gestapo agent's jacket from the chair, he draped it around Sarah's shoulders as she began to stir.

Manny knelt beside her, stroking the wet auburn hair away from her forehead. 'Sarah, it's Manny,' he spoke softly.' Bergman and Sam are here.'

Sarah stared defiantly at him, shrinking back a little, a look of disbelief on her blooded face.

Manny could see she thought it was a trick.

She shook her head, blinking her eyes, trying to clear her blurred vision.

'Sarah, it's not a trick,' Manny said gently.

'Manny,' she whispered through swollen lips, the defiant look left her face as she whispered his name again.

'We'll dress her in the guard's uniform,' said Manny. 'The Colonel and I will carry her.'

'OK, while you're doing that, I'll see if everything's going to plan.' Pistol ready, Bergman slid along the wall, moving back towards the entrance.

He hadn't gone far when someone whispered, '*Shalom,*' Bergman replied, '*Passach.*'

Isaac walked out of a cell on his left. 'Everything's OK. The guards have been taken care of, we're waiting for you. Have you got Sarah and Bellamy?'

Bergman nodded. 'Yes, I'll get them.' He looked at his watch. So far everything had gone to plan, but he said to Isaac, 'We've fallen behind schedule, start the engines and be ready to move out.' Without another word he returned to the others.

Sarah, her arms draped around Bellamy and Manny's shoulders, bravely tried to walk. They pass dead soldiers in the corridor and on the front steps, the car and half-tracks waiting in the courtyard, engines ticking over.

The Colonel boarded a half-track, as Sam went to leave the vehicle, but David stopped him, whispering something in his ear as Sarah was gently helped onto the rear seat of the car by Bergman, who carefully moved in beside her. Manny slid onto the front seat. Isaac let out the clutch and they moved off, followed by the half-tracks, turning right out of the prison and heading north through the city.

Manny looked at Isaac. 'We've an hour and ten minutes, can we make it in time?'

'Yes.' Isaac glanced quickly at Sarah then turned to face the road. 'Did they?'

'No,' Manny whispered so Sarah couldn't hear him. 'But they did some bad things to her, and she never cracked. I'm glad Sam didn't go in with Bergman, he would have shot up the place.' Manny turned his head, looking tenderly at Sarah. 'She'll recover in time, but first we have to get her and the idiot who caused all this back home.'

'Won't be long now,' said Isaac, putting his foot down on the accelerator.

An open-topped staff car and lorry passed, going in the opposite direction. The passenger in the staff car stared at them.

Manny's eyes followed them. 'Shit, that's the Commandant of the prison.'

The staff car turned into the prison, coming to a stop by the open gate. Its passenger leapt out of the car, waving his hands at the lorry driver, gesturing angrily for him to back up. A soldier jumped from the lorry and ran into the prison.

'What did you say?' asked Bergman.

'SS-Hauptsturmführer Koltz has returned. He's seen the open gate and probably the dead soldiers, put two and two together, and come up with us.' Manny looked back once again adding, 'Can't you go any faster as Herr Kolz wants his prisoner's back?'

They sped through the town. Isaac suddenly swerved the car as bullets flew towards them from two trucks straddling the road ahead.

The two half-tracks passed the car, coming to a stop in front of it. The men leapt from them, using the armoured vehicles as cover, returning fire. Two of the Paras were killed.

Manny turned, looking behind just as the prison Commandant and his men come to a halt, cutting off their retreat and sending a stream of bullets in their direction. Bergman and Isaac returned fire. Manny's mouth formed a straight angry line: time was against them.

'Sarah, we're trapped; you know this town – do any of the side-streets by-pass this section so we could get behind the vehicles blocking the road?'

She tried to focus and shook her head, trying to clear her fuzzy brain and her vision as Manny repeated the question. She looked quickly around, 'No, I'm afraid there's no other way,' she replied.

Firing his Russian Tommy-gun, Manny took a peek towards the vehicles blocking their way, then at his watch. They had better get out of here soon; otherwise they would miss their rendezvous. He let off another burst, again taking a quick glance around looking for an escape route as the enemy's fire becomes more intense.

'Moshe, Saul, over here,' he yelled.

In a crouching run, the two men left the cover of the half-tracks, coming to a slithering halt beside Manny. 'Help Bergman and Isaac, I need to speak to Sam.' As the two men added their weapons' fire to that of Isaac and Bergman's, Manny's up and running zigzagging across to the half-tracks bullets cutting up the road behind him, leaping for the cover beside Sam.

'For what do I owe this pleasure, not enough excitement where you are?' Sam said between gritted teeth, letting off a burst from his weapon.

'Funny, very funny; we've got to get out of here; otherwise we're never going to make the rendezvous in time.'

'Tell me something I don't know.' He let off another burst. 'How do you propose we do that when we're caught in a crossfire?'

Manny pointed at the two trucks. 'There's a slight gap between the two trucks. If we drive our two half-tracks side by side, we can crash through the middle of them. Have a look and see what I mean.'

Sam took a quick peek, letting off a burst from his Schmeisser. 'You're right. What about the car?'

'Leave it, Moshe and Saul could give covering fire while Bergman, Isaac and I bring Sarah over.' He patted Sam on the shoulder. 'Let the men know what we've planned, I'll be back.'

Without waiting for Sam to reply, he ran back across the gap as bullets flew all around him, slithered beside Bergman, letting off a burst from his Tommy-gun, explaining his plan to the others.

Moshe and Saul gave covering fire as Manny, Isaac and Bergman helped Sarah across to the half-track, boarding it ready to move off. Manny moved behind the steering wheel, started the engine yelling to Moshe and Saul to come over. The two men let off a long burst from their weapons and ran across the gap between the vehicles with Manny and the others giving covering fire.

Halfway across, Saul yelled, 'I'm hit.'

Moshe looked back to see his friend crawling along the ground. He turned, running back and heaving Saul onto his shoulders fireman-style, and ran zigzagging to the half-track with bullets following them. Willing hands grabbed the wounded man, hauling him into the half-track as it moved off. Moshe leapt onto the running board of the moving vehicle and onto the seat beside Manny, smacking a fresh magazine into his weapon, adding his firepower to Manny's, who was driving one-handed, firing his gun with the other.

The two half-tracks gathered speed as they hurtled side by side towards the two trucks. Bullets flashed past, or ricocheted off the metal plating. German soldiers leapt from behind the trucks as the two armoured vehicles simultaneously crashed through the blockade.

Manny looked back; the Commandants were giving chase, but it didn't last long. Under the withering fire from the Paras, its tyres burst and the car flipped over and over, coming to a stop, crashing into a wall.

The light began to fade as the two vehicles stopped at an entrance to a field. Moshe got out of the vehicle, opened the gate, scrambling onto the running board as Manny drove into the field. Before the two vehicles had come to a halt, Sam jumped out of his vehicle, running over to the other half-track.

'Sam, wait a moment.' Manny stood in front of him hands on his shoulders stopping his cousin going any further. 'Sam, she's been tortured.'

There was a question in Sam's eyes.

'No, she hadn't been sexually abused, although they did some nasty things to her breasts. I'm sure they'll heal in time, as will her other wounds. Don't ask her any questions. What she needs right now is for you to cuddle her.'

Sam nodded silently, patted his cousin on the back as a thankyou and moved to the vehicle, sliding onto the seat beside Sarah.

'Hello angel.' He placed an arm carefully around her shoulders, gently kissed her swollen lips, her eyes and cheeks. 'I love you.' She began to sob with relief as the man she loved wrapped his arms around her, holding her close. She sighed, resting her head on his shoulder, knowing she was safe in his arms.

Manny, Bergman, and the men run along both sides of the field placing lamps at regular intervals. Taking a small two-way radio from the half-track, Manny switched it on, pressing the transmit button. 'This is Vesta, this is Vesta, are you reading, Over?'

'This is Cigar, reading you loud and clear. Could I have a light please?'

Manny gestured to the men, who lit the lamps.

'See you; be with you in two shakes of a nanny goat's tail.'

They heard the drone of a plane coming closer. Everyone raced back to the half-tracks as a Junkers 52 transport appeared in the darkening sky, its wheels down, port engine smoking and making a noise like a car backfiring as it came in for a perfect landing. The half-tracks raced beside it as the transport turned about at the end of the field, its propellers turning lazily. The side door opened and a ladder was lowered. Sam carried Sarah over to the plane. Eager hands reached down, helping her inside, with Sam behind making sure she didn't fall.

Manny and Moshe booby-trapped the half-tracks as the men helped the wounded and carried their dead comrades onto the plane, laying them on the floor and covering them with their jackets before moving to the seats along either side of the fuselage as medics tended the wounded.

Manny, the last aboard, brought up the ladder and closed the door. The plane began to move. He walked along the fuselage towards the cockpit, patting his men on the shoulder or knee in a congratulatory gesture, smiling at Saul and the four men having their wounds attended to before entering the cockpit to sit on a seat just behind the pilot. 'Thanks, Joshua, we couldn't have done this without you.'

'We're not out of the woods yet. My radio's jammed with messages from German air traffic control.' Joshua pushed the throttles forward and the aircraft leapt at ever-increasing speed along the ground; he pulled back the stick and the JU52 lifted off the ground. He pointed to the spare headset.

Manny put it on, hearing a high-pitched exasperated voice saying. 'Come in JU52, this is Hammer Control, do you read, do you read, over?'

Joshua ignored it for a while, and then pressed the talk button on his radio. 'Hammer Control this is JU52 George Papa Mike. You're transmission is breaking up, must maintain radio silence, over and out.' He switched the radio to another frequency then turned to Manny. 'How's Sarah?'

'She'll be OK, but it is going to take time.'

They crossed the coast and out to the North Sea. 'Keep your eyes peeled for fighters, German and British.' Joshua said, searching the sky around them. Nearing the English coastline he spoke into the radio. 'This is Cigar, do you read?'

'Reading you loud and clear, Cigar, what's your position?' a voice into their headsets asked. Joshua gave his position.

'Coming in behind you, Cigar.' A Spitfire appeared on their port side, and another on the starboard.

'Nice to see you, old chap,' one of the pilots said; the Spitfire on their port side wagged his wings.

Joshua and Manny looked over to the pilot who was waving, they waved back. 'Ditto,' replied Joshua.

The Spitfires peeled off as Joshua brought the JU52 into land; an ambulance raced alongside. They taxied towards a hangar, coming to a stop in front of its doors.

Colonel Bellamy had been silent the whole trip, thinking that he was being taken to Berlin. Relief showed on his face as he stepped down from the aircraft, stretching out a hand towards Manny beside him. 'Thanks very much.'

Manny looked at the hand, then without warning punched him on the chin, knocking the colonel to the ground.

'You were a fucking ignorant son-of-a-bitch. Through you that young lady, who was sent to rescue your sorry arse, was tortured; and we had to mount another operation to rescue you in case you jeopardised the ally's invasion of Europe. Three of my men are dead and four wounded. If it were up to me, I'd have thrown you out of the plane without a parachute when we were over the North Sea.'

A truck pulled up beside them. An American Army captain with MP armband and four armed MPs appeared from the rear of the vehicle surrounding the colonel.

'Colonel Bellamy, you're under arrest on the orders of General Eisenhower.' The captain moved forward, handcuffing the colonel.

Manny smiled grimly. 'I think the war's over for you. You're lucky my cousin didn't kill you.'

'Cousin?'

'That's the man who went with the woman in the ambulance. She's his fiancée.' As Bellamy got to his feet Manny kicked him in the groin. The colonel doubled over, gasping for breath, falling to his knees. 'That's so you'll never be stupid enough to fuck anyone again.'

The MPs were silent as they picked Bellamy up by the handcuffs and dragged him unceremoniously towards the truck.

Epilogue

AFTER a week's recuperation in Reading, and not being able to get to London to see the girls, Manny and his men were bored with lazing around and wanted to get back into action. He visited his four wounded men and was told they would be rejoining him in a couple of weeks.

Before leaving, Manny, Isaac and David, visited Sarah who was recovering from her ordeal at a nursing home in Hertfordshire. Sam was with her, having been granted two weeks' compassionate leave.

Sarah's face still showed a faint hint of bruising.

'The doctor said she might be able to go home in a week,' said Sam.

'How come you were captured so quickly?' Manny asked.

'I went to the Wüstestätte where I was to meet my contact.' She shrugged her shoulders. 'Just my luck, a boy from my old school recognised me, the bald-headed Gestapo agent. He followed me and I was arrested, thankfully before I met my contact. He told me the only reason he was in Bremen was to pick up an American colonel for interrogation.'

Her voice quivered slightly as she added, 'I tried to walk casually away, but he grabbed me, wanting to know what I, a Jewess was doing in a place like the Wüstestätte. I told him it's for the music, he just laughed. The rest, as they say, is history.'

She stood kissing the three of them on the cheek. 'If you hadn't come to rescue me, I don't know what else they would have done to me. Thank you.'

Sam moved to her side, placing a caring arm around her waist. 'We both thank you. I owe you one.'

'Don't be stupid,' said Manny. 'You don't owe us anything. As Isaac once said, we're family; this was what families do for each other.'

Manny's story continues
in the sequel to this novel:

It Would Have Been Enough